ASSASSINS IN THE SHADOWS

By

David Traynor

This book is a work of fiction. Places, events, and situations in this story are purely fictional. Any resemblance to actual persons, living or dead, is coincidental.

ISBN: 1-4033-4488-4 (e-book)
ISBN: 1-4033-4489-2 (Paperback)
ISBN: 1-4033-4490-6 (Dustjacket)

Library of Congress Control Number: 2002108209

This book is printed on acid free paper.

Printed in the United States of America
Bloomington, IN

1stBooks - rev. 10/17/02

--ONE--

The Yabrer, a rusting freighter flying Qatar colors, churned slowly through the Red Sea waters off Yemen bearing north towards the Suez Canal.

Inside the bridge, the captain of the ship, a colonel in the Palestine Authority's security force was talking with Yassef Abdul, his second-in-command.

"The Chairman will be pleased with us, Yassef. There are sufficient arms and munitions on board to continue our struggle against the Jews for another six months."

"That is good, Colonel. We must be able to defend our land against them. Their occupation is unacceptable."

"Where does your family live?"

"In Jenin."

"We have lost so many from there."

"I know. I lost my nine year-old niece two weeks ago when the Israelis invaded our neighborhood. She was shot to death right in front of my sister."

"That is tragic. Your niece will be avenged, Yassef. Every drop of our blood will be avenged. These weapons will help us kill ten Jews for every one of us who is slaughtered."

"I want revenge for my family."

"You will get revenge. It is the will of Allah."

"When are we expected to deliver the shipment in Haifa?"

"Tomorrow evening."

Suddenly, without warning, there was a loud blast from an artillery gun and the howling sound of a canon shell as it landed in front of the ship's bow.

The two Palestinian officers had been too engrossed in their conversation to have noticed the fast approaching Israeli Navy cutter.

The second-in-command quickly trained his binoculars on the ship and saw the messages being sent to them.

"Captain, they're ordering us to stop the ship. They are coming aboard. What do you want me to do?"

The Captain watched as Israeli commandos started to assemble on the deck of the cutter.

The heavy mesh climbing ropes had already been dropped over the railing and several high-speed inflatable boats that had been hoisted over the side by winches were ready to be dropped into the water.

He counted at least thirty heavily armed troops who were preparing to board his undermanned ship. Besides him and Yassef, there were only four crewmen on board.

There wasn't any way for him to physically resist the Israelis.

The Captain wondered how anyone would know about the shipment.

Did someone inside the Palestine Authority tip off the Israeli intelligence?

The penalty for anyone helping the Jews was immediate public execution.

Dozens of Palestinians had been executed in the refugee camps for helping the Israelis identify members of Al-Aqsa Martyrs Brigades, Hamas and Arafat's Fatah movement.

The colonel thought about his options to save himself.

There would be a great deal of trouble for him when he got back to Ramallah, even though this wasn't his fault.

The best course of action was to obey the orders to stop. He will talk with the Israeli soldiers.

Perhaps he could convince them that he knew nothing of the weapons in the cargo containers.

"Stop all engines!" He said to the second-in-command.

"Yes, Colonel." Yassef said, dejectedly.

The cutter lay just aft of the freighter with their canons trained directly at the bridge.

The commandos scrambled down the rope mesh as soon as the boats hit the water.

Within minutes, they were clamoring up the gangplank onto the deck of the freighter.

The Colonel was there to meet them.

"What's the problem?" He said in Arabic.

The Israeli officer commanding the boarding party replied in Arabic.

"We have reason to believe that you're carrying contraband arms. We're going to conduct a search of your cargo. Tell your crew to open the cargo hole and then come back up on deck."

"We have nothing to hide. We are just carrying some electrical equipment. You can see my manifest."

"No. We see for ourselves what you're carrying. What's your destination?"

"Haifa."

"How many crew?"

"Six, including my second-in-command and me."

"You and your second officer wait over there, so we can keep an eye on both of you."

"Sergeant, conduct the search."

The colonel thought that he would deny any knowledge of the arms being in the ship.

The ship was traveling light.

Other than the smuggled goods, there were only a few containers of electronic equipment and parts.

How could they prove that he knew anything?

He had orders from his superiors to pick up some cargo in Yemen.

He was only a soldier doing his duty.

Twenty minutes went by before the sergeant came back up on deck and reported to his Lieutenant.

"Sir, we found an arsenal down there. Hundreds of automatic weapons, mostly AK-47s, a thousand cases of ammunition, shoulder-held rocket launchers, land mines, grenades. It must have cost these guys a few million dollars for the stuff."

The Lieutenant turned to Palestinian Colonel and said contemptuously, "So, you didn't know that you were carrying contraband weapons?"

"Absolutely, not. My orders were to pick up electrical equipment from Yemen and bring it back to Haifa."

"Did you bring any cargo from Haifa down to Yemen?"

"No."

"Didn't you think that was unusual? You normally deliver cargo to Yemen and pick up cargo to bring back to Haifa."

"I didn't think much about that, because my orders were explicit and I don't question my orders."

"You better get your story straight before we get back to Haifa, because there'll be a lot of people who will want to talk to you about your shipment."

"Sergeant, take two of the men and escort the Captain up to the bridge.

"Have him make way to Haifa immediately.

"I'll stay here with the rest of the men.

"I want to make a complete inventory of the shipment before we get there."

"Yes, sir."

After they left for the bridge, the Lieutenant radioed the Captain of the cutter.

"We found the weapons and munitions. There's a lot more here than we thought. I'll know exactly how much they hauling after I finish an inventory."

"Was it headed to the Palestine Authority?"

"It seems that way. This stuff could have done a lot of damage back home. Some of these weapons have enough range to reach Tel Aviv."

"Wait until Sharon hears about this. He'll be furious. Did you have any resistance?"

"No. They only have six crew. All were unarmed. The Captain denies knowing about the shipment."

"I wouldn't expect him to admit anything. He'll be in trouble with his own people for messing this thing up.

"They've spent a lot of money to buy these weapons. They are not going to be happy when they hear about this."

"We'll stay on board until we reach port."

"That's fine. We'll be along side you all the way back. Good job, Lieutenant."

"Thank you, sir."

--TWO--

After signing off with the commando leader, the Captain radioed Navy Headquarters and reported the seizure of the Yabrer and the contraband arms and munitions.

A few minutes later, an intelligence officer in the Mossad, Israeli's secret service, called the Director of Operations in the Central Intelligence Agency and informed of the event.

"Jim, this is Shev. I have good news. We've just seized that Palestinian freighter we been monitoring.

"We've hit it big this time. There's around four million dollars worth of arms and munitions on board.

"It was headed right to the Palestine Authority. They won't be able to talk themselves out of this one."

"That's really good news, Shev. What are you planning to do about it?"

"We plan to conduct an exhibition of the arms, the ammunition and the other ordinance on the dock in Haifa.

"We've announced a press conference and have invited members of the United Nations to inspect this shipment.

"We want them to take a look at this stuff up close and personal.
"This is big news, Jim. This shipment appears to have been approved by Arafat himself.

"We have him in a corner now, Jim.

"He'll probably deny knowing anything about the shipment, but we prove that he authorized the financing of the deal.

"Don't you think that Arafat might claim that someone in the Authority acted without his authorization?"

"Probably, but that's not going to make it any better for him because it would make it appear that he has lost control of some of his operatives.

"Either way, it doesn't help him."

"Shev, when is he going to realize that the solution to the problem is political and not military?

"You guys aren't going to walk away from your home.

"I don't understand the man."

"Well, Jim, we have a lot of people here who believe that Arafat has never wanted peace.

"He wants us to vanish into thin air and as long as we are here, he will continue to attack us."

"I don't know how you will be able to stop the cycle of violence, Shev. It seems so hopeless from this side of the pond."

"Most everyone here and in Palestine is fed up with the bloodshed and they want peace.

"They're getting a little frustrated with Sharon's and Arafat's seeming inability to reach any kind of an understanding."

"I hope it works out. But anyway, congratulations on your capture of the arms shipment. That should give you lots of political collateral."

"I think it will, Jim. Have you found out anything about the source of these weapons?"

"We have some suspicions, Shev.

"Our ATF people have been hearing some noise from your area that the brokers might be Americans."

"Are you serious?"

"Like I said, it's only noise right now, but the prospect that our people are dealing for the Hamas doesn't settle very well with us."

"I can imagine. Is there anything I can do to pin that down for you?"

"I suppose there is.

"I'm sure that you have some people in place inside the refugee camps.

"If there are any sound bites that you pick up implicating our people, I'd like to hear about it."

"I can do that, Jim. We're going to grill the Captain of the freighter that was bringing the shipment back to Palestine. We've already identified him."

"Yeah?"

"He works for Arafat and his top security guy. He's just the delivery boy, but we might get him to admit being the link to the Palestine Authority's top people.

"The more pressure we put on Arafat the better. He's losing control of his own people, which is good for us."

"Would he know who was involved with the arms deal?"

"Do you mean whoever brokered the deal?"

"Right."

"Maybe. If we can find out who brokered the deal for the Palestine Authority, we may be able to find out who their contact was on the sale side."

"You'll keep me up to date, then?"

"As soon as I hear anything, I'll give you a call."

"Thanks, Shev."

Jim Devine hung up the phone, sat back into his chair and thought for a few moments.

The call from his counterpart in Israel was unsettling for several reasons.

There was a pipeline established from some unknown source that was feeding arms and munitions into the Palestine territory.

That was going to create more havoc and devastation in Israel because the arms and explosives were being delivered into the hands of the militant Islamics and the suicide bombers.

The weapons and ordinance that was seized on the Yabrer were multinational in origin.

The AK-47 automatic weapons were Russian made.

The Stingers, the shoulder rocket launchers, were manufactured in China.

The hand grenades were made somewhere in the Eastern Europe area.

Who was putting the package of weapons together?

Whoever it was had the capital and the contacts to put the deals together.

The ATF had given him a heads up that there was a remote possibility that American operatives could be involved.

This was a very disconcerting possibility.

Why did they suspect our own people?

They had run down the Russian and Chinese brokers. They claimed they weren't involved.

Their operatives hadn't been spotted with any of the Hamas or Hezbollah intelligence agents.

The Israeli intelligence had heard from their informers that the men seen with the arms brokers for the Hamas and Hezbollah were Anglo-Saxon types.

They thought that the men looked like Americans.

It had been discontinued after two years because it successfully put people on the ground inside those radical groups.

There hadn't been any operation sponsored by the agency since that time.

The seizure of the ship could provide leads to the identity of the broker or brokers.

As Director of Operations, Devine was responsible for several departments including counter-intelligence.

Although most of the intelligence gathering process relied on electronic eavesdropping and intercepts, an effort had been made to establish human intelligence gathering.

The agency had authorized an operation several years earlier for the purpose of establishing contact with the radical militant groups in the Middle East.

The idea was to have counter-intelligence agents pose as arms brokers for some fictitious Saudi family. The agents would adopt false identities as Canadian citizens.

They created layers of offshore corporations to hide the flow of money and rent office space throughout Europe and the Middle East ostensibly as an import-export trading company dealing in spices.

Before being assigned as Director of Operations, Devine had worked in the Office of Near Eastern Analysis.

He knew that area well. Devine realized the restrictions that Congress had placed on the agency in the early eighties after the Iran contra fiasco.

Electronic surveillance was an efficient method to gather a great deal of intelligence, but the magnitude of the number of intercepts became staggering over the last few years.

Two million intercepts an hour were flowing into the intelligence agencies and much of the data needed to be translated accurately.

The sheer volume of the messages and conversations was bogging down the system. The agencies were incapable of analyzing all the data.

The deputy director of counter-intelligence had run the covert arms brokering operation.

He had been responsible for managing and financing the business for his undercover agents.

Agency money was used to purchase ordinance and munitions from foreign brokers, mostly Russians and Chinese, and drop ship the cargo at neutral ports in the Middle East.

The money was flowing through a series of offshore bank accounts and accounts in several European countries like Monaco and Liechtenstein that had extremely lax banking regulations.

Once the money flowed through those banking systems that lacked tracking systems, it became impossible to follow.

During the two-year existence of the operation, millions of dollars flowed freely and undetected to the agents' special bank accounts from the bank account of the militant Islamics.

The operation was successful in a little over two years. The demand for small arms, automatic weapons, grenades, mortars and Stingers increased dramatically as the Middle East boiled over.

A seemingly endless number of militant Islamic factions were dealing with the undercover agents who were able to compromise several of their members into providing intelligence data.

Devine's predecessor, who had resigned from the agency to take a senior executive position in the private sector, decided to terminate the operation because it had achieved the goal of developing a human intelligence network.

The undercover agents involved with the operation had been relocated to the European area and assigned to more conventional duties at several United States Embassies.

--THREE--

Devine decided that it was time to do some investigation on his own.

He opened the top secret classified files on the old operation because he wanted to learn the identities of the agents who had been involved in it.

There were eleven agents who had been assigned to the operation over the two-year period.

One agent that Devine recognized immediately was Rich Ranfield, his Deputy Chief of Counter-Intelligence.

Ranfield had been assigned as an undercover broker for six months before he was brought back to the States and assigned as a supervisor in the department.

Devine thought he might have heard something about the scuttlebutt that American operatives were brokering arms and munitions with the Hezbollah and the Hamas.

Devine picked up his phone and called him.

"Ranfield, here."

"Rich, this is Jim Devine. Do you have a few minutes to talk?"

"Yes, sir, I do."

"Good. Rich, I thought that you would be able to help me with a possible situation that might be developing in the Middle East region."

Ranfield sensed the drift of this phone call immediately.

He would have to be very careful how he would answer his boss's questions.

Ranfield wouldn't want the Director to get too close to what was happening in the Middle East.

"What's that, Jim?" He asked in an innocuous tone.

"I received a call from Alcohol, Tobacco and Firearms last week. It seems that a few of their special operations people have picked up some intelligence involving certain arms brokers in the region.

"I was wondering whether you are tracking the foreign arms brokers who deal with the militant Islamics?"

Ranfield thought that the question was loaded.

If he didn't track the foreign arms brokers, he would be faulted for failure to monitor the contraband trade with the militants.

If he did track them, he would know about the current situation, which he couldn't tell Devine about. He decided to go down the middle of the road.

"Well, Jim. We've had a pretty good handle on the Russians and the Chinese. They do business in the open. They don't bother to conceal their dealings with the militants.

"The brokers in the Eastern European countries are fairly fragmented. They act as sub-contractors for the big guys for small stuff, like grenades and mortar shells."

Devine recognized that Ranfield really didn't give him any leads with his answer.

"Have you heard any talk from your contacts inside the Hezbollah and the Hamas that their arms buyers are dealing with American brokers?"

Ranfield was taken back. He had to think about what he was going to say and he'd have to reply to Devine quickly.

He hesitated for a moment and said, "No, we haven't heard anything like that.

"Maybe the ATF is getting old data from our operation that we shut down five years ago."

"Maybe, Rich, but they seem to believe that this is a current situation. Their sources are indicating that Americans are running an arms business in the Middle East now."

"I think that we would know about that if the information were credible.

"There's only a handful of arms brokers that can handle the amount of business that's going on and they're very competitive to keep doing business with the militants."

"Rich, I was reviewing the operation you referred to a minute ago. I read that you had been assigned as an undercover agent for six months.

Did you establish relationships with buyers for the Hamas and the Hezbollah?"

"Actually, I did. That's what we were supposed to do. We tried to develop relationships with their buyers in order to gather intelligence. They were extremely suspicious of us.

"They thought they were dealing with a bunch of Canadians who worked for an undisclosed Saudi family.

"The Hamas and Hezbollah agents didn't trust us for a minute. "After I was assigned back here, there were some other agents who were able to get information from paid informants inside the groups."

"Are those agents who were assigned to that operation still on duty in the Middle East region?"

Ranfield was becoming more apprehensive as Devine's line of questions was getting too close for comfort.

"I believe that some of them are still assigned in the region. They're probably working in one of our Embassies."

"Rich, this is what I'd like you to do.

"I want you to conduct some sort of surveillance on the agents who were part of that covert operation five years ago who are still on duty in the Middle East now.

"I've got to run down these rumors fast. The people on the Hill better not get wind of this before we find out that the rumors are credible."

"I wouldn't think so, Jim, but I'll check on that as soon as I get off the phone."

"Good. Let me know what you can find out about them.

"If we have people dealing with those militants and some other intelligence agency finds out before we do, then we're all going to be in big trouble."

"I understand, Jim. I'm getting right on it. I should be able to get back with you late tomorrow with a report."

"Okay. I'll look forward it. And Rich, thanks for the rundown."

"No problem, Jim."

--FOUR--

After Ranfield hung up the phone, he sat back in his chair and mulled over the conversation with his superior.

This was not good news.

Who knows where the scuttlebutt got started.

Regardless of the source, the rumor was out there in the intelligence community.

Americans were running an arms operation and high-level people were getting upset about it.

Ranfield realized that there wasn't any way to shut down the rumors.

They had to be dealt with, whether they were true or false. The damage had already been done.

There was a perception in the intelligence community that Americans were dealing with the enemy. That perception was going to be a reality.

Ranfield decided that he had to do something to stem the tide that was swamping the agency in general and Devine in particular. Devine was getting too close to his people in the field.

It was only a matter of time before he would find out about Whitestone and Maxwell.

They were the only agents in the Middle East region who were involved with the original covert operation. Now, they had become a liability to Ranfield and his associate.

Ranfield decided that it was time to contact him.

Devine was getting too close to uncovering the operation. He needed some direction as to what to do now.

He picked up the phone with scrambler capability.

Ranfield needed to talk on an open line without his people intercepting the conversation.

Talking in code was too slow and sometimes misinterpreted.

He dialed the unlisted number.

"Yes." A voice answered.
"It's Ranfield."
"I know."
"There's a problem."
"Really?" "Devine wants me to put surveillance on Whitestone and Maxwell."
"Why?"
"AFT has heard some noise that some Americans are involved with dealing arms with Hamas and Hezbollah operatives."
"Do they think they're Americans in the intelligence community or that they're just rogue independents?"
"Right now, they don't know. Devine wants me to monitor our people. That means..."
"I know what that means, Rich.
"We do have a problem.
"We can't let Devine get close to Maxwell and Whitestone.
"I'm not sure that we can trust either of those guys to keep their mouths shut.
"Are you with me, Rich?"
"Yeah, that's why I called you. What do you think we should do?"
"I don't want to take any chances, Rich.
"We can't afford to have those guys connecting us to the operation.
"That would mean big trouble for you if they find out that you're managing the arms business right under their noses."

Ranfield agreed.

"I'd hate to think about what the agency would do if they did find out about it. I don't think that I would get off as easily as the Iran contra people did."
"One of the problems we have now, Rich, is protecting our assets in the foreign accounts.
"We have at least a couple of hundred million dollars scattered in offshore banks."

"Do Maxwell and Whitestone still have their own bank accounts?"

"Yes, they do, Rich. They have access to them anytime. What they don't know is that we can access their accounts without them ever knowing about it."

"Do you mean that you have the authorization to transfer funds out of their accounts?"

"That's the way I set it up in the first place. If something went wrong, I'd still be able to get their money. It was insurance for us in case we ever had a security problem with them."

"Do they know about our accounts?"

"No way. That wasn't going to happen. I've put so many firewalls around our assets that no one will ever get to them."

"They probably know that we've set up accounts for ourselves."

"I'm sure that they do. That's what concerns me.

"If Devine runs those guys down and gets them to cooperate in exchange for a slap on the wrist type punishment, they'll connect both of us to the arms operation."

"Do you want to close the operation down?"

"I think that would be a good idea. The questions we have to figure out are timing when to close it down and how to do it."

"By the way, did you hear about the seizure of the Palestinian ship carrying a big load of ordinance and munitions earlier this morning?"

"Yes, I received the report from an associate right after it happened."

"Did you pick up on the coincidence that the shipment was picked up in Yemen at the same wharf that Whitestone uses?"

"Yes. That wasn't a coincidence.

"I saw the deposit of over four million dollars into Whitestone's account in Liechtenstein last week.

"From what I was told, that would be about the right amount for the all the stuff that was aboard that ship."

"Did your associate know whom Whitestone made the deal with?"

"Yes. It was one of the regular brokers from Hezbollah. He was acting as an intermediary for the Palestinian Authority.

"They needed the firepower to put up a fight when the Israel's invaded the refugee camps."

"After this seizure, the Palestinian Authority is going to need the firepower even more."

"That gives me an idea at least as far as Whitestone is concerned. Are you still able to contact him?"

"Yes. I can reach him at our Embassy in Tel Aviv. Our communications are secure."

"Good. You tell him to set up a meeting with the same Hezbollah broker. The Hezbollah will be anxious to buy more ordinance for Arafat. Find out exactly when and where the meet is to take place."

"Okay, then what?"

"Then, I want you to authorize the assassination of Whitestone after that meeting takes place."

"Do you want me to get an outside contractor?"

"No. I want you to use one of the agency people."

"You know the policy. We're not supposed to be assassinating individuals."

"I know the policy, but I also know that we can rationalize exceptions."

"Why use one of our own to do the job?"

"Think this through with me. Devine is getting close to finding out that there is an illegal arms business going on. Right?"

"Right."

"The only two people who can implicate us are Whitestone and Maxwell."

"Agreed."

"We can prevent that from happening by eliminating both of them. By using one of the agency shooters, we can make it appear as if he was part of the rogue arms operation, possibly that he was even running it."

"This sounds risky. If I issue orders for the kill, the shooter will eventually be debriefed and the agency will know that I issued unauthorized orders. They'd hang me."

"We're not going to let it get that far. We're going to wait until the jobs are finished and then the shooter will have a fatal accident before there is any debriefing."

"Did you just say jobs?"

"Yeah. We've got to take out Maxwell, too. We want Devine to find out after these two have been eliminated that they were the only agents involved with the illegal arms operation."

"What about the shooter?"

"Devine won't be able to trace the orders because you can make the orders disappear."

"I can do that."

"He won't know exactly what role the shooter had with the operation, but he won't have a trail to follow. There will be no one alive to connect us to them."

"What about Maxwell?"

"Where is he these days?"

"He's working in our Consulate in Florence. I'm in contact with him every week."

"Can you arrange to setup a time and place for the shooter to take him out?"

"Yes. He checks into the import-export office twice a week around the same time in the morning. That shouldn't be a problem. When do you want me to get this rolling?"

"As soon as possible. Since Devine suspects there are intelligence officers running the business, he's going to keep on top of the situation until he gets answers. We're going to provide him with some credible information that the operation was limited to Whitestone, Maxwell and the shooter."

"And if this doesn't work, then what?"

"I'll draft some preliminary plans for our exit strategy. The worse case scenario for us is that we go to ground outside the country and enjoy spending our hard-earned money."

"I hope this works out."

"It will. Report back to me as soon as the projects have been completed."

After he hung up the phone, Ranfield put in a call to Whitestone's secure phone line at the United States Embassy in Tel Aviv. It was seven o'clock Tel Aviv time, but Whitestone usually stayed in his office until ten.

The agent picked up the line after the first ring.

"Special Agent Whitestone speaking."

"This is Ranfield."

"Hello, Rich, how are things back at the ranch?"

"We're in good shape, here. John, I heard about the Israelis commandeering that Palestinian freighter this morning. Do you know anything about that?"

"We were surprised to hear it. We don't know if the Israelis were randomly boarding ships around the Red Sea or that they received some intelligence about it."

"Have you talked with your contacts at the Mossad?"

"Yes. They have some people in Jenin and Nablus.

"Supposedly, there was some talk that a big shipment of guns was coming in soon.

"They did tell me that they have been monitoring the freighters coming from Yemen because that's a port the Palestinians use regularly to pick-up contraband munitions."

"We know. The shipment looked like it had your footprint on it, John."

"That's possible, Rich."

"I've got an assignment for you. The Palestinians still need ordinance.

"Contact your broker and set up a time and place for a buy. You'll probably be able to get more than the four million you got from the last deal."

"They're trying to get more long-range stuff, Rich. Can we get any long range mortars?"

"That shouldn't be a problem. Take the order for as many as they want. I have a source in Pakistan that can ship the goods. Remember, let me know when your meet is set up."

"I will, Rich. Thanks for the call."

After he hung up, Ranfield thought that Whitestone wouldn't be thanking him for the call if he knew what Ranfield was arranging for him.

He opened up the files of the people in his counter-intelligence group to determine who would be the best candidate to carry out the assignments.

The vast majority of the shooters were full-time agents.

It would be difficult to assign any of them to these jobs because their supervisors monitored their activities and they were only used in special situations.

It would too risky to use them.

Ranfield knew that there were some part-time shooters still under contract with the agency.

He checked through their files and found a former agent that would be perfect for the assignment.

Ranfield knew the procedure for contacting the shooter and issuing the orders.

There was a blind drop at a New York Post Office for the agent to pick up a dossier with the time and place for the shoot, a physical description of the target and locker key to pick up a weapon in the airport closest to the target area.

There were no payments to be made to this particular shooter. Ranfield thought there must have been some compensation package that was approved by the agency that hadn't been specified in the shooter's file.

There were no debriefings of the assigned shooter after the completion of the assignment.

The best part of assigning this part-time shooter was that he would return to the United States without the protection of the agency and would be vulnerable to an assassination by accident.

Since there had been very little contact between the agency and this particular shooter, the agency wouldn't learn of the accident for months afterwards.

Any connection between the assignations of Whitestone and Maxwell and the accidental death of the shooter would take some time to figure out.

The agency might make the connection, but there would be more questions raised than answered trying to figure out who eliminated the apparent operatives of the illegal arms brokerage business.

The intended result would create a disconnect between the eliminated agents and Ranfield. The plan was a good plan, but it was going to be risky using one of the agency's own shooters.

--FIVE--

In the early morning light, the long shadows cast by the high walls in the quiet center hall of the Uffizi Gallery engulfed Leanne with feelings of peace and comfort.

This old museum seemed like a large sepulcher preserving precious relics from the fifteenth century.

For now, it was a sanctuary in which to reflect and to meditate on the deadly business that lay ahead.

Traveling throughout Europe as an international art dealer, she often spent quiet times like this ambling through the Lourve in Paris, the Prado in Madrid and the Uffizi.

Still, this was her favorite place.

This architectural masterpiece was the essence of beauty and tranquility.

Under the watchful eyes of the Medici Court, the Uffizi Palace was constructed around the Church of San Pier Angelo, a small eighth century Romanesque building on the banks of the Arne River.

Leanne's tepid interest in art as a teenager became her passion by the time she graduated from Yale's School of Fine Arts.

The Venetian and Florentine masters, whom she considered to be primary contributors to the Renaissance movement, fascinated her.

Now, Leanne was surrounded by chapel-like rooms dedicated to individual masters, such as Botticelli, del Sarto and Tintoretto.

For the next twenty minutes, she wandered aimlessly through the two-floored gallery, visualizing the mission, mentally preparing for each phase of the plan.

As she approached the main staircase, a booming baritone shattered the silence and her concentration.

"Ahah, there you are! I knew that you'd be here early to visit our ancient friends!" He said, as he waved his arm in a wide sweeping gesture towards the gallery rooms.

"And how is the most beautiful art dealer in the world today?"

She couldn't help but laugh.

Vincente Vaspari had become a good friend over the last five years. Always charming and complimentary, easy to like, a loyal customer, without a mean bone in his five-foot-four, three hundred pound body.

"Oh, Vincente," she said, playing with him, "You do flatter me too much."

"My dear Signorina," he said, grabbing her by the shoulders and kissing her on both cheeks, "that is simply not possible."

"It's good to see you. You look well. How's your family?"

"Like me, Leanne, it's growing!" He said, holding his stomach and laughing at himself.

"My Theresa is expecting another beautiful girl sometime in December."

"That's wonderful news. Won't this be your fifth child?" She asked, affectionately.

"Ah, you remember everything, Leanne."

"Well, I have more good news for you."

"Yes?"

"One of my wealthiest collectors passed away last month on his eighty-fourth birthday."

"A sad irony. I'm sorry for you."

"Yes, but his passing was expected. He called me after being diagnosed with inoperable cancer.

He wanted to distribute his entire collection of paintings. Vincente, there is a Tiziano, a Botticelli and a Veronese in the collection."

Leanne noticed Vincente's face becoming florid with excitement. Pausing for effect, she leaned forward and said "Vincente, they're yours. He's given them to the museum."

"Incredible! Fabulous news! You are an angel! How can we ever thank you enough for your thoughtfulness."

Teasingly, she said, "Well, I'm sure there will be ample opportunity to repay me the next time I offer paintings to you!

"Seriously, Vincente, you deserve the gifts. You've done such an excellent job managing the restoration of the museum.

"You have brought the elegance of the past to millions who will be passing through here."

"Thank you. It was truly a labor of love for everyone involved. We are all very proud of this old church."

"The paintings will be shipped to you next week by a bonded courier."

"That's wonderful! I don't want to seem rude, Leanne, but this is such exciting news.

"I was wondering, would you mind if I told the Curator about this now? Is that all right with you?

"Will you forgive me?"

"Of course, Vincente. I understand.

"It's not every day that someone donates four million dollars worth of paintings to the museum. Anyway, I have to catch an eleven-thirty flight."

"Well, promise me that we'll have dinner the next time you're in Florence." He said, bounding up the stairs to the Curator's office.

"I promise, Vincente. Chiao!"

"Arriverderci "He called back

She glanced at her watch. 8:35.

It was time to go.

Leanne moved from the dim halls of the Uffizi into the bright sunlight of the June morning. She strolled towards the Vio Veneto Bridge, a popular attraction for international tourists.

Some were searching for bargains on everything from souvenirs to Italian jewelry, some sat at crowded sidewalk cafes, munching on freshly baked croissants and sipping steaming hot coffee and others simply watched people walk by.

She scanned the street for anything unusual or out of place. The pace of the tourists shopping on the street seemed normal.

Many were walking in groups while others browsed through the shops. The cars parked on both sides of the street were empty.

There were no panel vans or service trucks that could be used for surveillance.

Leanne looked like a typical young Italian businesswoman keeping appointments with the buyers for the shops along the bridge.

She wore a white silk blouse, short tailored black skirt and black high-heel shoes. With her long dark hair piled high in a twist and large designer sunglasses covering her eyes, she blended indistinguishably into the flow of tourists walking the streets.

In less than ten minutes, she came within a block of the vacant six-story warehouse that she reconnoitered the previous day.

Convinced that there wasn't anyone following her, she walked to the rear of a small cafe adjacent to the warehouse, exited unnoticed into the back alley and turned towards the building's loading dock.

As she walked closer to the rear door of the warehouse, Leanne slipped on a pair of thin surgical gloves and unlocked the door with a master key.

She entered the building and closed the door behind her.

A pair of men's work boots was on the floor, just as she had left them the day before.

Leanne took off her heels and put on the boots-- better to leave boot prints than heel prints for the police to find on the dusty warehouse floors.

She covered her head with a shower cap--no loose hairs for investigators to pick up.

A lighted bulb hung from the ceiling.

Since the power was on, she would use the freight elevator instead of walking six flights of stairs.

Once Leanne reached the top floor, she walked into a small room with a single window facing the street.

A lightweight cloth covered the window. The two crates and the clean towel were where she placed them.

Sitting on the towel with her back resting against the larger crate, Leanne reached into her oversized shoulder bag, pulled out a black lightweight metal case and snapped it open.

Inside, several precision metal pieces fit snuggly in a contoured styrofoam mold.

Within thirty seconds, she had assembled a high power Remington sniper rifle.

Leanne glanced at her watch. It was a little after nine o'clock.

She checked her pulse. It was sixty-eight.

There was enough time to rest and get to her pulse down to her optimum rate of fifty-seven for the shot.

Leanne needed the low pulse rate to avoid spoiling the shot by jerking on the trigger.

The slightest disturbance to the trigger could ruin the shot.

Her orders estimated that the target would be arriving at his office between 9:30 and 9:35. He would park in a garage up the street and walk directly south to the entrance of the office building.

Leanne used the larger crate as a bench rest. The metal bipod under the barrel immobilized the front of the weapon and she secured the stock by strapping it tightly into her shoulder.

The day was windless.

The clear skies allowed good visibility to the target area. It wasn't necessary to adjust the sights.

The range to the target was some six hundred yards. Sitting on the smaller crate, she sighted in on the target area.

She figured that it would take about twenty seconds for the target to walk from the garage to the front of the office building.

With a second spotting scope, she trained it on the garage door and waited.

It didn't take long. Within minutes, she saw the target come out of the garage door.

He fit the description in the photo sent to her. Male, Caucasian, early thirties, five feet- eleven, one hundred and ninety-two pounds, dark curly hair, clean shaven, no glasses.

She put the spotting scope back down on the crate.

Counting down the twenty seconds, she closed her left eye, looked through the scope on the rifle and moved the crosshairs to a space on the sidewalk in front of the building.

Shallow breaths now. Inhale... exhale...

In a few seconds more, he should be walking into the sights.

Small breathes. Inhale a little... exhale a little...

The people in the scope seem to be moving in slow motion.
The target slowly entered the scope.
His head moved into the crosshairs.
She held her breath.
He held the front door open for a woman in a wheelchair.
Steady.
The target hesitated...he seemed to be frozen in the sights.
She squeezed....and the bullet blew his face away.

Blood splattered everywhere as the screaming woman watched as the body crumpled to the ground.

The distance between the warehouse and the street muted the screams and cries of those witnessing the assassination.

Leanne heard none of it.

In seconds, she broke down the weapon, placed the rifle parts into the case and shoved it into the shoulder bag.

Leanne walked quickly down the six flights of stairs, put the high heels back on and stuffed the shower cap and gloves into the side of her bag.

She opened the back door just enough to look into the alley. It was empty.

It was time to take a taxi to the airport.

There was one more mission to accomplish.

--SIX--

The headquarters for Hamilton-Montague was located in Lower Manhattan, just south and diagonally across the street from the New York Stock Exchange.

The old historic financial district traced its roots all the way back to the days of Alexander Hamilton and to the bank that he had founded after the Revolutionary War.

Although the vast majority of the brokerage and financial services firms had moved out of the district, Hamilton-Montague had maintained their headquarters in close proximity to the Exchange and the New York Federal Reserve Building.

After the fixed commission schedule for stock transactions was eliminated in the early seventies, the fierce competition for business forced firms to convert from manual operations to computer systems.

The transition to computer-driven operations resulted in chaos, confusion and errors.

Many firms suffering from enormous financial losses had to consolidate with more successful firms in order to survive.

The massive consolidation of brokerage firms in the seventies prompted an exodus from Lower Manhattan to cheaper, more technologically friendly space uptown.

Hamilton-Montague, however, decided to stay put in the office building they had owned for over sixty years.

Up on the fortieth floor of the leading investment banking firm on Wall Street, Brent Maxwell the young Director of Investment Banking was running a meeting with his large team of associate investment bankers.

"Thank you for coming on such short notice. I want to brief you on the purpose of this meeting.

"Our President, Henry Ingersoll, had me in his office for two hours this morning reviewing the Investment Banking Group's quarterly report."

Maxwell paused and glanced around the long oval walnut conference table. He had attention of his associates because their compensation was based on production.

Although he was relatively young to be the Director of Investment Banking, the associates respected his ability to structure financings and to manage the relationships with their blue-chip corporate clients.

They knew their corporate clients stayed with Hamilton, Montague because they trusted Maxwell's financial judgment.

"I want to share with you Henry's observations and his questions concerning our business prospects moving forward.

"Overall, Henry is pleased with our quarterly results.

"Our top line revenues have grown sixteen percent and our net revenues have grown twelve percent sequentially from the last quarter.

"Year over year comparisons have shown that we have increased our revenues twenty-two percent while our net has grown eighteen percent.

"We've increased productivity by cutting down on business travel, ramping up our video conferencing system and bringing in some productive new associates."

Maxwell glanced at the three young bankers he was referring to.

"Our margins have increased to nineteen percent which is sequentially better by ten percent.

"Obviously, our performance has been influenced by the needs of our corporate clients to raise capital. With interest rates continuing to decline, I anticipate our customers will accelerate their plans for expansion.

"That being said, Henry has given our group very favorable ratings, so it looks like we'll be getting our bonuses at the end of the year."

Maxwell saw a room full of smiling faces after that statement.

"However, despite our good report card, the Board of Directors has asked Henry whether our group should be soliciting the IPO business of the new start-up technology companies.

"The Board seems to be enamored with the numbers that our competitors are putting up this year. Given this environment of irrational exuberance, the demand for these new issues is much greater than the supply.

"So, we're having this meeting to discuss the feasibility of underwriting new issue tech stocks. I'll start with my thoughts and then we'll open up the discussion for everyone.

"Internet technology is new to all of us. As underwriters, it will be difficult for us to determine whether any of these business plans will succeed. Clearly, there is a technological revolution happening, but we don't know how the applications will play out.

"No one really knows at this point how any of these companies are going to generate revenue and profits.

"The advent of these new economy companies and how they relate to the now old economy companies is still a huge question mark. "How will the internet companies interface with clients like ours?

"I don't know the answer, our president doesn't know the answer and our Board of Directors doesn't know the answer.

"I want this meeting to be an open and frank forum about the capital markets today and how we can increase our market share of future corporate financings.

"I'll open the floor now for any of you to discuss whether we should solicit these new internet companies."

Jason, one of Maxwell's more senior bankers, spoke up first.

"Brent, you and I have seen the explosion in these IPO stock prices which began in late last year.

"The capital markets provide money for corporate America. As investment bankers, it is our responsibility to analyze and perform due diligence on the credit worthiness of our corporate clients.

"If we're doing an equity deal, we're responsible for determining the company's prospects for making any money.

"Our clients are established companies that have been Fortune 500 companies for years. They have a history of financial success.

"We have never taken on losers, because we have never wanted to sell risky credits to our institutional and individual investors.

"These internet company IPOs are more than risky credits for our investors, Brent. They're lawsuits ready to happen."

"Jason, I can't disagree with you. I've spoken with the CEOs of several of our major clients. These people run real businesses. They sell goods or services for a profit. They look at these dot.com companies and don't see them selling anything.

"Skeptical doesn't adequately describe their thoughts about the business plans for these companies. These young new executives have little, if any, management skills."

Barbara spoke up next.

"I've heard that comment from some of my contacts in the retail business.

"They don't follow the financials that these companies file with the SEC, as we do, but they can't imagine how a twenty-some year old chief executive officer without management experience will be able to execute a business plan."

One of the newest associate bankers, Ken, jumped in on that observation.

"The business plans for these companies are absurd."

Maxwell smiled, slightly amused at the enthusiasm of his latest hire, who was closer in age to the young men and women who were going to run the new companies than he was.

"Well, let's hear it, Ken. What do you think?"

"Brent, the business plans are insufficient to create a successful enterprise. Their platform is in cyberspace, which is okay, but most of their plans are designed to provide free services from their websites.

"We've already seen companies providing information free from everything from health care to how to make Indian cuisine.

"There are a few exceptions. Ebay, Amazon, Priceline.com and some others generate revenues by charging a percentage of the transactions.

"The problem with the online sellers is too much competition.

Maxwell concurred.

"I agree with you, Ken, but I want you to continue your thoughts about the flaws in the business plans.

"I'm sorry, I got off the point. A major flaw is the assumption that revenues will be generated by the sale of advertising space.

"Establishing a brand name is essential to attracting visitors to any website. Providing content is necessary for visitors to come back to the website. They will sell advertising space only if those two elements are in place.

"I look at these companies the same way as Ken does." Barbara said.

"These dogs are chasing their own tails. They're running around trying to get each other's advertising money. If they don't get ad money, they're going to burn through their cash and crash."

"Graphically put, Barbara." Brent said.

"If that happens, they won't be able to come back to the capital markets for more money." Jason said.

"I fail to see the long-term advantages for this firm to be involved with these companies."

Tom, another senior banker, offered his opinion.

"Brent, there's no question that the fees and commissions generated by bringing these IPOs are substantial. All of us have friends at other investment banks on the street who've been bragging about the ten million dollar bonuses they've been getting.

"The entire financial system has changed course and that raises serious questions about integrity, honesty and greed in the capital markets. ,

"These markets aren't going to go up forever. There will certainly be a correction and it'll be painful.

"Barbara has suggested a potential problem for those underwriters if these companies fail. Shareholders will come back at them with class action suits for restitution.

"My opinion is that our competitors have either gotten sloppy in their financial analyses of these companies or they are knowingly selling worthless shells to an unsuspecting public."

"Tom, let's keep on this trail because I've already heard from friends of mine at the SEC that they suspect a form of collaboration between the street's investment banks, their research departments and certain institutional accountants. Nothing actionable as yet, but certainly it's on their radar screens."

"Brent, the insiders know what's going on. A pattern seems to have developed in the capital markets that suggests collusive arrangements between venture capitalists, investment bankers and their research departments and institutional accounts."

"Tom, before you go on, I want whatever we discuss here today to stay in this room. We are examining possibilities that may exist in the market. We are not the SEC.

"We are only speculating about practices that may exist now which would affect how we move forward with our own business. I don't think anyone in this room has first hand knowledge of the practices at other investment banks.

"We'll treat this discussion as speculation. Go on, Tom."

"Well, speculatively speaking, Brent, I'll lay out a hypothetical scenario of my view of the investment banking system today in the most of the major firms. This is based on hearsay and circumstantial data."

Everyone around the table exchanged knowing smiles, including Maxwell.

"Young entrepreneurs needed seed money to get their businesses started. They couldn't get money from banks because they had no collateral.

"They couldn't get money from us because they had no history of revenues or profits and we weren't going to sell unproven companies to the public.

"In comes the first player in the game, the venture capitalist. The venture capitalist as the phrase implies is a wealthy investor who is willing to financially back businesses that have ideas but don't have the money to get them up and running.

"In exchange for the money, the venture capitalist usually receives about eighty percent ownership of the company, while the operators retain about twenty percent.

"This seed money enables the operators to get the business started, at least partially, so there will be some financial data available to bring them public.

"The second player in the game is the investment banker. Once the company shows some traction in whatever space they're operating in, the investment banker signs them on as clients and brings them public with an IPO.

"The investment bank pays the venture capitalist and the operators the five hundred million dollars, or whatever, for the sale of the stock to the investing public and in turn receives monster fees for managing the deal and monster commissions for trading the stock in the aftermarkets."

"The third player in the game is the investment bank's research department and the individual analysts assigned to the internet sector of the market.

"The word shill has been bandied around lately describing the role of the analyst relative to the questionable creditworthiness of the new issue internet stocks.

"The information that the research analyst puts out to individual and institutional investors has become critical for the success of the public offering.

"The last player in the game is the institutional account. My opinion is that the institutional accounts have played a role in helping to create a feeding frenzy among individual investors in the aftermarkets of the initial offerings.

"I base that on the pressure placed on institutional portfolio managers to attract new money to their funds. Since there are thousands of mutual funds out there, the competition to attract investors money has become more intense than ever.

"Portfolio managers are paid for the amount of assets under their management. The best way to attract new money to their funds is to demonstrate excellent rates of return on the money that they manage.

"The rates of return on these new internet IPOs were averaging four hundred percent on the first day of trading alone. I can't calculate what the annualized rate of return would be, but it got the attention on the individual investors."

Brent interjected.

"These deals didn't have any restrictions for holding the allocated stock for any period of time. They could flip them on the same day they were priced.

"This wasn't like the old days when syndicate managers were concerned that if institutions bought the IPO and the prices went down in the aftermarket, they'd sell their allocated shares and drive the prices down even more."

"That's right, Brent." Tom continued.

"There is speculation on the street that some investment banks were ensuring the prices of the new issues would skyrocket on the first day of trading. The talk was that they'd pump up prices in the aftermarkets by placing large buy orders at prices higher than the allocated stock price.

"That way, individual investors wouldn't be able to buy stock until it opened at much higher prices than the allocated price. Guess who would be selling stock at the higher prices? The institutional investors who had bought the stock at the much lower prices."

"That's quite an indictment, Tom. One of my friends at the SEC is very concerned about some of our competitors pumping up stock prices."

"I know, Brent, but that's what we're dealing with. Is this the kind of business that we want to be involved with? I don't think so.

"The short term rewards of fees and commissions for bringing internet companies public does not outweigh the possible loss of our client base and our reputation as a reliable investment advisor."

"Sally, this touches on the question of whether the portfolio managers are sharing the profits with the investment bankers that brought the stock public. I imagine they could do several different ways."

"Yes, they can. I've heard some of the firms want to share in the profits that the institutional accounts realize by charging excessive commissions when the institutions sell their stock back to the firm's trading desk."

"That would mean, Sally, that there were prior agreements as to how the profits would be split up, probably based on how much stock the firm allocated to the portfolio manager."

"That's what I've heard. The performance those portfolio managers realized was incredible. Investors were pouring their money into their funds and managers earned big bonuses for the new money under management."

"I think that I've heard enough about the supposed practices of our competitors. Greed has caused prices for the stocks of the internet companies to skyrocket. Greed by institutional and individual investors and our competitors.

"There is no analytical matrix that I know of that can justify the prices investors are paying for these stocks. The analysts are shilling for the investment banks to keep this game going, but the game will not go on forever.

"These firms will pay a price for their shenanigans sooner or later. There will be an accountability for the losses that will inevitably result when this bubble bursts.

"We, as a firm, cannot afford to damage our reputation or our relationships by becoming involved with this type of business. Tom is right. We should continue doing what we do best and that is to service our accounts with accurate information and timely service.

"Our relationships are our most important priority. Your responsibility is to nurture, maintain and broaden those relationships moving forward.

"I'll report back to Henry and discuss what we have talked about today. We will stay the course we've been on for the past five years. I'll tell him we will continue to do the things we do best.

"For now, we may seem like the turtle, but in the end we will win the race.

"Thank you all for coming. This meeting is over."

--SEVEN--

Sunlight flooded through the cabin window of the blue and white El Al 760 Airbus as it climbed into clear skies headed towards the Middle East.

The three other passengers in the first-class cabin were too preoccupied with their laptop computers and magazines to notice her.

As she gazed down on small clusters of clouds, she reflected on the morning's mission.

It had been successfully accomplished.

The weapon left in the locker at the Florence airport by one of the agency's operatives had been properly sighted.

That would seem like a small detail to most civilians, but competitive shooters rely on their sights to hit the small black bull's-eye on their targets.

Shooters will test their sights by aiming at the bull's-eye and firing several shots at the target.

The holes on the target appear as a small tight grouping, usually appearing slightly off-center from the bull's-eye.

The sights on the sniper rifle can be moved fractionally up or down and moved left or right to bring the group to the dead center of the target.

Someone from the agency had sighted her weapon before it was put in the locker, because she didn't have the time to find a rifle range in Florence to sight it herself.

The agency took care of all the details for this type of an assignment.

Her sights had to aligned perfectly to make a head shot from six hundred yards away.

She had an assignment similar to the Florence mission nearly six years earlier when she was working full-time for the agency.

The agency ordered Leanne to take part in the rescue of an Army officer who had been kidnapped by Islamic extremists in Iran.

The militants claimed the officer was a spy and demanded that the Israelis release several political prisoners in exchange for him.

When informers told the agency where the officer was being held, they put together a hostage rescue team and dispatched it on a covert mission to Iran.

Although there were heavily armed special operations people on the team, the agency wanted her there if they needed any long-range night shots from a sniper rifle with a silencer.

She single-handedly took out the six militants standing guard outside the small hut where the American officer was being held.

The special operations people were able to break into the hut without resistance and kill three more militants inside.

The American officer was rescued and brought back to the United States unharmed. She received a special Letter of Commendation for her part in the successful rescue.

It seemed strange that she had never been assigned to a direct assassination mission in the nearly ten years she had worked for the agency full-time and part-time.

Direct assassinations by agencies in the United States intelligence community hadn't been allowed since the late seventies when Congress decided that there wasn't enough control over the agency's covert intelligence operations.

There were too many rogue operatives in the various intelligence agencies breaking laws and dealing with countries on the enemies' list of the United States.

Leanne wondered if the Islamic militants' attacks on American interests throughout the world had changed the policy.

Since the 1988 Lockerbie bombing, factions of Islamic militants had attacked United States Embassies in Africa, kidnapped and killed American tourists, attacked the World Trade Center with a rented panel truck full of explosives, killed American soldiers in Somalia and hijacked airplanes.

It seemed plausible that the policy had been changed because of the attacks on American interests by Middle Eastern types. The target in Florence wasn't Middle Eastern. He was Anglo-Saxon.

Unless he was connected in some way to one of the Islamic militant's faction, it wouldn't make sense to take him out.

It also seemed odd that she would have two assignments in the same day.

That was very unusual.

There had to be some connection between the two targets that prompted the agency to assassinate both of them on the same day.

What were they thinking about?

Leanne opened her carry-on bag and pulled out the dossiers she picked up at the blind drop at the New York City post office.

The picture of the target in Tel Aviv indicated clearly another Anglo-Saxon type.

She was starting to get anxious about this mission.

If these targets weren't Middle East terrorists, then, who were they and what was the reason for killing them?

The agency wouldn't tell her because there would be no need to tell her.

Leanne wondered why they assigned these jobs to her since they knew there was only four months left on her contract.

Leanne would be finished with this business once she resigned from the agency.

The covert operations weren't meant for her anymore.

She had become increasingly more uncomfortable with the business of taking people out.

Leanne thought they would have wanted to wind her down, not give her more jobs.

Maybe they saw this as her last hurrah, which would be fine with her, because she rather not work anymore before the wedding in December.

As she glanced down at her left hand, Leanne thought that her ring finger looked barren without her engagement ring on it.

Leanne missed wearing the four-carat emerald cut diamond set beautifully on a wide platinum band.

The ring wouldn't attract much attention in New York City, but out in this part of the world it would certainly stand out.

It would attract the unwanted attention of strangers which she didn't want happening on this mission.

The ring was an unnecessary accoutrement while she was on a mission as a contract assassin for the Central Intelligence Agency.

Leanne was very attractive and was noticed by men whenever she traveled around the world buying and selling paintings and other works of art.

She was able to downplay her appearance by wearing ordinary outfits with muted colors and covering her long hair with simple styled hats.

A pair of plain black-tinted sunglasses hid her strikingly beautiful cat-green eyes.

The wedding had been scheduled to take place in St. Francis of Assisi Church in Darien, Connecticut in December, a mere two months after her contract with the agency expired.

Her financee, Brent Maxwell, a wealthy investment banker in New York City, still didn't know she worked for the CIA.

She felt that it would be difficult enough trying to explain to Brent why she wanted to work for an intelligence agency in the first place. Leanne didn't think there was any need to tell him while she was still under contract and still sworn to secrecy.

Even though she only worked a few days a year for them, her missions were covert and top secret. Only a few people at the agency knew about her role as a part-timer.

Everything she did as a contract shooter was to remain top secret for the rest of her life.

Eventually, Brent would want to know about her background and why she decided to accept the offer made to her by the agency. The time wasn't right, yet.

Brent was from an old money, aristocratic family. Leanne was from a small, poor South Carolina farming family.

Leanne hoped he would understand why she was recruited by them and why she felt that it was the right thing to do at the time.

Her migraine started to kick in again. She had the same symptoms after every mission.

The headaches started after her first mission, even though she didn't fire her weapon. Leanne ignored them for over a year, until they continued to worsen.

The doctors at Langley had diagnosed the problem as post-traumatic stress. They said this was a normal reaction for most people involved in a combat type operation.

Her missions were much different than her competitive rifle matches at school.

There was a lot of pressure and tension in the matches, but she had never suffered from any headaches after a competition.

Whenever she worked with a special operations team on a quick strike mission, there were casualties and usually deaths.

Leanne was in as much danger as any one else on the team. For her, this was a very traumatic experience.

She had been taught to project the experience of killing an enemy, but the psychological training sessions hadn't adequately prepared her for the real time experience.

The doctors scheduled sessions for her before and after she went on combat missions in order to monitor her reactions to the event. They were concerned that her condition would worsen, because she was subconsciously rebelling.

If Leanne was a psychopath, she would probably enjoy doing what she was doing or even a sociopath, she wouldn't think there was anything wrong with what she was doing, then she wouldn't have post-traumatic symptoms.

The doctors observed that Leanne's reactions to her missions were becoming increasingly more severe.

In addition to the headaches lasting longer and becoming more painful, Leanne was beginning to become nauseous and was manifesting signs of anxiety.

The doctors were very concerned about her situation because recovering from these traumatic events was taking increasingly longer which prevented her from working.

They thought that Leanne's condition might deteriorate to the point where she wouldn't be able to function as a sniper any longer.

They had given her painkillers, but the headaches kept getting progressively worse, often lasting for days.

Six months before she retired from full-time duty with the agency, her superiors decided to assign her to a position in the research department.

The doctors convinced them that if Leanne continued to participate in traumatic operations, she would suffer serious psychological damage.

Leanne thought for a moment.

This assignment seemed to be getting stranger than ever.

They had to know the headaches could affect her shooting. That's why they had been spacing out her assignments over the past few years.

Leanne always had time to get rid of the throbbing in the front of her head before executing the next assignment. These two assignments don't make sense for another reason.

Since they knew she suffered post-traumatic stress symptoms after an assignment and that the headaches could adversely affect her shooting,

The next hit was scheduled for six o'clock in Tel Aviv.

That certainly wasn't enough time to calm things down.

The throbbing could present a problem for getting off an accurate shot.

Leanne's thoughts were interrupted by the voice of a flight attendant on the intercom.

"Your attention, please, ladies and gentlemen, in approximately twenty minutes we will be arriving at Ben Gurion International Airport."

Time to prepare for her arrival.

Leanne checked her handbag to make sure she had the key to the locker inside the airport terminal.

She had put the sniper rifle used in the morning kill in a drop near the Florence Airport.

An identical case with another disassembled sniper rifle was waiting here to be picked up from a locker inside the terminal in Tel Aviv. The weapon had to be on the ground at the location of each assignment.

She'd never be able to get the weapon through extraordinarily tight security at the Tel Aviv airport.

Thirty years earlier, different factious militants started hijacking planes to negotiate the release of their members held as political prisoners in jails throughout Europe and the Middle East.

In order to prevent hijackings of any of the planes in the El Al fleet, the Israeli government devised the most stringent airport security system in the world.

Everyone passing through the airport was searched, screened and questioned who they were, what was the nature of their business and the reason why they were entering and leaving the country.

The system had worked.

There hasn't been a single Israeli plane hijacked since 1988.

Any person deemed slightly suspicious was interrogated at length and often detained by Israeli security personnel.

Leanne had been in the country several times interviewing aspiring painters who wanted her to sponsor an exhibit at her art gallery in New York.

Leanne had an acute awareness of what would sell in the New York market and she traveled throughout Europe and Middle East searching for new talent to market through her gallery.

A female security guard came up to her and started asking the usual questions.

Yes, she's entered the country several times over the past few years on business.

She's an art dealer from New York and she plans to interview several artists in Tel Aviv.

No, she doesn't intend to stay very long, only for the day.

She had reservations on a flight leaving tomorrow evening for the United States.

The destination of the flight was JFK International Airport. Yes, she had left the United States from JFK.

Leanne showed her return ticket to the security guard. She had been in Florence visiting a curator at the Uffizi Gallery on business. He is one of her regular buyers of Florentine and Venetian works of art.

They finally passed her through.

She didn't resent the thorough examination, because she understood that the Israelis were surrounded by their enemies.

Leanne walked into the main terminal and saw the row of lockers towards the front of the building. Stopping briefly at a newsstand, she scoped out the crowd flowing in and out of the building.

The place was filled with security personnel in plain clothes. Security people dressed as custodians were constantly checking trash cans, and any unattended packages and bags in the terminal building.

She waited several minutes and walked over to the lockers. The drop was in locker forty-seven. She deliberately did not glance around her to see if anyone was watching her.

Leanne knew that she was being watched by someone hanging around the lockers to see what was being put in and taken out of them. There were hundreds of security cameras positioned throughout the terminal scanning the lockers and the people using them.

She was not going to behave in a suspicious manner. She was merely an American art dealer picking up a portfolio of sketches and drawings dropped off by local artists.

Leanne opened the large locker and pulled out a black leather portfolio bag in which the thin lightweight metal case had been placed.

A few minutes later, with the portfolio bag hanging from one shoulder and holding her carry-on bag, she walked out of the terminal and hailed a waiting taxi.

Leanne wondered if her own people were with her on this leg of the mission.

Usually, on jobs like this, she worked by herself without a backup. This part of the world was a dangerous territory. The escalation of the violence between the Palestinians and the Israelis was getting out of control.

With long dark hair, high cheekbones and tanned complexion, she could easily pass for someone who lived in the Middle East.

She had seen the white delivery truck following the taxi since leaving the airport. Maybe she could spot the tail when she got onto the streets.

When they drove to within a few blocks of the hotel, Leanne told the driver to stop and let her off. She paid the fare and glanced back through the rear window.

Leanne watched as the van moved slowly by the taxi.

There were two men sitting in the front of the van. The one on the passenger side looked straight at her. He was American and the driver was Middle Eastern.

They were her people.

So, they did have back up for her in case there was any trouble. As they stopped for a red light at the next intersection, she felt relieved that they were there with her.

After milling with the crowd as it was moving towards the hotel, Leanne stopped briefly in a few shops seemingly to browse, but actually to check if she was being followed.

This was standard procedure for her. This territory had been so volatile that it became impossible to predict violent events. Even with her bodyguards in the white van, Leanne still needed to protect herself from being noticed.

Ten minutes later, she walked through the lobby of the hotel and directly to the elevators. The agency had made a reservation for Room 356 for a fictitious company.

Since she planned to be in that room for only a half-hour, there would be no way to trace her later.

Leanne slid the card key into the slot, pushed the door open and entered the elegant suite.

After placing her shoulder bag on the floral quilted bedspread, she walked to the windows and glimpsed through the slightly parted sheer curtains.

The target area was a small restaurant located about forty yards down the street and across from the hotel.

She had walked by there, just minutes ago.

Leanne thought that this was unusual. The restaurant was so close to the hotel that a high-powered sniper rifle really wasn't necessary for this mission.

A target standing forty yards away could be sighted without using the high powered scope.

She scanned the street. It was narrow and very congested with late afternoon shoppers and commuters.

Leanne thought that this was probably the best shooting site given the conditions.

After assembling the weapon, she flipped the front bipods and set the rifle on the expensive writing desk thinking that this was the closest she'd ever been to a target.

Maybe they thought that she wouldn't mess up such a short shot, even though she would be bothered by her headache.

At such a close range, the high powered scope would seem to bring the target's head within inches of her eye.

Time to kill.

--EIGHT--

Hamilton-Montague, the most prestigious investment banking firm on Wall Street, had their headquarters on Broad Street just south of the New York Stock Exchange.

Unlike many of their competitors, who had moved up to midtown Manhattan or over to the World Trade Center, they stayed rooted in the heart of the historic financial district.

The outside of their seventy-year-old brick building was fairly nondescript compared to the glistening office buildings up on Avenue of the Americas.

An ordinary brass and glass front with revolving doors guided visitors into a large marbled foyer fronting an imposing security station.

Up on the forty-second floor, Brent Maxwell, the firm's young Director of Investment Banking sat engrossed in front of his computer making last minute changes on a big financing deal.

Looking to raise eight billion dollars for plant expansion, Universal Motors, one of their largest clients, insisted that Maxwell, not an associate, direct the deal. The company's Chief Financial Officer had already approved Maxwell's proposal, issuing four billion ten-year and four billion thirty-year corporate bonds.

The structure of the deal wasn't complicated. With interest rates at historically low levels, it made sense for corporations to borrow money from institutional investors at such low levels.

Borrowing money from institutions was cheaper than borrowing money from banks through their revolving lines of credit.

Institutions had the flexibility to structure their borrowings for a much longer period of time than their loans from the banks. It wasn't unusual for companies to borrow money by issuing bonds or other fixed income securities with staggered maturities.

Corporations needed capital to finance a myriad of projects that required the use of funds for different periods of time. Since these corporate borrowers paid a higher rate of interest on the longer maturing bonds, the popular and less expensive maturities to issue where between two and ten years.

General Electric and IBM were renowned throughout Wall Street as the two most astute corporations in timing the issuance of debt securities. They always seemed to finance when interest rates were historically low.

Since their credit ratings were among the highest issued by the rating services, such as Moody's and Standard and Poor's, the interest rates paid by them was nearly as low as the rate paid by the United States government for their United States treasury bonds with similar maturities.

The demand for high rated corporate bonds by the big fixed income bond funds was high because investors had been switching money out of the collapsing tech market into bonds.

High-grade bond funds were scrambling even more for investment grade bonds, because so many corporations had seen their credit ratings fall to junk status.

The problem for Maxwell was not getting the deal sold, it was selling enough bonds to fill the demand. High quality corporate bonds were becoming scarce in the marketplace.

His phone rang. He remembered that he had told Angie to hold all his calls.

"Yes, Angie?"

"Brent, I know you didn't want me to interrupt you, but there's a gentleman here who says he's with the government and that it's urgent."

"Did he say what he wants?"

"No. He only said that it had to do with Jeff."

"With Jeff? I wonder what... did he show you any identification?"

"Yes, Brent. His photo was on the card he showed me. His name is James Devine and he is with the Central Intelligence Agency."

"All right, Angie. I'm just about finished with this, anyway. Would you show him in here, please?"

A few minutes later, Angie opened Brent's door and introduced the agent.

"Brent, this is Mr. Devine, he's with the CIA."

The two men shook hands.

"Do you want me to close the door, Brent?"

"Yes, please, and Angie, would hold all my calls?"

"Of course." She said, as she closed the door behind her.

"Angie said that you wanted to talk with me about my brother, Jeff?" Brent said.

"Yes, I do. Mr. Maxwell, I'm the Director of Operations with the Central Intelligence Agency. Your brother worked in our counter-intelligence group that reports to me."

"What do you mean, he worked for you? Did he resign or something?"

"No. I've got some really bad news for you, sir."

He paused... "We just got word that your brother was killed this morning in Florence."

"What?! Killed?! What are you talking about?!"

"I'm very sorry, sir. Jeff is dead. He was shot down walking to work in front of his building. He was murdered."

"Is this some sort of sick joke?" He demanded.

"I'm sorry, I wish it were a sick joke. Jeff has been working for us in counter-intelligence for the past several years. He had been on assignment lately in Europe stationed at our Consulate in Florence."

"I can't believe this!"

"I'm really sorry to break this to you, but I wanted you to know as soon as possible. I wanted to tell in person. I didn't feel that you should have received just a phone call."

Brent was stunned. He hadn't heard from Jeff since last December when he had called to wish him a Merry Christmas. He didn't say that anything was wrong.

He knew Jeff well enough to know that he wouldn't tell him anything about his work, even if he were in trouble. Brent wasn't surprised when Jeff told him that he decided to join the CIA.

Since his childhood, Jeff played hard, constantly looking to do things that gave him a rush. Remembering back to the times when he played with his brother, who was two years younger, Brent was grateful that neither one of them were killed.

To say that Jeff pushed the envelope wouldn't adequately describe the things he would do to experience the thrill and excitement of dangerous stunts.

Jeff was a great athlete with tremendous agility, balance and quickness. He loved the extreme sports, like snow and skate boarding, even though he was an All-State football and lacrosse player at prep school in Massachusetts.

Brent remembered how Jeff would constantly challenge him to do stunts on the moguls that usually left them both with monster bruises or separated shoulders.

By the time Brent went to the University of Virginia in Charlottesville on a lacrosse scholarship, Jeff had firmly established himself as the wild man of the family.

His parents were glad to see their young turk head off to the tranquil, scenic campus where he could party, play ball and make some great connections with children of other wealthy families.

His parents were more concerned about Jeff surviving than getting good grades.

Jeff followed his older brother Brent to the University and became one of the very few athletes to play on the football and lacrosse teams during his four-year stay.

"What happened?"

"Like I said, he was murdered."

"You said he was shot."

"Yes. He was assassinated."

"I don't understand."

"Someone wanted to kill your brother. Jeff was shot in the head by a sniper."

"How do you know that?"

"We could tell from the bullet and the type of wound on your brother's head."

Brent was starting to feel sick to his stomach. The graphic descriptions were upsetting him.

"This is so unbelievable to me. I'm having a very hard time with this. Jeff and I were very close."

"I know, Mr. Maxwell. I can understand how you feel, because I lost my oldest brother in Vietnam. I still have trouble accepting that he's dead. That's one reason why I came here to see you in person. It was as much a shock to us as it is to you."

"You know, I think what bothers me most was that he was assassinated. Somebody deliberately wanted to kill him."

"That's right. Someone did want your brother killed. He was definitely the target."

"Can you tell me what he was doing?"

"Do you mean about his job?"

"Yes."

"Well, he was stationed at the Consulate in Florence and was doing routine administrative work. He wasn't involved with any special operations that would put him in any physical danger."

"So, you're telling me that there wasn't any apparent reason why someone would want to kill him?"

"That's right. At this point, we don't know why your brother was killed."

"Do you have any idea about who would want to kill him?"

"No. We're not going to know the identity of the killer until we establish a motive for the killing."

"A sniper killed him?"

"That's right. Our people have already found the place where the shooter took the shot."

"How far away was it from Jeff?"

"The shooter shot from a window on the sixth floor of an unoccupied warehouse. The distance from the window to the front of the building where your brother was standing was over six hundred yards."

"This may be a stupid question, but I'll ask it anyway. Was that a difficult shot to make?"

"For a civilian, without any marksmanship training, the shot would be impossible to make. It would be a difficult shot for even someone like me. You're talking about a six hundred yard shot at a moving target.

"This was done by a professional hit man."

"Are professional assassins easy to find?"

"Not really. All the security forces in the world have snipers, like our SWAT teams here in the states. All the intelligence agencies throughout the world have snipers."

"So the fact that this guy who shot Jeff was a professional really won't help you find out why someone wanted to kill him."

"That's right, especially if the shooter was an independent contractor."

"What do you mean?"

"Well, if I wanted to hire an assassin for a job, someone who isn't working for any particular intelligence agency, someone who is just freelancing, then I would have to work through an intermediary."

"Like a broker?"

"Right. The price for the job would depend on who the target was and how much risk there would be to the shooter of being caught after the target was taken out."

"Does your agency have information about any of these people in your database?"

"As a matter of fact, we do. We set up relational databases on foreign operatives who work in Europe and Middle East.

"I can't tell you the sources for our information. That's top secret, but I want you to know that we might be able to profile this shooter."

"What filters do you use?"

"If they weren't so obvious, I wouldn't tell you. You could probably have figured it out by yourself. Shooters are an independent lot. They are self-reliant, highly disciplined, organized and sometimes display certain idiosyncrasies.

"I can understand that first part, but I don't get what you mean about the idiosyncrasies."

"Shooters are very individualistic. It's as if they want you to know that they were the shooters."

"Do you mean like trademarks?"

"Exactly. It could be a lot of different things. The caliber of the bullet, the type of rifle and the length of the shot are all clues for us to help profile a shooter."

"You said that you have figured out where the shooter took his shot?"

"Yes, the shot was taken from the sixth floor of an unoccupied warehouse."

"How did find that out so quickly?"

"I'm sorry that I have to be so graphic, but there is no other way to explain these things to you."

"That's all right. I want to know everything."

"I can understand that. We were able to determine the shooter's location based on the angle of the bullet's trajectory and where your brother was positioned at the moment he was hit."

"That sounds like the Kennedy assassination in Dallas."

"Yeah, except Kennedy was moving a lot faster than your brother and Oswald wasn't an expert long-range sniper."

"Did you find anything at the warehouse that would indicate who the shooter was?"

"So far, our forensic people haven't found anything. I mean, we haven't found fingerprints, hair or anything that would give us any DNA samples."

"That's too bad."

"We keep checking, because we know that the shooter walked across the first floor, took a freight elevator and after the shot, walked down six flights of stairs."

"How do you know that?"

"The place was pretty dusty. We followed the fresh footprints up to the room and back down.

"That's the only hard evidence we have right now. We'll keep looking, but we'll have to get lucky to find anything else. Like I said, this guy was a professional."

"What about the characteristics of these independent contract shooters?

"Did he leave any trademarks that you might match up to the people in your database?"

Devine looked at Maxwell a little differently after that question. Maxwell was a quick thinker, just like his brother.

"I'll set the scene for you, Mr. Maxwell."

"Please call me Brent. No one calls me Mr. Maxwell, except Angie, and that's only when we're with clients."

"Okay, Brent. The sightline from the warehouse to the front of building where Jeff worked sometimes was narrow, maybe ten yards wide. Inside the room on the sixth floor, the shooter had placed two heavy wooden crates, one larger than the other, next to each other."

"That sounds like the shooter was using the larger crate as a bench rest."

Devine was taken back a little.

"How did you figure that out?"

"My father was a fighter pilot in the Marines. Before he went to flight school in Pensacola, Florida he had to qualify on the rifle and pistol ranges in order to graduate from Officers Basic School at Quantico, Virginia."

"I don't get where you're going with this, yet."

"His scores earned him expert medals for rifle and pistol because he really loved to shoot.

"After he finished his contract with the Marines, he became a competitive shooter. My dad used to drag Jeff and I out to his competitions.

"He used the same set-up that you described in the warehouse. That would replicate a bench rest that a competitive shooter would use."

"Brent, if you ever need another job, give me a call. I can always use someone like you."

"I think the shooter was probably a competitive shooter at some point in his life. My father said that competitive shooters in the United States are a close knit bunch."

"That's true. I'll look into that when I get back to the office. I should be hearing something soon from forensics about the bullet and the type of rifle that the shooter used."

"Is there anything that I can do now?"

Devine paused, then looked at Maxwell and said softly, "I wanted to ask you about the funeral arrangements for Jeff."

"I don't know. Do my parents know yet?"

"No. We haven't able to reach them. We called their house in New Hyde Park, but they weren't there."

"They're away on vacation with my aunt and uncle. They have a beach home in Duck on the Outer Banks."

"Do you want me to call them?"

"No. I appreciate that you came up here today to tell me in person. I have their phone number. I'll give them a call. I'd rather tell them myself. You don't have to."

"Brent, your brother was killed in the line of duty for the Central Intelligence Agency. He's eligible for full military honors at his funeral and burial at Arlington National Cemetery."

--NINE--

Between sips of bitter black coffee, John Whitestone haggled with his contact from the Hezbollah over how much money would be paid for a new shipment of arms and munitions.

The small cafe on a busy street in Tel Aviv had been a frequent meeting place for them to negotiate their arms deals.

Their discussions included the types of munitions and arms that were needed and available. The militant Islamic had memorized his shopping list before the meeting.

Whitestone had access to an extensive number of automatic weapons, short and long range mortars, rocket launchers, ammunition, land mines and grenades.

The Hezbollah, a militant Islamic group operating out of southern Lebanon, usually needed long range rockets to continue their attacks on Israel from the southern border of Lebanon.

Today was different.

Whitestone and Habib, his regular broker for the Hezbollah, were hashing out the details for an important shipment of arms and munitions for the Palestine Authority.

Whitestone had gotten a call from his contact in the CIA to set up this meeting with Habib.

The last deal that Habib brokered for Arafat had ended in a disaster.

The Israelis had seized a Palestinian freighter in the Red Sea carrying four million dollars of arms and munitions that had been picked up from an obscure seaside town in Yemen.

"Habib, did you get any flack after the freighter was seized by the Israelis?"

"Flack?" They thought that I told someone about the shipment. They were going to kill me."

"Why did they think that?"

"I don't know. They had never been betrayed by anyone in our organization before now."

"What did you tell them?"

"I told them that I had negotiated with you for several years and never had a problem. We've done business without anything like this ever happening."

"Well, it was a surprise to me. Do you think that the Israelis knew that the freighter was carrying the stuff or that this was a random inspection of the ship?"

"I think that it was a random inspection. The Israelis know that there are only a few ways to smuggle weapons into Palestine. There are tunnels between Egypt and Palestine, but they're so narrow you can only get so much ordinance through them."

"I agree with you on this one. That was a substantial order we brokered. I thought that the only way we could get that shipment to Arafat was by ship."

"That wasn't a good day for us. Listen, Arafat's people are putting a lot of pressure on us to re-supply them. Is there anything you can do for them?"

"It's going to cost you. I can't just rub two sticks together and make your shopping list happen. What do they want this time?"

"They want the same things they ordered the last time, plus they want some long-range mortars."

"That's great, long range mortars. They're not easy to get Habib. How many are they looking for?"

"Fifty."

"Fifty? Are they dreaming?"

"Sometimes, I think so. What's it going to cost them?"

"Double for the mortars, thirty- percent premium for the stuff they ordered the first time around."

"You're brutal. How am I supposed to explain those kinds of prices to them?"

"Tell them that it wasn't you fault that the Israelis seized their ship. Why don't you tell them that it wasn't any of your people that leaked information about the shipment?

"Why don't you suggest that maybe it was one of Arafat's own security people inside the Palestinian Authority who tipped off the Mossad?"

"I'm not going there with that one. I'll tell them that they'll have to pay extra to get the delivery this quickly.

"When will you be able to get the special order to the wharf in Yemen?"

"Best case would be three weeks. I can't get it to them any sooner than that."

Normally, negotiations between these high-powered arms brokers would last for hours. During the past four years, Whitestone had learned how to haggle with the most difficult of the brokers.

They would never trust him, but they certainly wouldn't trust the transaction if there weren't the normal and expected insults, declarations of lack of trust and the feigned indignant posturing.

Their ancestors had honed the trading and bartering skills of these current day brokers.

Sellers chronically complained that they were giving goods away, while buyers whined that sellers wanted far too much money for inferior merchandise

This flow of attack and counter-attack was a familiar dance between Whitestone and Habib.

There wasn't a merchant in the Arab world that would ever accept a first or second offer for his merchandise.

Today, there was a greater sense of urgency than a few months ago.

Every faction in Palestine was screaming for weapons and ammunition. The Hamas, Islamic Jihad Infidel, Tanzim militias and the Palestine security forces wanted the ordinance.

They were engaged in a war with Israel.

Despite repeated attempts by the United Nations and the League of Arab Nations, there were still no signs of peace on the horizon for the region.

"You're getting a great deal, my friend." Whitestone said.

"Thirty shoulder rocket launchers, two hundred rockets, four hundred Kalisnakov automatic rifles, twenty cases of ammo and the mortars. For four and a-half million? You're stealing money from me!"

They needed the weapons soon. They had to punish the Israelis. Whitestone knew it and so did Habib. Whitestone could see it Habib's dead brown eyes.

"All right, all right. But we can't pay you any more than three million five. We don't have the money." Habib said, lying in his teeth.

"You're tough, Habib. My final offer. Four million, two-fifty Take it or leave it."

Habib hesitated. He had to go back to his people with a deal. Arafat was putting too much pressure on his brothers in the Hezbollah to buy the weapons. He could not fail.

"Three million, seven-fifty. That's all I can do." He said, while throwing his hands in the air in mock despair.

"I'm walking, Habib. I'm not going to give this stuff away for nothing. I need to make something on this deal."

Whitestone got up from the table.

"By the way, Habib, you pick up the tab for the coffee and bagels."

"Wait. All right, I'll pay four million. They will kill me when they find out how much I've paid." Habib said finally.

Whitestone walked back to the table and sat down.

"I don't want you to get killed by your own people. Four million American dollars. Do we have a deal?"

"Yes. Agreed. I'll wire the money to your account tomorrow morning."

"When I receive confirmation of the deposit, I'll make arrangements for your people to pick up the shipment at the regular place. The wharf in Yemen."

"Okay. We'll be in touch with you again soon."

"I'm sure that you will, Habib." Whitestone said, shaking hands before leaving the crowded cafe.

Calmly positioned at the Queen Anne writing desk, Leanne sighted the target area immediately in front of the cafe, fingered the sensitive trigger and waited for the target to appear.

The front of the cafe was getting congested.

Mostly teenagers were waiting in line now to get in.

She would have to make a quick decision to identify the target. There wouldn't be much time to get off a clean shot with so many people milling around the front door.

Perhaps only a second or two.

The next ten minutes tested her control and recognition abilities. Each time a man had walked out of the restaurant, she had to decide in a millisecond if he was the target.

Even though she had been sighting the target area for only a few minutes, the tension and suspense waiting for the right target to appear made it seem like an eternity.

Again, the front door opened.

This time, two men walked onto the sidewalk.

She recognized the taller man as the target immediately.

Wait.

Both men had stopped and were shaking hands.

The tall man's head was in the crosshairs.

Leanne started to squeeze...

Suddenly, there was a huge explosion in front of the restaurant. Instinctively Leanne ducked, as the force of the blast blew out the windows in her room and showered her with glass.

She looked onto the street.

Leanne saw the fires that were raging from mangled shells of cars and smelled the dense acrid smoke that filled the street.

She wasn't able to see what was happening in front of the restaurant.

As the smoke slowly cleared, she saw the extent of the devastation on the street below.

There was a gaping hole in the front of the restaurant.

Bodies were strewn in senseless patterns, some piled on top of each other.

People were screaming as they ran for safety. Some stood dazed with blood streaming down their faces.

Without discrimination, the shards of glass and shrapnel had become millions of lethal weapons cruelly slicing into men, women and children in this narrow, congested killing field of fire.

The street had become a ravaged war zone leaving death, destruction and despair.

Leanne hadn't fired her weapon.

The explosion had taken her shot away.

Peering intently through the scope, she tried to see the front of the restaurant.

Small shiny cars had been transformed into crumpled and blackened metal caricatures that were now barricading the street.

Trams had become grotesquely twisted shells tossed randomly into the street.

Where was the target?

Sirens from police and fire rescue trucks could be heard wailing within blocks of the blast.

Panicked survivors were screaming and crying as they ran from the scene.

Rescue teams would be too late for many, but soon enough for some.

Following the first rescue unit to arrive, she watched as a young female medic frantically, but carefully, felt for pulses.

Still, no sign of the target.

There was blood everywhere.

Medics picked up amputated limbs hoping they belonged to survivors.

Leanne saw a hand reaching out for someone, anyone. It sat severed, with its entrails in a small pool of blood.

A small child seemed to look for her mother with eyes that would never see again.

Two young Israeli medics had become veterans since attending to victims of the violence escalating between them and the Palestinians. They knew the dead with a knowing glimpse of the eyes.

The eyes of the dead.

The eyes that waited no longer.

The eyes that cried for their lids to be closed and to sleep until the Day of Judgment.

Was she seeing the impossible?

A medic was gesturing urgently for help.

A second one hurried over.

Together, they rolled a mangled corpse off a man pinned underneath it.

Was the man moving?

No.

Was it the target?

It was difficult to tell.

How could he possibly survive this?

He was standing so close to the blast.

Leanne watched as the medics applied tourniquets to stem the blood gushing from severed arteries in his upper thighs.

She couldn't see the man's face.

They were blocking her view.

A third medic, carrying a stretcher, was jogging through bodies scattered on the street to get to them.

While one medic held the plastic containers filled with saline fluids, the other two lifted the victim onto the gurney.

It was him!

Leanne got a quick glimpse of him as he was being taken to the ambulance.

She wasn't able to get a shot off because there were too many people in the way.

With it's sirens screaming, the ambulance slowly weaved through the debris-laden street taking Whitestone to safety.

He was gone.

She had failed her mission.

--TEN--

On such a clear day, the view from high up on the south side of the gleaming skyscraper was spectacular.

In the distance, he could see the Statue of Liberty and the Veranzano Bridge that spanned from Brooklyn to Staten Island for over two miles.

He gazed disinterestedly at the glistening New York harbor waters flowing lazily through The Narrows and winding down around the upscale Bay Ridge section of Brooklyn and into the Atlantic Ocean.

Right now, he could care less about the panoramic view or how slowly the tides were flowing or whether the tides were coming in or going out.

He was much more concerned with the results of the missions in Florence and Tel Aviv. He had taken some calculated risks to execute the plan, but he felt that they had been necessary.

He felt no animosity towards Whitestone or Maxwell. They had turned out to be excellent recruits and they did a good job running the field operations of the arms business.

There was just too much going on in the investment banking department at Montieff, Lancaster.

The operation that he had put in place had been another stroke of genius by a master manipulator.

The agents didn't know anything about how he had infiltrated the large investment banking and brokerage firm or how he had managed to perpetrate such a massive fraud on the investing public without any of the regulatory agencies knowing about it.

His problem was that they knew him. He had been their supervisor when he was deputy director of counter-intelligence and ran an authorized covert operation to gather intelligence in the Middle East.

They had been operating undercover as free lance arms brokers with false Canadian passports.

After two years, when they had established a network of informers within various Islamic militant factions, the agency decided to shut down the operation.

He was responsible for wanting to continue the arms operation without telling the agency about it.

The operation had made a great deal of money for the agency and had helped to fund other covert operations.

Each of them had made their own money by skimming some of the profits for themselves without the agency seemingly knowing anything about it.

He knew that other field agents in the past had run small operations for themselves without approval from their Director.

It seemed to many of the agents that the agency suspected they were freelancing on the side but tacitly allowed them to do it.

It was his idea to restart the business with their own money since they had made a few million dollars during the two-year operation.

He approached Whitestone, Maxwell and Ranfield with the concept. Every one of them liked the idea.

They could make much more money by themselves if they were able to finance the deals with their own money rather than by being funded by the agency.

He briefed them on a plan for the business.

They could operate from any of the Consulates or Embassies in Europe and the Middle East. He would manage and coordinate the business from the states.

The militants and terrorists seemed to have an insatiable appetite for all kinds of ordinance. They were to act as brokers for the weapons. Unlike the authorized operation, he planned to stockpile inventory in different countries around the Middle East.

That would create greater profit margins.

He would also be responsible for the logistics and administration of the business. The arms operation was going to be a strictly offshore venture without any ostensible connection to the United States.

The profits would be split evenly among themselves. Each partner would have their own secret bank account in certain small countries that had little, if any, banking regulations.

Their money would be safe and secret.

The three agents liked the profit sharing arrangement and the ability to keep the money tax-free. If they ever wanted to bring the money back to the states, they knew how to do it without getting caught.

The operation would be their secret. No one else would know about the deal. They agreed unanimously to go along with it.

Each of them was trained in the tactics used to bring money from illegal operations outside the country into the banking system.

Several laws, like the Bank Security Act, were designed to counter those attempts to launder billions of dollars into the United States.

They had experienced tracking down money launderers in the drug business, but they couldn't prevent all of the drug money getting into the states because there were so many ways to do it.

They learned that laundering money into the United States was relatively easy to do, because the concept was so simple.

Money launderers were converting the dirty, illegal money into tangible assets. The cash was used to buy gold, diamonds, expensive works of art, fine wines, and other expensive assets.

Then, they were shipped to the United States and sold to legitimate dealers for clean currency.

They were familiar with the Financial Crimes Enforcement Network, which had been established in 1990 to detect money laundering in banks and other financial institutions.

They discovered that the operators trying to bring serious money into the states were avoiding the domestic banking system and creating new inventive ways to physically smuggle the money into the country without detection.

The problem for the enforcement agencies was the volume of money successfully laundered through the United States was in the trillions of dollars.

After running the operation smoothly for several years, he decided to resign.

He had dreamed up a new operation that was going to make the profits from the arms business look like chump change.

He felt that the three of them would be able to run the business by themselves and more importantly, he wanted to get some distance from them.

He needed the time and space to pursue his next objective.

After he resigned, Ranfield was brought back from field operations and promoted to his former position.

Ranfield was going to run the arms operation from his desk at Langley.

He didn't want to be involved with the arms operation anymore, because he needed to spend all of his time to pull off what he hoped to be the biggest fraud in the history of Wall Street.

The object of this next mission was to accumulate billions of dollars by surreptitiously gaining control of a major Wall Street firm.

He had devised a business plan that was flawless, but he needed a support team in order to execute it properly.

He needed an organization that would enable him to build an international empire.

There was a lot riding on what was supposed to happen. Failure could possibly mean the loss of his fortune or worse, his death.

The cell phone rang. He glanced at the desk clock. It was time for the report.

"Yes." He said quietly.

"European project is done. Yesterday morning. No complications."

"And the other one?"

"He's still with us?"

"Why? What happened?"

"Just as he was leaving the cafe, a car bomb blew up. He was seriously injured. We're going to bring him back here for surgery tomorrow."

"Where and when?"

"He's scheduled to land at Dulles at ten in the morning. They'll be bringing him to Bethseda Naval."

"Any security on him?"

"No."

"How 'bout our observer?"

"No problem. Left the scene heading back."

"All right. I'll take care of things from here now. You understand?"

"Yes."

The car bombing didn't surprise him. That particular shopping mall was very popular and always packed with civilians in the early evening.

A suicide bomber would be able to take out hundreds of unsuspecting shoppers.

Violence between the Palestinians and the Israelis had been escalating for months with no end in sight. Earlier attempts to co-exist peacefully failed, due to a longstanding hatred and distrust for each other.

What did surprise him was the timing of the blast.

That was an unfortunate coincidence.

The mission should have been completed, but it wasn't. Now he's alive and he is still a problem.

He was determined to solve the problem on Sunday, on the day of the Hospice Cup yacht race in Annapolis.

There would be plenty of time to get up to Bethseda Hospital and back before the start of the race.

He punched the buttons on the cell phone, starting with an international area code.

After a single ring, a voice answers with a faint accent, "Yes?"

"Cobra. We have complications."

"Yes?"

"I may have a problem with one of our assets. She's loose."

"Where is she?"

"Coming back to New York. We need to tie that up."

"Has she been contacted?"

"No."

"We'll have someone waiting for her."

"We can't let the pigeon fly away."

"I'll take care of it. Are you still planning a vacation?"

"Yes."

"Soon?"

"Yes. It's starting to get stormy here."

--ELEVEN--

Around ten-thirty on the following morning, after the weekly investment department meeting had ended, Maxwell received a phone call from the long time Manager of Hamilton, Montague's Wire Transfer Department.

"Good morning, Brent, it's Kevin O'Reilly." He said with the distinctive accent of a first generation New York City Irishman.

"Kevin, how are you?'

"Just fine, just fine. I want to convey my condolences on your loss. We just received the office memo just a few minutes ago telling us about your brother and I wanted to call you as soon as possible to tell how sorry I was when I saw it."

"Thanks very much. I appreciate your concern."

"The memo said that he was a Navy pilot. I was in the Navy, too, but I only got to seaman first class. That's quite an honor to be buried at Arlington, Brent. My wife and I will be going down to the funeral next Saturday."

"That's very thoughtful of you, Kevin."

"That's the least we can do, Brent."

"Thank you."

"Brent, there's one other thing that I have to tell you about. It happened just a few minutes ago and I thought that I should get this to you as soon as possible."

"What is it?"

"At ten twenty-one this morning, a Credit Swiss bank in Zurich wire transferred thirty-six million, two hundred and forty-three thousand, five hundred and seventy-six dollars and seventeen cents into your personal brokerage account."

"What did you say?!"

"I said that over thirty-six million dollars was deposited into your personal account here at the firm."

Maxwell was practically speechless.

"This is incredible. You said it came from a Credit Swiss bank?"

"Yes. It came from a branch office in Zurich."

"Thirty-six million dollars. Who authorized the transfer?"

"There wasn't any individual's name on the transfer instructions, Brent. Since the amount was so large, I thought that you would want to know about it right away."

"Of course, I appreciate that, Kevin. I have no idea who would send that kind of money to me."

"All I can tell from the transfer instructions is the amount of transfer, when it was sent and which bank it came from. We can tell from the routing number that it was a Credit Swiss bank in Zurich."

"And there wasn't any corporate or individual's name on it?" "No, sir. Just the bank's number. That's all I know, Brent. Like I said, I wanted you to know about this right away."

"You did the right thing, Kevin. Thanks."

Brent sat back and tried to absorb the news.

Someone just gave him thirty-six million dollars. Thirty-six million dollars was very serious money.

Who in the world would have thirty-six million dollars and why would they give it to him?

His parents had that kind of money. He had talked with them right after Devine had left his office the day before. That was a rough conversation for all of them.

His mother was devastated by the news.

She only had the two boys.

Jeff wasn't the black sheep of the family by any means. He was the challenging one, who loved adventure and lived his life to the fullest.

Every day was special for Jeff and exasperating for his parents, especially his mother who loved him dearly.

His father was equally distraught.

Although Jeff decided to follow his instincts and join the CIA, his father had a special bond with Jeff because they had both been Navy pilots.

Were his parents somehow connected to this money?

Nothing was mentioned about it during their conversation. They would have said something about it to him.

The timing of the wire transfer bothered Maxwell.

This was so close to Jeff's death, but he couldn't make the connection.

He wondered about what was happening to him.

A Director in the CIA tells him that his brother was murdered for no apparent reason and now his wire transfer clerk tells him that thirty-six million dollars has been deposited into his account.

There must be a connection between Jeff's death and the money. This couldn't be just a coincidence.

There was no such thing as coincidence in the intelligence community.

Jeff had told him that.

Angie, his secretary, interrupted his thoughts.

"Brent, you have a long distance call from Zurich. There is a gentleman on the line. His name is Werner, Hans Werner. He says that he is in charge of the trust department at Credit Swiss Bank."

This is odd, Maxwell thought. A phone call from the bank so soon after the money had been transferred to his account.

Things have happened so quickly since he had learned about Jeff's killing.

Maybe he would find out who was behind all of this.

"Angie, put him through, please."

Maxwell picked up the phone as soon as the connection was made.

"Hello, this is Brent Maxwell."

"Yes, good morning, Mr. Maxwell. This is Hans Werner. I am with the Credit Swiss Bank here in Zurich. I am in charge of the Trust Department. On behalf of Credit Swiss bank, and myself we extend our deepest sympathies on the loss of your brother."

"My brother? You knew Jeff? How did you know him?"

"Mr. Maxwell, your brother was a client of our bank. In 1996, he retained the attorneys in our bank's trust department to establish a trust fund for him."

"A trust fund? I don't know how much you know about Jeff's financial affairs, Mr. Werner, but Jeff really didn't need to establish a trust fund with your bank."

"I can assure you, sir, that I know very little about your brother's financial affairs.

"We did not manage his assets."

"We were retained by your brother to establish the trust and act as custodians for the assets he deposited periodically in the trust."

"That seems odd, Mr. Werner, because my brother currently has several trust funds in his name in custody with our family's bank, Chase Manhattan in New York City."

"Mr. Maxwell, I really don't know why your brother retained Credit Swiss Bank instead of Chase Manhattan. He expressed his wishes to our legal staff and they prepared and executed the necessary documents."

"I still don't understand why he did that."

"Nor do I, Mr. Maxwell. However, he did indicate that his business necessitated his staying in Europe for extended periods of time. Perhaps, he felt the need to deal with a bank that was closer to his business activities than to your family's bank."

Maxwell wondered what the trust officer meant about Jeff's business activities.

He couldn't be referring to his position in the agency.

Jeff wasn't making the kind of money that would fund a trust with thirty-six million dollars.

"Did my brother indicate in what type of business he was engaged?"

The trust officer thought it was strange that this man would be questioning him about his brother's business. Certainly, he should know what his brother did for a living.

There must have been a reason for his client to keep his financial affairs confidential. Obviously, he didn't want his family to know what he was doing.

The bank official had dealings with hundreds of foreigners who had established relationships with his bank.

Many were legitimate businessmen, but many were criminals who were parking money in their bank accounts.

"No, he did not. Whatever it was, it seemed to be highly successful, don't you think?"

Maxwell thought that the phrase "highly successful" was a gross understatement for someone like Jeff, who was on the government payroll, to accumulate thirty-six million dollars.

He was beginning to get worried about what Jeff had been doing in Europe and why he hadn't told his family about it.

"Excuse me, Mr. Maxwell, are you still on the line?"

"Sorry, I was just thinking about something."

"Of course, I understand. However, I must continue to discharge my duties as the custodian of this trust."

"Certainly, please continue."

"Under the terms and conditions of the trust, your brother Jeffrey Maxwell designated you as his sole beneficiary upon his death."

"Only me? He didn't include my parents?"

"You are his sole beneficiary. We transferred the funds earlier this morning immediately after we were notified by phone of your brother's death yesterday by his attorney, a Joseph Sullivan, a senior partner with Blackwell and Reed, in New York City."

"What? Joe Sullivan called you?"

"Yes, Joseph Sullivan. Is there something wrong?"

Maxwell thought that it would be better to talk with Joe directly, rather than with this trust officer. He wondered what the connection was between Joe, Jeff and the money.

"No, no, please go on."

"Pursuant to the instructions in the trust document, we have wire transferred all the assets from your brother's trust account to your personal account with Hamilton-Montague."

"I was notified about that transaction a few minutes ago."

"We received confirmation of the transaction at ten thirty-one Eastern Standard Time this morning, four thirty-one in the afternoon our time.

"Furthermore, your brother insisted that while he was alive the existence of the trust and the financial transactions in the trust must not be disclosed to anyone, including you.

"Well, I certainly didn't know anything about this until you called. The deposit came as a complete surprise to me. Up until this conversation, I had no idea who had sent this money to me."

"We acted on your brother's instructions. They were quite explicit. He empowered the bank to act merely as a custodian and administrator of the trust."

"So, you didn't manage any of his assets?"

"That is correct. He also instructed us that he did not want us to send him the usual quarterly statements concerning the value of the assets in the trust."

"Did he tell why he didn't want them?"

"No, he did not."

Maxwell began to realize how carefully Jeff had built a wall of secrecy around this mysterious trust of his.

He wouldn't even let the trust officers at Credit Swiss manage his assets. At least he could have allowed them to invest the money in short-term money market funds.

He had been very cautious setting up this trust.

These unusual instructions not to manage his assets and not to send statements were designed to avoid detection.

This was meant to be kept secret from day one. Maxwell wondered about the connection between the secret account and his murder.

Was Jeff murdered to gain control of his money?

Did someone stumble onto the existence of the account and then decide to steal Jeff's money?

That might be one possibility, but there were too many unanswered questions at this point to make any definitive conclusions.

"Mr. Werner, considering the value of the assets that were in the trust, don't you think that it was highly unusual that my brother didn't even want to earn interest on his money?"

Werner was sitting in his office three thousand miles away waiting for this question from his client's brother.

This American is an investment banker.

He understands money and he doesn't understand why his brother chose not to invest in short-term funds.

"Mr. Maxwell, I feel that I can not comment on that. I do not know why your brother chose this option."

Werner thought that Maxwell knew why.

His brother didn't want to draw attention to the existence of the account.

Werner wanted to end this conversation.

There was no sense in continuing this any longer.

"Our last responsibility will be to terminate the trust. Our attorneys have begun to draw up the termination documents. As soon as they are finished, we will send them to you.

"Have you any further questions?"

"Yes. I do. When did my brother retain your bank to set up this trust?

"Let me see. Your brother signed the retention papers on July 15, 1996. The trust documents were executed here in the Zurich office the following month on August 20. 1996."

"Did he fund the trust then?"

"Yes."

"What was the amount of the initial funding?"

"One million American dollars."

"Thirty-six million dollars is a great deal of money to accumulate in five years, Mr. Werner. Do you have a record of the transactions in the trust account?"

"Yes, I do. Would you like me to send you the quarterly statements and the list of transactions?"

"Yes, I'd like to see them. Do you have them on file?"

"Of course. I will fax them to you as soon as our conversation is finished."

"Thank you for calling, Mr. Werner, you've answered some of my questions, but you've also raised some others."

"I am glad to have been of service. You might want to contact your brother's attorney for more information. I have his phone number here if you need it. Please contact me anytime if you have any additional questions concerning the trust."

"Thank you, Mr. Werner, for your help."

What was going on?

Where did Jeff get that kind of money?

Why did he create a secret trust in Zurich when his family trust money was being managed by Hamilton-Montague?

Maxwell wondered why the trust people at Credit Swiss were merely acting as custodians, not as money managers. Jeff didn't want anyone to know anything about the trust.

At least, he didn't want anyone to know about it until after he died. That seemed odd.

Jeff would have known that a transfer of this much money would sound alarms with the Treasury officials.

This transfer would have been picked up on the radar screens at the Financial Crimes Emergency Center.

Jeff knew about the people at the Center. He and Maxwell had talked about them when Jeff was going through training.

Maxwell had explained that Hamilton-Montague, other Wall Street firms and other financial institutions were part of the network that fed information about all their financial transactions into the Center's tracking system.

Whenever a transaction filtered through the system that appeared to be unusual or suspicious, the Center would respond with an immediate investigation.

If they checked on deposits or withdrawals over ten thousand dollars, they would certainly scrutinize this transaction. This was going to command their attention.

Jeff knew that this would happen and had probably counted on it.

But why did he set it up this way?

It must be some kind a signal or a warning.

Maxwell thought Jeff might be trying to lead him to his killer. It would make sense if he ever had a problem with someone who wanted to kill him.

Maxwell thought that this was a contingency Jeff put in place in case someone killed him.

Maxwell needed to call Joe Sullivan, his long-time family friend and attorney.

Sullivan answered his own phone.

"Hello, this is Joe Sullivan."

"Joe, its Brent."

"Brent, how are you. I'm so sorry about Jeff. This was such a terrible shock to all of us. Are you all right?"

"Not really, Joe. I still can't believe this happened. I feel numb."

"I can't believe that he's gone. He was such a tough guy. I keep remembering him playing ball at Virginia."

"Yeah. I know. Joe, have you got a minute? There's something that's come up here at the office."

"Sure, Brent. What is it?"

"I just got a call from a trust officer in Zurich. He told me that Jeff had set up a trust. Do you know anything about that?"

"I'm familiar with that, Brent. Jeff called me about five years ago and told me that he wanted to create a trust naming you as sole beneficiary in the event of his death.

"He said he would be depositing funds to the trust from time to time and wanted keep the trust in a European bank that was relatively close to his station in Florence."

"Did you know about some of the conditions he put in the trust documents?"

"I knew very little about the trust except he put it together with their attorneys over in Zurich. Jeff wanted me to handle things from this end in the event of his death."

"You mean, when Jeff died, you were supposed to tell the trust people at Credit Swiss?"

"That's right. That's all that I was supposed to do. Jeff was concerned that if he was killed while he was on duty, that no one would know about the trust account. He was worried that you wouldn't be able to get the money."

"Doesn't that seem strange to you, Joe? Jeff and I have never needed any money. Our trust funds are each worth over twenty million dollars.

"Why would Jeff be worried that the assets of this particular trust fund wouldn't get to me?"

"That seemed a little odd to me at the time, Brent, but I didn't question Jeff about it."

"Do you know anything about the assets in the trust or where he was getting the money to fund it?"

"No. I assumed that he was putting his paycheck or something into it."

"So, you didn't know how much money was transferred to my account this morning?"

"No, Brent, I don't."

"Try thirty-six million and change."

"What? Forget my paycheck theory!"

"Right. Jeff set this transfer up as a signal. He knew that the transfer would alert authorities monitoring any money laundering activities and he knew I would get involved if he was in trouble. Why else would he create the appearance of an illegal transaction."

"I think your right, Brent, because normally a beneficiary named in a testamentary trust unlike this trust would not receive the assets from the trust by wire transfer.

"I believe that Jeff fingered his murderer by using a wire transfer. Have you gotten a call from the CIA about the transfer?"

"No.

"You will, soon. You can count on it. Has anyone at the CIA come up with any leads yet?"

"No, nothing so far. They said that it could be a retaliation killing. It seems that an Iraqi intelligence agent was killed last week and this could be a reprisal, but I'm not sure that I buy that."

"Why not?"

"Jeff was stationed in Europe. I don't see the connection between Jeff and a Middle Eastern intelligence agent."

"I see what you mean. Did Jeff ever tell you what he did for the CIA while he was overseas?"

"Not really. He was always vague about what he did. He told me that he was involved in secret operations. They were dangerous and I would be put me in jeopardy if I knew anything about them.

"I didn't press him to tell me anything more. I almost forgot. The bank is sending me a copy of all the transactions in Jeff's trust since 1996. Maybe that will help figure out what he was doing."

"Good. Please keep me informed Brent."
"I will. Are you going to the funeral tomorrow at Arlington?"
"Of course. Take care, Brent."

"Angie, I am expecting a transaction report from Credit Swiss Bank in Zurich. Please bring it to me as soon as it arrives."

--TWELVE--

The ringing of the phone pounded through George Wilson's hangover. As the woman next to him stirred, he pushed back the satin sheets and picked up the phone.

The Chief Executive Officer of Montieff, Lancaster grunted into the phone.

"Yeah."

"Morning, boss, it's your wake-up call."

"Okay, give me twenty minutes. And Tony, extra black coffee and a cream cheese bagel for the ride downtown."

"No problem. I'll be right out front when you come down."

Wilson rolled out of bed naked and shuffled into his custom designed bathroom feeling that his stomach was going to throw up the three hundred dollar dinner into his vanity toilet.

He stuck his index finger down into the back of his throat and retched the filet mignon, asparagus tips and cabernet sauvignon into the toilet.

The five rounds of orange schnapps laced with Absolute vodka after dinner was going to take too long to get through his system.

This was the quickest way to get ready for work, although the headache from that much booze would stay with him throughout the rest of the day.

When her boss had closed the bathroom door, Kimberly got up and went to a separate bathroom in the three-story apartment.

Kimberly wanted her own shower. She had enough of his little pecker the night before.

Kimberly felt that it was drag doing him, but as long as he kept promoting her and giving her expensive presents, she would keep doing it.

After an exhausting night of trying to get him to keep it up, Kimberly always looked forward to the weekends.

While Wilson was back with the wife from Friday night to Monday morning, she would be able to date guys she really enjoyed screwing.

Kimberly knew the routine by heart, since she had already been in his trophy room two dozen times before.

After leaving the apartment, Kimberly hailed a cab and headed downtown to work, before George had finished shaving.

The schedule worked out for both of them.

George was a weekday warrior working out with a bunch of the women from the office.

The young single girls were preferable to him because they were more eager to please their charismatic leader than older more successful married women.

On Friday nights, he'd head back up to his family in Connecticut on his Darien estate for a weekend of rest.

He'd get in a few rounds of golf at the club with his regular foursome and take his wife, Beverly, out to the obligatory dinner on Saturday night.

Beverly and George had a working understanding about their relationship which had begun fairly well, considering that this was a case of wealth marrying wealth.

Their families were distantly related to one of the country's old robber barons of the nineteenth century and their marriage continued the pattern of trying to keep their vast fortune in the family.

After a few years of marriage, they began to drift apart.

The commute for George wasn't difficult since he was driven back and forth between Darien and lower Manhattan in the firm's limousine.

He could work from the back of the car with his laptop with access to the firm's wireless network.

The workday for brokerage and investment banking firms in the United States had become longer and longer as markets for trading stocks around the world created continuous twenty-four hours conditions.

George would leave the Darien mansion by five forty-five and came home at ten o'clock in the evening, tired and increasingly indifferent to the insignificant social events in his wife's day.

It got to be boring for him.

Beverly spent her weekdays as a veritable Wall Street widow. As time went by, with George drinking more and more, she really didn't look forward to sleeping with him anymore.

If he had fallen asleep on the ride home, he'd literally fall into his bed without even talking to her.

Beverly started to resent his indifference towards her and his disinterest in what she did during the day, especially with her charitable activities.

It didn't take very long before either of them had any interest in having sex, at least not with each other.

Soon, they discovered that there were plenty of opportunities for sex outside the marriage were far more enjoyable and satisfying than anything they had ever done together.

George decided that he was going to stay at their three-story townhouse apartment on the Upper East Side on Fifth Avenue between Eighty-Second and Eight-Third Street during the workweek.

The commute to work would be shortened by an hour each way and he felt he would have more time to play with his young, hard body, girl friends.

The arrangement suited Beverly just fine.

Several of the young studs hanging around the country club had already started to hit on her.

Beverly was curious as to what these boys ten years younger than her had to offer and whether she had the stamina to stay with them.

What a wonderful opportunity, she thought, since George was away for the entire week, she had a chance to awaken her dormant sexuality.

George was all too familiar with the consequences of leaving his wife alone for the week in the decadent atmosphere of that country club. While playing golf at the Club, Beverly noticed other lonely wives whose husbands were away all week and whose children were sent away to exclusive boarding schools.

They found it easy to be attracted to young men who only wanted to have sex with them.

Wilson would understand that, because he had been one of those young sexual opportunists when he came home for summer vacation.

George probably expected her to play with the boys during the week.

This would be a fair trade-off with her.

Divorce was out of the question, because there was too much money involved and their parents would never have allowed it.

If they did divorce, they knew they would be disowned.

George thought this arrangement would afford his wife a healthy distraction to the current state of their relationship. His wife would be sexually satisfied and feel that someone actually had an interest in her, although only briefly.

Beverly thought the arrangement would work out well because she could continue doing what she enjoyed doing.

She would work on the Boards of her charitable institutions, work on lowering her handicap and get laid at least three times a week with someone who would enjoy her body.

George wouldn't be coming home until Friday night, so she wouldn't have to tolerate his presence for five whole days and four long nights.

No longer would she have to try to interpret his drunken mumbling about the stock market and all those idiots he had working for him.

Beverly really didn't care about his work. George didn't earn the right to be the head of the firm anyway. He just happened to be the family's heir apparent to the position of Chief Executive Officer.

George had become a boring, vane and uninteresting companion for her.

Their attitude towards people who weren't their kind of people was the only thing they had in common.

But, even though Beverly knew that she was a snob, she thought that George's denigrating and repulsive attitude towards less fortunate people was just awful.

George treated them as if they weren't clean. The unwashed masses, he called them.

George was different than his wife because he was hypocritical. Ostensibly he'd make a fuss over people like his employees and the clients of the firm, while inwardly he despised them.

He possessed the same gift of many charismatic politicians who remembered names of people in their family and what they did for a living.

George didn't give a shit whether one of his research analysts had her second or third baby, but the fact that he remembered their names made the employee feel part of the firm's family.

He was a master at inspiring the workforce.

"Morning, Mr. Wilson, how are you feeling today?"

"Are you serious, Mike?" Wilson retorted with the hint of a smile.

The burly doorman was holding the front door of the apartment open for him with a knowing smirk on his face.

Wilson looked awful. His normally ruddy complexion was ashen this morning.

The doorman couldn't help but laugh.

He had seen Kimberly with Wilson going up to his apartment last night and had just gotten her a cab a few minutes earlier.

"Your guest left the building a few minutes ago."

Mike wondered how Wilson could keep up the pace with all these young chicks he was bringing home during the week.

Either he had an insatiable desire for sex or he was popping too much Viagra.

Either way, his little pecker was probably going to drop off pretty soon.

"Thanks, Mike. I can tell that you enjoy keeping score by that silly grin on your face."

"I like keeping score at all the ball games, Mr. Wilson. It's kind of a hobby of mine, especially baseball."

"That's very funny, Mike."

"I'm serious. I'm a big Mets fan. Every time I go to Shea Stadium, I bring my two boys and my scorebook."

"That's great! Mike, I appreciate your concern about my social life." Wilson said, with a tinge of sarcasm.

"Why don't you take the boys out to Shea this weekend? They're playing the Giants. There is a night game on Saturday and an afternoon doubleheader on Sunday. You can use my box right behind the visitor's dugout. Maybe the boys can get an autograph from Barry Bonds."

"Are you kidding? That would be great."

"Good. You can pick up the tickets from the Will-Call window before the game starts."

"You're the best, Mr. Wilson. I'm really going to enjoy that."

"Okay, Mike. I've got to go and make some money."

"You have a great day, Mr. Wilson. I'll see you tonight."

--THIRTEEN--

Tony waited with coffee and a bagel on a corrugated paper tray. He opened the door to the limo and said, "Nothing but the best, George."

He nodded down at the food on the tray and handed it to Wilson when he sat down in the backseat of the limousine.

"Thanks, Tony, this will be food for my thoughts. I've got to draft the weekly inspirational message to the troops."

"Go get 'em, tiger." He said, his eyes full of mischief as he teased George about his Princeton tigers.

Tony Russo wasn't an ordinary driver contracted by a temporary outsourcing employment agency.

The security for senior executives has been beefed up after there were several attacks by highly disturbed and disgruntled investors and former employees against office managers in retail brokerage offices around the country.

Every financial services firm in the United States adopted a policy of heavy security for their headquarter offices requiring photo identification cards in order to enter their high rise office buildings.

Many senior executives at the investment banking firms chose not to have personal security.

Chief Executive Officers, who presented a high profile not only in the investment community, but also throughout the business world opted for it.

Rage in the workplace had become almost daily news. Anger at being fired, demoted or perceived disrespect often ended in tragic shootings and suicides.

Wilson was looking for someone who was more than just a limousine driver.

He found Russo through a friend of the family who was a member of his country club in Darien and often in one of Wilson's foursomes on the weekend.

His oldest son, Tony, was looking for work in the securities business but was having difficulty getting hired because of disabilities he had incurred in the Gulf War.

After graduating from Penn State with a degree in economics and a national championship ring as a back-up tight end on Joe Paterno's football team, he became an officer in the Army Special Forces.

Like many others involved in that conflict, they were afflicted with strange unexplainable symptoms after they returned from the war. Many of the veterans, like Russo, became somewhat dysfunctional and were unable to hold down steady jobs.

Russo was still physically impressive at six-foot, four and two hundred and thirty pounds of muscle. He was an expert in weapons, hand-to-hand combat and managing teams of special forces in combat situations.

Wilson was convinced that Russo's background and experience would make him an ideal candidate to coordinate the security at the firm's offices at Seaport Plaza.

Two weeks later, Wilson hired Russo as Head of Security and his personal driver and bodyguard.

Over the next few years, Wilson and Russo developed a friendship that was unique between a chief executive officer and a lower level employee of his firm.

There were no secrets between them.

Russo knew everything about his boss and for that matter he also knew a lot about the five thousand people who worked for the firm throughout the world.

Early on, Wilson learned that Tony Russo was his own man.

He had a great deal of confidence in his abilities and he was a competitor.

Like most successful college athletes, Russo thrived in competitive situations.

The good athletes learned early in their athletic careers that losing wasn't the end of the world, it merely provided the motivation to get tougher to win the next game.

Wilson had bigger plans for his protege than running security for the firm.

For the time being, though, Russo would continue as his driver, bodyguard and head of security.

Once a week, George drafted a rousing reassuring memo to the firm's employees worldwide usually based more on fiction than fact. Since writing was one of his favorite pastimes, he happily seized the opportunity to provide motivational material to a captive audience.

If nothing else, the messages were entertaining.

Before Jack came on board, with the firm struggling to make money, the weekly exhortations effectively glossed over his incompetent leadership.

Now, with revenues rocketing higher quarter after quarter due to efficient execution of Jack's business plan, he could and would take full credit for the firm's success.

He sat in the back of limousine, dictating quietly into the handheld recorder.

After finishing a few sentences, he'd rewind and review his words of excellence.

George would spend the trip from the apartment to the office creating a masterpiece of inspiration to his captive audience of five thousand employees, most of whom actually looked forward to reading his lyrical slush.

Wilson had the capability to elegantly inspire his employees with an entertaining message of fiction and fluff in a rambling uplifting style of writing.

He convinced them that the company was actually making money and achieving a greater share of the securities business every succeeding quarter.

George thought of himself as an amateur poet and writer with the skills necessary to motivate his employees.

His interest in writing was piqued during his stay at Princeton in several literature classes where he became intrigued that he might be published in the school's literary journal.

Like many other children in wealthy families, George did not have the motivation to work hard at anything. Everything was given to him, so everything he had was taken for granted.

Although he was undersized and uncoordinated, George was very bright.

That much was in his genes.

His father was the Chairman of the Board of a large multi-national property and casualty insurance company with headquarters on Pine Street, only a few blocks away from George's office.

His father was a Harvard man, graduating summa cum laude from the college before finishing Harvard Business School third in his graduating class.

George's grandfather brought George's father into the insurance company right after business school and put him on the fast track.

The sponsorship by the family brought him to the boardroom as the chief executive office of the company by the ripe old age of thirty-three.

George's father displayed executive and leadership skills unparalleled in the history of his family, guiding the company through the cycles of natural disasters from hurricanes, tornadoes and floods that often decimated the bottom line of other property and casualty insurance companies.

His father became legendary in the business by changing the direction of the business from merely being reactionary to the loss of property or life and limb, to encouraging clients to engage in preventive maintenance in their workplace to reduce their potential liability.

The claims rates plummeted, the profit margins increased and the company's stock rose at predictable fifteen percent annually.

His mother attended Wellesley College located just east of Boston and graduated with a degree in English Literature. Some of her poetry and romantic fiction was published in the school's literary journal.

She went to Harvard for a graduate degree, but her ultimate ambition was to go back to Wellesley as an associate professor of English Literature.

George thought that it was his Mother's influence that first got him interested in reading and then writing.

When he was a child, she explained that language was a powerful tool. Although he didn't fully understand it then, he came to appreciate it later when he wrote reams of required assignments at Princeton.

George combined his lack of motivation to work hard with a lack of any drive to accomplish anything.

When he was a teenager, his parents sent him away to an exclusive, outrageously expensive prep school in Connecticut not far from his home in Darien.

Near the end of his first semester and just before the Christmas break, he was expelled after drug paraphernalia was found in his room. His parents appealed the school's decision, but to no avail. George was booted out.

The early heave-ho turned out to be a blessing in disguise for him because he hadn't completed the semester. In effect, there was no record of the incident and no transcript.

His parents rationalized that George was merely demonstrating a temporary period of immaturity while trying to find himself.

Besides, they thought that smoking marijuana wasn't really that serious.

George went home with his parents and toiled away on the family's yacht and kibitzed on the golf course until the following fall. His parents paid the tuition in full, in advance and shipped him down to St. James, another prep school for children of the wealthy in the East Coast.

George's life style in the first year at St. James didn't change a bit. This time he never got caught. There was more action around Annapolis than the landlocked prep school in Connecticut.

There was easy access to sailing, because his father was a member of a local yacht club.

One of the family's boats was in the club's marina located in the old harbor.

Drugs, booze and girls were plentiful yearlong in the trendy Capital of Maryland.

Many of his new friends at school were children of friends of his parents.

He was with his own kind of people.

George liked to write when he was school. The pleasant surroundings and the beauty of the Chesapeake Bay inspired him. At least, that was what he thought.

Mostly short stories, but even some poetry.

Although he had little life experiences to write about, he wrote about his world as seen from the eyes of a teenager.

His submissions to the school's newspaper were rejected. George still felt that he had talent.

In his second year at the school, one of his short stories about sailing in the Chesapeake Bay was accepted by the editor of the school's slim literary publication.

Now, George knew that he had talent.

George wondered, when he was sober, what he was going to do after he left prep school.

His father's plan was to bring him into the business world, but at this point in his life, he really didn't know what that meant.

Long term in the life of a sixteen-year-old usually was limited to what was going to happen by the end of the week.

There never was any worry about money then or in the future. George would always be wealthy.

This wasn't the time to be seriously thinking about what he was going to do with his life.

There was partying to do. Mostly sailing the family's racing yacht on weekend trips down to St. Michael's with a bunch of his friends from school.

They would bring along the girls and the booze and get stoned without any concern for getting busted.

Sailing allowed George to wile away a great deal of time while he attended St. James.

As he became a more accomplished sailor, he had some fleeting thoughts about racing seriously.

He decided to join the sailing team.

Soon he discovered that there was a modicum of physical labor required in competitive racing.

After three weeks, George decided that competitive racing wasn't as much fun as social sailing, so he quit the team.

Four years later, he graduated without distinction, without participating in school activities and falling well below the minimum indices required by Ivy League schools for admission.

His father wanted George to go to Harvard, while his mother favored Princeton. his grandfather's alma mater.

Although his father was furious about his dismal academic record, he told George he was going to send him to another prep school in New Jersey as a post-graduate student.

George would elect to take core courses in science, history and mathematics.

His father informed him that he would exercise his fourteen hundred plus SAT brain to achieve a perfect 4.0 and then he might be admitted to Harvard or Princeton.

It seemed that his father had known that their admissions committee would consider the one-year post-graduate transcript independently of the St. James transcript.

The grade point average, the class standing and the SAT scores would exceed the minimum score for those indices.

The plan worked because George made the effort.

George made the effort because his father had threatened to disown him and he meant it.

He was accepted at Princeton at the end of the school year.

The family breathed a collective sigh of relief, while George looked forward to attending a school that had an infinitesimal expulsion rate.

The opening sounds of the William Tell Overture coming from George's cell phone broke through his concentration on inspiring the thousands of his employees.

"Yes?"

"It's Jack. Where are you now?"

"Going through Central Park. What's up?"

"We have a problem."

"What do you mean?"

"Not on the phone, George."

"I was going to the Athletic Club for a sauna and a rub."

"Forget about it. I want you in here now."

He hung up on him.

--FOURTEEN--

The Boeing 747 looked like a hulking heron as it surged into the skies over Tel Aviv. Leanne luckily sat next to an empty seat in the first class cabin that was almost full.

The flight from Tel Aviv to JFK normally took six to seven hours.

Like other passengers who frequently flew on these long trans-Atlantic flights, first class was the only way to travel.

Leanne wanted to be as comfortable as possible on such a long trip and be able to relax, read and sleep in the wide cushy seats with the extra leg room.

As the plane leveled off at thirty thousand feet, Leanne had already drank her first Mimosa.

She thought that it wasn't a very good idea to mix alcohol with her medications and drugs, but she wanted to get some sleep before she got home.

Physically and emotionally, Leanne was drained.

The assignments had been stressful and enervating.

Competitive shooters use up a great deal of emotional energy trying to make each succeeding shot perfect.

These missions exacerbated Leanne's stress levels since there is only a one-shot opportunity.

There isn't any room for error.

There is only success or failure.

Tension and stress to make the right shot wore a shooter down, even though there isn't any physical activity involved.

The time change from Tel Aviv to New York was seven hours, so she calculated that leaving Israel at two-fifteen in the afternoon would bring her into JFK at nine-fifteen in the evening.

Since the flight time was seven hours and the time change was seven hours, she would arrive in New York at the same time she left Tel Aviv.

Leanne always had some trouble with trying to figure out the difference in the time zones.

Whatever they were, she was going to be tired when she got back to the states.

Her persistent migraine was symptomatic that something was bothering her.

It was her job.

Leanne felt that she had changed a great deal since joining the agency.

Until she started at Yale, her experience had been limited to living on military bases with her father, a career Marine Corps enlisted man.

It was only recently, after five years of active duty with the Central Intelligence Agency and five years as a part-time contract assassin, that Leanne realized she didn't want to do this any longer.

Especially after she had fallen in love with Brent Maxwell.

The horrific memories of the scene on the streets of Tel Aviv haunted her.

It seemed that the moment of destruction had let loose long suppressed emotions.

Leanne had become more and more disenchanted with this killing business.

Leanne had come to realize that her attitude towards life had changed gradually since she had joined the agency ten years earlier.

She was a service brat, a term used to describe the children of parents in the military who move from base to base throughout their careers.

She wasn't a brat in the sense that was she disobedient or lazy, because her father would never allow it.

Her mother was sixteen years old and five months pregnant with her when she got married to her father.

Leanne's mother and father came from a rural area in northeastern South Carolina.

Her grandparents tried to make a living raising chickens on their small farms, but it was difficult.

They spent long hours trying to make ends meet. They weren't dirt poor, but they were close to it.

When her sixteen-year-old father found out her mom was pregnant, he decided to join the Marine Corps.

Their parents offered to have them stay on the farm and raise the child there.

The problem was that they were hard pressed to get enough food on the table for their own families.

Her father figured if he joined the Marines, which he wanted to do anyway, and married his sweetheart, then he would be getting a regular paycheck and his baby would be delivered free at the base hospital.

They got married three weeks later in a small white Baptist church that stood alone on a country road.

Leanne's father enlisted the following day and reported to boot camp the week after.

Her mother stayed home with her parents until it was time for her to drive the two hundred-some miles to have the baby.

Leanne was born on a hot, steamy day in August 1968 at the Base Hospital at Camp Lejeune, North Carolina while her father was completing his basic infantry training a few miles away.

Leanne's father became the stuff of legends in the Marine Corps. Part of his basic training program was a course on marksmanship. His instructors duly noted the uncanny shooting skills he exhibited on the rifle range.

As he progressed from basic training through the Infantry Training Regiment program, his supervisors recommended that he be assigned to the Marine Corps sniper school located on the base.

There was a need for snipers.

In the early stages of the Vietnam War, American ground forces had experienced unforeseen casualties caused by teams of deadly accurate Vietcong snipers.

They caused considerable damage because their primary targets were unit commanders.

It was a mismatch at first.

Infantry units on patrol, armed with short-range automatic weapons and rocket launchers were helpless against snipers who had the capability to shoot accurately from a thousand yards.

The Marine Corps decided that there was a need to neutralize these enemy snipers to not only limit the number of casualties caused by them but also to alleviate the psychological damage that was being inflicted on the forces on the ground.

He honed the shooting skills that he had acquired back on the farm shooting rabbits for dinner until he became an expert sniper.

As soon as he completed his training, he was flown directly to Saigon, and trucked to an area that was experiencing significant Vietcong sniper action.

Within a week, her father was sent on a mission to infiltrate a Vietcong controlled region, hunker down into a camouflage position and hope to detect an unsuspecting enemy sniper.

He was alone on these missions, awake for sometimes twenty-four hours a day, waiting patiently without moving an inch while constantly scanning areas in front of him searching for any telltale signs of movement by his Vietcong counter-part.

Her father was immensely successful in the field on his own.

He recorded several kills that resulted in depleting the number of enemy snipers in the infantry regiment's region.

The deadly game that was played between her father and the enemy snipers demanded incredible patience and determination in unbearable weather conditions.

Detection meant instant death.

After his first few kills, he had lost any element of surprise. Her father, the hunter, had become the hunted. They never found him in that region again.

He was assigned to another hot spot further north.

As he was traveling in a personnel carrier to the command post of his new sector, an enemy land mine exploded under the vehicle tossing it high in the air and setting it on fire.

Leanne's father lay trapped and unconscious under the flaming truck while an intensive firefight was going on. When the fight broke off, both sides had sustained heavy casualties.

He had suffered severe burns on thirty percent of his body as well as breaking bones in both his legs. As soon as they could safely land in the area, a medical evacuation helicopter and rescue team took him to a nearby field hospital.

His fighting days were over.

Once his badly mangled legs were repaired, he would need extensive rehabilitation to walk again with full mobility and without pain.

The burns were another story.

They were extensive.

The doctors told him he probably would not fully recover from them even with several years of skin graft operations.

They told him he was too disabled to remain on active duty in the Marines, even though he wanted to stay on as a sniper.

His commanding officer had a better idea than simply an Honorable Discharge for her father.

He issued orders assigning him to the sniper school at Camp Lejeune as an instructor on limited-duty status.

They sent him back home to South Carolina in time to celebrate Leanne's first birthday with her mother and grandparents.

The act of killing increasingly disturbed her, despite the justifications by her superiors and her own rationalizations that it was only part of the job.

The long quiet times on the trans-Atlantic flights gave her hours to reflect on her life.

Leanne wondered why she ever got into this business.

She believed that she should be loyal to the United States of America.

That's the way she was brought up by her father.

That's what military people believed. They should put their lives on the line for their country.

The agency persuaded her that she would be serving her country and protecting it against its enemies.

They had known her background at Camp LeJeune and knew she would be easy recruit as a sniper for counter-intelligence.

Leanne was in the image of her father.

It was only after she went through college and graduate school that she realized how much her military upbringing had shaped her priorities.

She really didn't know any better, because she had no frame of reference except life in the military.

Leanne smiled slightly as she remembered skate boarding with her boy buddies around the Marine reservation and outscoring them on the rifle range.

She couldn't stand the killings any more.

When Leanne was on active duty in the agency, she knew clearly that there were bad guys that had to taken out, especially those people who had kidnapped our agents.

Acting as a part-timer, she had been given very few assignments during the past five years and none of them involved assassinating individuals.

Leanne wondered what the targets in Florence and Tel Aviv had done to justify direct assassinations. If there was going to be a debriefing, maybe they will tell her.

One thing she knew for certain....she had to get out.

There could be no life with Brent with this hanging over her head.

Leanne picked up the phone from the back of the seat in front of her and dialed Brent's cell phone number.

"Hello." He answered.

"Hi, it's me. I'm on my way back now."

"That's good news. I've missed you."

"I've missed you too. How are you?"

"Not very good. I got some bad news yesterday."

"What happened?"

"I found out my brother was killed."

"Oh, I'm so sorry, Brent. That's terrible. What happened?"

"I still can't believe it."

"Brent, tell me what happened?"

"He was murdered."

"Murdered? That's awful. Where are you now?"

"I'm in the office. There wasn't anything for me to do, so I just stayed here making arrangement for his funeral."

"I wish I could be there with you right now. I hate to see you by yourself, Brent."

"None of my family lives around here. Most of them live around the Boston area."

"What about your parents? Where are they?"

"They're coming back from their vacation today. They were with my aunt and uncle down on the Outer Banks. They'll be going to the house in New Hyde Park so I'll probably see them up there tomorrow."

"How are they holding up?"

"They are devastated. Mom had her moments with Jeff, but she had a special place in her heart for him. I guess she thought of him as her bad little good boy, always getting in some trouble and then working out of it somehow."

Leanne felt it was good that she was able to get Brent to start talking about his brother.

She had never met Jeff. Brent had told her that he worked in some government-sponsored think tank down in Washington, D.C. as a senior research fellow.

Brent had told Leanne the name of Jeff's research organization, which sounded vaguely familiar, but she didn't recognize this one because there were hundreds of think tanks in the Washington area with similar innocuous and meaningless titles.

Brent had also said that he and Jeff were very close.

They were two years apart.

Brent was older.

They had gone to the same schools together, first to Phillips Academy, an exclusive prep school in Andover, Massachusetts and then to the University of Virginia, in Charlottesville, Virginia.

They were both very intelligent, good athletes and good looking, although Brent thought that Jeff was better than he was at getting the girls.

Leanne really couldn't believe that anyone was better looking than Brent.

He was the complete package.

Brent was a big, strong man with curly dark hair, soft blue eyes, high cheekbones and a warm smile.

He was very thoughtful, kind and extremely wealthy.

Brent was great in bed. So strong yet so gentle, he made love in such a reassuring way.

Leanne had never before felt the emotions that she started to experience after she went to bed with Brent. They were so different from her earlier sexual encounters.

Before Brent, she had occasional sex with guys in her regional public high school near Jacksonville, North Carolina and later, up at Yale University in Hartford, Connecticut.

It was simply sex without feelings.

It was very different with Brent.

He was very considerate of her, unlike other guys she had slept with.

He was able to elicit feelings from her that she didn't know she had. She felt wanted and loved.

Brent was able to transform the physical act of lovemaking into an experience that allowed her to feel her natural instincts as a woman.

Feelings that everything was going to all right, feelings that he was there to take care of her and feelings that he was going to protect her.

He did not rush in bed.

This event was not a race to the finish line.

He took his time to help her become relaxed and comfortable. Simply by holding her in his arms, Brent was able to reassure her that he cared for her.

Leanne appreciated Brent's patience with her and his understanding that she needed a lot more time than he did to experience a fulfilling climax.

There hadn't been any declarations of love for each other when they went to bed for the first time.

Neither one of them knew at that point whether they loved each other or not.

Their feelings had been getting stronger, but they were still somewhat reluctant to say the words to each other.

"Brent, I'm so sorry. I feel so helpless just sitting here in this plane so far away from you."

"It's okay, Leanne, I understand. It's just that this all came as such a shock to me. It really hasn't sunk in yet."

"I understand how you feel, Brent. It was so sudden."

"Leanne, I'm so frustrated that I'm sitting here doing nothing. I wish I could find out who killed Jeff. I'm so angry right now. If I could find the bastard that did this to Jeff, I'd probably want to kill him myself."

"Is there anything I can do?"

"No, Leanne. We can talk more about it when you get home tonight."

"All right."

"What time do you get in?"

"I should be there by nine fifteen."

"I've scheduled some extra meetings today. I'm just trying to get my mind off what has happened."

"I understand."

"I won't get out of here until at least eight o'clock tonight. I have a meeting with Henry Ingersoll after the markets close this afternoon. I think he's concerned about me."

"I'm concerned about you too."

"Is it all right with you if I send Victor out to the airport to pick you up?"

"Of course, it's all right."

"Do you want to go out for dinner, tonight?"

"That's sweet of you to ask, but I'd rather have some quiet time with you."

"Well, we can order something in."

"That sounds good to me. I'm a little tired right now and I'm trying to get rid of a headache that's bothering me a little. I should be fine when I get home."

"I'll order something from Georgio's. What would you like?"

"I'm not very hungry right now and I'm sure that you won't feel like eating very much later. I guess something soft that will settle well."

"Let's share something. I'll order their Fettuccini Alfredo for delivery. I have enough wine for us at the apartment. Does that sound all right?"

"That's fine. I'm looking forward to a decent shower when I get home."

"I might have a better idea...."

"Oh, yeah?"

"Why don't we hit the jacuzzi? Doesn't that sound good to you?"

"It certainly does. I'll look forward to that."

"I really missed you, Leanne. I know that it's only been a few days, but it seems like you've been gone forever."

"I've missed you, too. I love you very much."

"I love you, too. See you tonight."

--FIFTEEN--

Brent sat back in his leather swivel chair and recalled the first time he met Leanne. It had happened two years ago.

The Board had approved a multi million-dollar plan to renovate the five floors used by the Investment Banking Group.

They didn't want to spare any expense to make the space look rich and luxurious.

After all, many of their corporate clients were paying millions of dollars in fees to his investment banking firm and they expected the offices to be lavishly decorated.

Leanne had been hired as an expert art consultant to advise the firm what kind of paintings and pieces of fine art and furniture they should be buying.

The world of investment banking required an image of wealth and power. Image was an important intangible asset in the banking business because corporate clients could relate to their success.

The chief financial officers wanted to give their banking business to established and successful firms.

If they wanted to raise capital by way of a new issue or a secondary offering of stock, they demanded the deals to be done quickly.

If they wanted to raise capital by issuing fixed income securities, like corporate bonds, they demanded and expected that the deal be done with the lowest possible borrowing costs.

The fee structures established by the investment banks enabled firms to generate enormous streams of revenue.

An individual investor would find it difficult to fathom what a typical corporate bond offering would bring into the firm.

Two percent of the money raised in a corporate bond offering was a typical fee structure arrangement.

Although two percent seems like a small number, it equated to a tidy ten million dollars in revenue for the firm doing a single five billion dollar bond offering.

The competition between the investment banking firms on Wall Street created a battlefield on which they fought for the billions of dollars in fees and commissions that were generated by the constant need by corporate America for capital.

Investment banks plowed millions of dollars of these revenues back into their research departments, syndicate sales departments and trading desks in order to get thc business.

In any banking business, money is a commodity.

Bankers make their money by netting out the difference between their cost to borrow money and how much they get to lend that money to someone else.

Investment securities in some ways resemble commodities.

They are viewed in the marketplace on a relevant basis by different rating systems.

Government bonds are rated by agencies as AAA, while corporate bonds can be rated AAA all the way down to CC, or junk bonds.

The ratings determine the cost of borrowing for the corporations. In that sense, the market knows how to quantify the value of the corporate offerings.

For this reason, investment bankers are not able to alter the market's perception concerning what the securities are worth in the open market.

Investment banking firms soon realized that they were not adding value for prospective corporate clients.

The days of the old school ties were over.

No longer were five or six firms monopolizing the investment banking business as they had up until the early seventies.

The competition was fierce.

Every firm was looking for an edge to get new business.

Firms invested big money into their research departments, paying millions of dollars to individual analysts to research the largest corporations in America.

The problem was that they happened to be the same companies that generated most of the investment banking revenues for the Wall Street investment banks.

Investment bankers could then add the value-added research service to the marketing efforts.

Corporate clients expected the backing of the firm's research department in order to help raise capital for them.

The old so-called "Chinese Wall" seemed to have crumbed down during the late nineties.

Questions of conflicts of interests by research analysts invariable were raised, as the fighting for the huge revenues generated by the investment banking firms became more intense.

The investment banks bulked up their trading desks as another value-added feature, because the corporate clients of the investment banks needed large, heavily capitalized trading desks to provide liquidity for trading their stocks and bonds.

Additional monies were put into the syndicate sales departments to control the distribution of the new securities to the preferred corporate clients of the firm.

Corporate clients didn't see the small, spartan and uninteresting cubicles in the research departments of the investment banking firms. Although there was plenty of publicity swirling around every ten-million dollar-a-year senior All-American analyst, the investing public didn't realize there were hundreds of interns, junior researchers and administrative staffers who were crammed in obscurity on the same floors as their famous senior analysts.

Analysts had become an integral part of the investment banking department's marketing team.

Their research reports bolstered the price of stock and bonds and responded to the pressure applied by institutional portfolio managers, their own investment bankers and the corporate clients to grind out reports that would keep the stock prices going higher.

Corporate clients rarely made an appearance on the capital markets trading floors.

They weren't very attractive.

The floors were filled with long rows of trading desks with an economic use of the space. Snacks and lunches were often brought to individual's position to allow them to be riveted to their desks throughout the trading day.

Leanne had become an integral part of the marketing effort at Hamilton-Montague, Brent Maxwell's firm.

With Maxwell's investment banking group generating close to a billion dollars a year in revenues, the firm decided to budget forty million dollars to renovate the entire investment banking department.

In order to create the desired image of wealth and power, the Board agreed to spend the money on real assets rather than mere paint and wallpaper.

Leanne Anderson had been selected from a group of interior designers and other art dealers because of her extensive experience and knowledge in the international art world.

She owned her own art gallery up on Fifth Avenue and Fifty-ninth Street and had a network of associates located throughout Europe and the Middle East.

Leanne had impressed members of the Board with her presentation on how she planned to achieve the desired image and the structure of her compensation package.

The plan for the renovation included the purchase of priceless works of art, antique furniture and expensive rugs.

These elegant trappings would create an ambience that would make clients feel a sense of confidence in the wisdom and judgment of their investment advisors.

Angie brought Leanne into the adjoining conference room for their first meeting to review the decorating plans.

"Brent, this is Leanne Anderson, our new consultant for the renovation project."

"Hello, Leanne, it's nice to meet you."

"It's nice to meet you too, Mr. Maxwell."

"Please, it's Brent."

She smiled slightly.

"All right, ... Brent."

"I listened to your presentation to the Board of Directors. It was quite impressive."

"Thank you. I think I understand the image that they want to achieve in your department. The whole concept is very exciting to me. Given the size of the budget for this project, I expect that it will not be difficult to create an esthetically magnificent appearance."

Maxwell was intrigued by her enthusiasm for the project. She seemed to be thoroughly engrossed in the execution of her plan.

"Yes, forty million dollars is a lot of money to spend on decorations, even for this firm, Leanne."

She smiled and then laughed lightly. Her smile was warm and infectious.

Maxwell smiled with her, but he sensed she was laughing at his description of the paintings as decorations.

"Brent, I think you're right. Forty million dollars is a great deal to spend on decorations, but these decorations are tangible assets. The firm isn't actually spending their money. They're investing in valuable works of art."

"I really don't know a great deal about that market. My parents have bought paintings from time to time, but I wouldn't call them collectors. They enjoy the Impressionists, but those paintings are pretty expensive.

"A long time ago, my father bought some of Andrew Wyeth's early works and a couple of Remington's paintings."

"Those were excellent selections. Your father must have an eye for good paintings."

"He appreciates talent. I'll probably invite him down here to the office when you're finished the project. I want you tell me more about the market for these paintings you're planning to buy for us."

"Sure. Any painting by a master will appreciate in value over time. The same principle of supply and demand that applies to your business is applicable in market for paintings.

"The difference between markets for stocks and the market for paintings lies in the products themselves. Stocks are issued by the millions. Paintings are unique.

"In your market, the supply of stocks is almost limitless. In my market, we have only one painting for sale. In your market, the demand for stocks fluctuates, while the demand in our markets grows constantly."

Maxwell listened to her explanation of the markets. Based on her presentation, he thought she would probably be a pretty good investment banker.

He smiled at her and said, "As an investor, Leanne, what would you estimate the firm's rate of return would be on the paintings they're purchasing?"

"That's a good question, Brent, but it's difficult to give you a generalized answer. The paintings are so disparate and so unique that the way to accurately answer your question is to address the value of each painting.

"There is always a demand for good paintings by masters who have passed away. Once the master painter dies, the market can quantify his works."

"So, let's assume that master number one and master number two were equally talented. Let's take two Impressionists as an example. Monet and Manet.

"And believe me, Leanne, I don't know very much about the history of art. I never took any art courses in school."

"I think I know where you're going with this example and you're right. The works of two painters with similar talent, in the same time period and with similar styles will command comparable prices assuming that the number of paintings they have done is about the same.

"Brent, demand always increases for good paintings. On average, the prices for good paintings over the last ten years has increased by ten to fifteen percent."

"Well, depending on the cost of the paintings and I'll use the low end of the range. If these paintings appreciated in value by ten percent annually, we would double our money in seven years."

"That's right. I think that's a pretty fair way to look at these decorations, Brent."

They laughed at the same time.

Leanne's presentation was very impressive.

She had demonstrated her knowledge of fine arts in general and the market for the paintings that the firm would be buying.

Maxwell couldn't help but notice her beauty.
She had long black hair pulled back off her face in a tight French twist. Her high cheekbones and creamy skin framed the oval cat-green eyes that seemed to look right through him.
Once Leanne fixed her eyes on him, they never left his.

Brent felt a little strange.
She had his total attention and it wasn't only for her presentation.

The ringing from his desk phone brought him back from his reverie of Leanne to the reality of his office.

--SIXTEEN--

"Hello, this is Brent Maxwell."

"Mr. Maxwell, this is Jim Devine. I'm sorry to bother you, but we've got to talk."

"Have you found out something about Jeff's murder?"

"No, not yet. A couple of things have come to our attention that we need to discuss with you."

"What kind of things?"

"We received notice from our financial surveillance group that a substantial deposit was made into your account yesterday. We traced the transaction back to an account controlled by your brother."

"I was surprised when I heard about that yesterday."

"We'd like to talk with you about that and anything you might know about Jeff's activities in Europe."

Maxwell did a mental double take.

Why would they want to know about Jeff's activities in Europe? This guy was the Director of Operations.

He should know what Jeff was doing.

"You told me that Jeff worked for you. I thought that you would know what type of assignment he was on."

Devine felt he didn't want to talk about this on the phone. He wanted to have a face-to-face meeting with Maxwell in private.

"We are well aware of his assignments, but we wanted to know how much you knew about them. I really don't think this is a matter to be discussed on the phone."

Maxwell was starting to feel a little uneasy. There was a tone in the Director's voice that sounded ominous.

"When do you want to meet?" Maxwell asked.

"As soon as possible."

"You mean today?"

"Yes."

"Well, let me look at schedule. I've got some very important meetings today."

"What we've got to talk about is a little more important than your meetings."

Devine was getting somewhat impatient with Maxwell. Jeff Maxwell was this guy's brother, but he was also one of Devine's agents. The agency wanted to find out who killed him as much as his brother did.

"Let's see, I can postpone my two o'clock conference call with two of my research analysts. I don't really need to talk with them today. It can wait until tomorrow."

"Does that mean you will be available to talk with us this afternoon?"

"Yes. I can meet with you anytime after two o'clock this afternoon."

"Good."

"Do you want to have the meeting in my office?"

"No. I think it would better if we had it somewhere away from your office."

Maxwell wondered why Devine didn't want to come to the office to talk with him.

"Where do you want me to meet you?"

"I want you to go to the Trinity Church. It's only a couple of blocks from your office."

"I know."

"I won't be there. Be inside the church at two o'clock sharp. You will be contacted."

"Why don't you want to come to the office?"

"There's no need for anyone to know about this, except you and I. Do you understand?"

"Not really."

"There's no sense for you to attract anyone's attention as long as we don't know who killed your brother."

"I still don't understand."

"You'll find out soon enough."

"Isn't the Trinity Church normally closed during weekday afternoons?"

"Yes, but the front door will be unlocked for you."

"All right. I'll be there."

Within five minutes after he had left the office, Brent walked up the worn stone steps in front of the centuries old church on Broadway facing Wall Street.

This was a favorite spot for tourists who could visit the nineteenth century gravesite of Alexander Hamilton located directly behind the famous house of worship.

This seemed like a strange setting for a meeting.

Brent opened the heavy weathered oak door and walked inside the church.

"Mr. Maxwell?"

Brent turned towards the sound of the voice and saw two men standing behind the last pew.

"Yes?"

"I'm agent Ferragamo and this is agent Hombrook."

The two men flashed their identification cards.

Using the light shining through the stained glass windows, Brent verified the agents' identities and shook hands with them.

"I have a question. Why all this secrecy? Why wouldn't you come to my office?"

"Let's just say that it's for your own protection." Ferragamo answered.

"What do you mean for my own protection?"

"There are some things I need to explain to you. It concerns your brother and who killed him."

"How does that affect me?"

"It may affect you or it may not. There might be a possibility that you could be in danger."

"What are you talking about?"

"Mr. Maxwell, whatever I tell you now has to stay between us. Do you understand?"

"Yes, but do I want to hear what you're going to tell me? I mean, is this some top-secret information that will get me trouble?"

"It has to do with finding out who killed your brother. We need to know what your brother might have been doing while he was working for us in Florence."

"I can't begin to tell you how much I want to find the scum that killed Jeff?"

"All right. What I'm going to tell you is confidential. This meeting never happened and you're not to discuss this with anyone."

"I understand."

"For the past six months, we have been trying to run down rumors about a certain arms brokerage business operating out of the Middle East, specifically out of Tel Aviv.

"Intelligence agents in the Alcohol, Tobacco and Firearms have picked up some noise from their informants that Americans are running the business.

"Up until now, we haven't been able to determine whether the Americans, if they turn out to be Americans, are just a bunch of rogue arms dealers working independently or whether they work for one of our intelligence agencies.

"You have to understand that United States intelligence community is very large and diverse. There are twelve different agencies with their own intelligence departments all under the supervision of the Department of Justice.

"Sometimes we don't communicate with each other very well. This situation is different. If these people running the arms operation are intelligence agents from the ATF, or from the FBI or from our agency, there's going to be hell to pay for not knowing about it.

"Can you understand that, Mr. Maxwell?"

"Yes. I can."

"It gets worse. It seems that these operatives are dealing with countries on our enemies' list. Weapons and munitions that are brokered by these people are ending up in the hands of militant Islamics in the Middle East.

"Some of the ordinance has been traced to Iran, Iraq and the Palestinian Authority."

"I don't see what this has to do with Jeff?"

"Jeff was stationed at the consulate in Florence, which isn't that close to Tel Aviv. However, Jeff was tight with another agent who happens to be working out of the United States Embassy in Tel Aviv."

"I don't see the connection."

"We didn't suspect a possible connection until you received the thirty-six million dollars yesterday."

Ferragamo notice that Maxwell's face turned a little pale. He couldn't figure out what Maxwell's reaction meant. He might be scared, but scared of what.

"I told Devine that I was surprised at that. Jeff never told me that he had set up a trust fund."

"When did you first find out about the money?"

"Like I said, yesterday. I got a call from our wire transfer department that the money had been sent in. Then, I got a call from a trust officer in Zurich telling me that Jeff had set it up in 1996. He wanted to keep it secret, unless he died while he was still working for the agency."

"Didn't that setup seem strange to you? I understand that your family is very wealthy. Why would you're brother do that?"

"I don't understand why he kept the trust a secret."

"We understand that Jeff has a substantial amount of money in a family trust fund, isn't that correct?"

"Yes. Jeff and I both have large trust funds."

"Do you have any idea how Jeff was able to accumulate thirty-six million dollars in a six-year period of time?"

"No."

"Do you realize that the appearance of this money might implicate Jeff with this arms operation that I've told you about?"

"In a way, I can see how it might, but you've got to understand that Jeff knew about the banking regulations. He would have known that any transfer of this magnitude would get your attention.

"You've got to remember that he wanted to send the money to me only after he was killed or died while he was on active duty."

"Does anyone else know about the trust?"

"Yes, our family attorney, Joseph Sullivan. I talked with him earlier today."

"Does he know that Jeff worked in the agency?"

"Yes. He's been a family friend for years."

"Do you have any idea what type of work Jeff was doing for the agency?"

"Not specifically. He did tell me that sometimes it was dangerous and that he didn't want to put me in jeopardy by telling me anything about it."

"That was good advice."

"I can't believe that Jeff might have been involved with this operation."

"Why do you say that?"

"Because Jeff was a wealthy guy. He didn't need the money. I assume that you're suggesting that the thirty-six million dollars was part of the revenues from this operation?"

"Yes, that's exactly what I'm suggesting. Where else could your brother get his hands on that kind of money?"

"Well, I can tell you that it didn't come out of any of his accounts that are managed by our firm. I've been managing his money for six years and there has never been any withdrawals from his account."

"Then where did he get the money?"

"I don't know."

"Why didn't he let you manage the thirty-six million, just like he did with his other money?"

"I don't know."

Ferragamo saw the look on Maxwell's face and couldn't help feeling sorry for him.

He could see that Maxwell was having plenty of trouble coping with loss of his brother. The thought that his brother was a bad apple wasn't going down easily for him.

"Look Mr. Maxwell, I know this has been a tough time for you, but we're trying to find out who killed your brother. We think we're getting close to a motive for his death."

"It has something to do with the money, doesn't it?"

"That's a possibility. There's something that I haven't told you about."

"What's that?"

"That agent that your brother was tight with?"

"Yeah?"

"He was nearly killed by a car bomb explosion in Tel Aviv yesterday afternoon."

"Jeff was murdered yesterday morning!"

"Right. We don't know yet if there was a connection, but it doesn't seem to be a coincidence."

"Do you think they might have been working together?"

"They might have. The informers specifically said that one of the operatives worked out of Tel Aviv."

"Let's assume for a minute that someone tried to intentionally kill the agent in Tel Aviv. What would be the motive for a person to kill both of them?"

"There are a few possibilities.

"One, their operation was making a lot of money and a rival dealer wanted to steal their business.

"Two, they might have cheated someone in an arms deal and they were targeted to be taken out.

"Our best guess is that someone heard the same rumors we heard and killed him to keep his mouth shut."

"I have a hard time believing Jeff was involved with this operation. Why would he let himself get caught up in it?"

"We've wondered about that, too, because he certainly didn't need the money.

"The other agent is from a blue-collar family. He might have wanted to get into an operation like this for the money.

"Jeff might have gotten bored. He had a reputation for taking risks that he didn't have to. I mean look, the guy had everything he could ever want.

"The reason he gave for joining the agency was for the action. You know, Mr. Maxwell, there are certain guys who like to push the envelope.

"When you're working in counter-intelligence and you're in the field rubbing elbows with a bunch of crazies, some guys get a real rush. It's exciting for them to live that way."

"I know that when Jeff was younger he would take a lot of chances on the ski slopes. He would do just about anything for a thrill."

"Maybe as your brother got older, he was looking for some bigger thrills."

"You know, as much as I hate to admit it, there was a side to Jeff that made everyone in our family a little anxious, especially my mother. Every time that he got hurt doing something stupid, she'd plead with him to stop doing the crazy stunts."

"We see a lot of guys like your brother in the special operations group. Some of those guys never retire. They just keep going until they get hurt or they get killed.

"They usually don't have any family life. Once they get a taste for combat, they can't let go and get back into civilian life. I take it that Jeff wasn't married."

"That's right, but he had plenty of girl friends. He was never serious enough to get married."

"Yeah, he fits the profile. I want to ask you a few more questions about the trust."

"All right."

"You said, that the first time you heard about it was yesterday. Is that right?"

"Yes."

"And that's when you found out that it was a secret account. Is that right?"

"Yes."

"Do you have any idea why he wanted to keep his trust account secret?"

"I think I have an idea why he kept it secret, now that you've told me about the arms operation."

"What's your idea?"

"I think he kept it secret for two reasons. The first is obvious. He didn't want anyone to know what he was doing, because he was doing something wrong."

"Illegal is a more accurate description for their operation."

"The second is that he created a mechanism in the trust to send me a signal. The money transfer was meant to tell me something. Knowing Jeff as well as I do, he might have expected to be killed.

"Eventually I would find out about his operation and why he was murdered.

"That transfer was meant to be a clear signal to me and to the agency that he was murdered. The killer must be connected to the arms operation.

"I think that your best guess is the motive for the killing. Someone wanted to shut them up because you were getting too close to them."

"I agree with you. We didn't suspect Jeff or the agent in Tel Aviv until the money hit your account. The only way that he could have accumulated that much money was through the arms operation.

"Imagine how much money those guys made. If Jeff's cut was thirty-six million, the group cleared over a hundred million dollars.

"Do you think that there are any others involved with the operation?"

"No, not unless more of our people show up dead.

"We're almost certain that Jeff was involved with gun deals. There are very few ways to accumulate thirty six million in three years, legally. Were these two working together? Probably. Why would your brother be involved? The action."

He was right.

Typical Jeff.

Always looking for something more exciting.

When he was a kid, he'd do crazy stunts water skiing, skydiving and clowning around with his hot air balloon. Like the times he'd drop down into the neighbors' yards and peek into their bedrooms.

"You know, Mr. Maxwell, if there is a killer out there taking these guys out, you could be in danger."

"Why?"

"Because your brother might have told you something before he was killed that might compromise the murderer. You see, the killer doesn't know how much you know. You might pose a problem for him if Jeff told you about his partners in the business."

"But who would want to cover up the operation?"

"The guy who ran it."

"Is that why we're in this church?"

"Yes."

"Do you have any idea who might be behind all of this?"

"No, but we have a few ideas."

"What do you want me to do?"

"Just keep doing what you normally do. Business as usual. You know nothing and you show nothing. You're a grieving brother and you're going to bury him. We'll contact you when we need you."

--SEVENTEEN--

Kent sat at the large conference table in his office poring over the SEC documents delivered up from the Compliance Department.

Montieff, Lancaster had been designated as a target in a civil investigation by the Securities and Exchange Commission.

Several large institutional accounts, including some well-known mutual funds and state pension accounts, had filed complaints with the SEC against the firm alleging stock manipulation and that the firm had engaged in charging excessive commissions.

The complaints read that the firm's institutional equity trading desks had charged excessive commissions on the purchase and sale of newly issued shares of "dot.com" companies in the after-markets of several initial public offerings.

They further alleged that the excessive commissions charged were in reality a method for the firm to share in the huge profits realized by the institutional accounts.

Kent leaned back on his chair, reflecting on the investor mania that had swept through the new issue markets over the past few years.

He had seen the beginnings of it in late1998.

Young entrepreneurs with new ideas for doing business on the net needed capital to ramp up their businesses.

The investment banks realized huge fees by bringing them public and institutional portfolio managers showed staggering rates of return in a single day of trading.

As a global economist, he agreed with the Fed Chairman when he said that the markets had become irrational.

The dynamics in the markets were setting up the future implosion of new issue tech stocks.

Early on, after reading the prospectuses of fledgling "dot.com" companies, it became apparent to Kent that most of them didn't have any products to sell.

Their only projected source of revenues was selling advertising space on their websites.

Kent realized that technology might possibly revolutionize how the economy functioned.

The theory underlying the great expectations for the new economy was that the next generation of technological advances would increase productivity by allowing businesses to become more efficient and reduce expenses.

The Internet had arrived and had become a global shopping mall in cyberspace.

Kent thought the concept, in principle, was valid, but that the applications were still vague and unproven.

In the early nineties, most old economy companies knew very little about how to use technology to improve their productivity.

Corporate America wasn't structured to either learn about what technology could do for their business or how to integrate solutions into the manufacturing process.

By the late nineties, young men and women who grew up with computers and who understood technology and the internet, discovered that Wall Street was eager to finance their ideas.

No one knew if the ideas would result in real businesses selling products or services and making money.

There were too many companies doing the same things. There was too much competition for the same set of eyes that was browsing the internet.

Investors thought these companies were going to be profitable because they had new ideas.

The rush for capital had begun.

Investment bankers foresaw huge streams of revenue flowing into their firms.

Idea people without any business acumen had become multi-millionaires.

Investors in the new issue stocks became millionaires on paper by day trading.

Was this the "Tulip Craze" all over again?

Were investors taken up with thinking the impossible, that prices on these stocks would go up forever?

It seemed that way when several Internet stocks went public in November 1998.

One of them, theglobe.com Inc, soared 900 percent on the first day of trading.

Kent remembered that the performance of that stock probably set off an IPO frenzy.

That's when the plan dawned on him.

A plan, if executed properly, would allow him to gain access to the trillions of dollars flowing through the investment banks on Wall Street every day.

A plan, if managed cleverly, would enable him to divert billions of dollars into his own personal offshore accounts.

There was a polite rap on his door.

"Come in."

It was Wilson.

"I got here as soon as I could. What's happening?"

"You made good time."

"You said it was important."

"It is. Get yourself some coffee and sit down. We have some things to talk about."

After he poured coffee for himself, he sat down at the conference table expecting the worse because Kent didn't look very happy. The familiar scowl was on his face.

"We've got a few problems here, George. The SEC has started an investigation into the investment banking department. They think that we've been somewhat misleading to the public. You know, those research reports that hyped the new issues. They want to find out if the reports were based on proper analysis or just fabricated in order to sell the deals.

"They're also a little peeved with our trading desks. It seems that the traders have had some informal arrangements with our institutional accounts that are irksome to them."

"What type of informal arrangements?"

"You know, sharing the profits?"

"The profits from what?"

"The new issues, George. The traders think they should be getting bigger commissions from the institutional accounts than the usual five cents a share."

"I don't blame them. They should get more than that."

"I can't argue with you on that, George. We've created a money machine for those portfolio managers and they haven't had to do anything except buy the new issues at the IPO price."

"I don't think that the institutions should bitch about excessive commissions now. They made billions on those deals."

"I know, but this kind of problem always crops up when people have lost money."

"Right. We're seeing that on the retail side now. We've been hit with all kinds of complaints, mostly unsuitability, some churning."

"When you take a look at the institutions that have filed the complaints alleging excessive commissions, you'll see portfolio managers and other fund managers who still have positions in internet stocks that have gone bankrupt.

"George, there were a lot of mutual funds that were created in the last three years to invest in Internet stocks. Those funds took a big-time bath."

"I know. My brother-in-law runs Imperial Funds up in Boston. He's had horrendous performances with his technology funds, especially the ones that can only buy internet stocks."

"Your brother-in-law wasn't the only fund manager who got caught up in the rush to create specialty funds. There were hundreds of funds designed to invest only in internet and telecommunication stocks and they have been hammered."

"He's had to close down most of those funds because they were practically worthless."

"Well, guess what, George. One of the institutions that filed a complaint against the firm was Imperial Funds."

"Are you kidding?"

"Relax, George, it's only business. He's got to do it. His Board of Directors probably got on his back for the funds' poor performance and wanted to get some money back for the shareholders."

"That won't bring back the shareholders. He told me that investors have taken out every dollar they had invested in the funds and he didn't think they'd be coming back anytime soon."

"It's ironic, George, that these institutions are suing the firm. We're the same firm that made their performance when they were launched.

"If it weren't for us, they would never have gotten any of the new issue stock in the first place.

"If it weren't for us, they would never have realized those huge first day gains when the stocks were free to trade.

"When investors saw their rates of return, they piled their money into the funds.

"They were stupid to hold onto the positions, but they were too greedy.

"They should have locked up their gains and sat on cash for while."

"Well, do you think that my brother-in-law is going to get any money from us?"

"Normally, I would think they wouldn't, but this isn't a normal situation."

"What do you mean?"

"You and I have to consider that special real estate deal we ran through the firm three years ago."

George became anxious every time he thought about that deal. At the time he agreed to do it, he had never imagined it would cause him so much trouble.

At the time of the transaction, it seemed like such a clever and easy way to pay off some gambling debts without having to sell any stocks in his brokerage accounts.

The size of his gambling debts had gotten out of hand.

If his family knew about them, he'd be embarrassed.

If his father knew about them, he would fire his son as the chief executive officer of Montieff-Hamilton.

"Why would you think that the examiners would even find out about the Northfields deal?"

"The SEC is going to want to see the transactions in the investment banking department."

"I thought that the Northfields deal went through the Real Estate Department."

"It did. We negotiated with the manager of the real estate department when we sold the property to the firm.

"Then, he structured our property into a Real Estate Investment Trust.

"That's when they filed the papers with the SEC to bring it public as a deal for individual investors."

"Do you think that the SEC is going to look into our real estate transactions? Aren't they going to be concentrating on the issues raised in the complaint?"

"Yes, they should be sticking to the manipulation and gouging issues, but I don't want to take any chances.

"Oh, great! So they are going to find out about it."

"They're not going to find out anything unless they really dig deep and you're not going to let that happen."

"I hope you're right."

"Listen, the complaints were filed by institutional accounts, not the SEC. There's a big difference between the two.

"The SEC is acting on behalf of our institutional clients. The investigation will be limited to the charges specified in the complaint, manipulation and gouging.

"A general investigation by the SEC into possible fraud or possible criminal activity is much broader in scope. There would be an extensive investigation into everything we have done.

"This SEC investigation will be limited to the issues of stock manipulation and excessive commissions.

"You're going to give them what they want, George."

"What do you mean?"

"What an idiot!" Kent thought.

If his family wasn't the majority owner of this firm, he'd never be the chief executive officer. If it wasn't for Jack's brainstorm, he would have been fired from his job four years ago.

"You're going to cooperate fully with the examiners. You'll give them complete access to all the transactions on the institutional trading desks and in the investment banking department from early 1997 to now.

"You'll give them access to everything they want to see. There's no need to get them upset by obstructing their probe.

"And finally, George, you're going to admit to all the cozy profit-sharing arrangements between our trading desks and our institutional clients."

"What, are you crazy?!"

"A little."

"Isn't that risky? Aren't they going to slam us for admitting to that stuff?"

"This will create a diversion for us."

"I don't understand."

"It's easy. Give them something. They had to do some work preparing for this investigation. You don't want them to walk away empty-handed, do you?"

"I guess not."

"Right. You want to give them something that allows them to close the case with a settlement.

"George, you'll only have one thing to do, so don't screw it up. You are going to spoon feed the SEC with the informal arrangements that our desks had with the institutional clients.

"They'll feel good about that and it'll distract them from thinking about criminal fraud and embezzlement."

George was starting to cringe thinking about the Northfields transaction again. If the SEC somehow stumbles onto that transaction, he would be in very hot water.

"They'll feel satisfied that they've done their job. It's not their probe, remember?

"This is simply an issue between you and the accounts. When they call you with their findings, you're going to plea no contest.

"You won't admit to anything, but you won't deny anything. Good old nolo contendere saves the day for you, George.

"It's that simple. You'll probably reach a settlement with them and pay a modest fine.

"Oh, then they'll tell you to stop the commission gauging. All you'll have to do is say you won't do it anymore."

"Will this be expensive?"

"Let me put it to you this way. You'll pay them a helluva lot less than you made in the investment banking group."

"What about the stock manipulation charges? Aren't they going to find out about how we were pumping up the stock prices in the aftermarkets?"

"They will find out about the informal arrangements with the fund managers because you told them.

"But, even though you told them about your understanding, it's still going to be hard for them to prove manipulation. Stock manipulation is difficult to prove because the SEC must find that there was intent by the firm and the institutions to manipulate.

"We may have wanted the stock prices to go up in the after markets just like the portfolio managers who bought the stock. There's nothing wrong with that.

"You have to look at how the system works, George, to see how difficult it is to establish wrongdoing.

"The investment banks were virtually guaranteeing big rates of return for fund managers. The institutional accounts got all the stock allocated in the IPOs.

"Individuals get none of the allocated stock. They had to wait and buy stock at four times the allocated stock price in the after-markets. They got hammered."

"But, there's nothing wrong with that. Everybody does it."

"That's right. The whole system of offering new issues had become a game. The winners were the institutional investors and investment banks. They were the only ones who made any money on the deals."

"The individual investors were the losers."

"Right, they paid three to four times more than the initial offering price in the after-markets."

"We priced the stock at some ridiculously low level and opened it for trading four to five hundred percent higher.

"There wasn't any restriction on holding the stock for any time period."

"No. That's because the trading desks needed that stock to be available to sell to the individuals paying the higher prices."

"Are you sure they aren't going to go any further into the other thing?"

"No. If you do what I just told you to do, you'll be all right."
"I'm still worried."
"I know, George, but you're such a good actor, you'll pull it off."

--EIGHTEEN--

The C-130's turbo engines were droning steadily when Whitestone awoke. He felt pain in his legs and he couldn't see. He reached up and touched the bandages covering his eyes.

A hand closed over his and a woman's voice said softly, "Commander Whitestone, I'm your nurse. My name is Lieutenant Massey. You were injured in a terrorist explosion in Tel Aviv. We're on our way back to Bethseda now."

"Nurse, how bad is it?"

"Your legs are damaged. Shrapnel severed the femoral artery in you right leg. We were able to stop the bleeding, but you'll need the vascular surgeons in Bethseda to repair the damage.

"You were fortunate that the Israelis were able to identify you. They contacted us immediately so that we could get you back to the states as quickly as possible.

"How do you feel?"

"I don't feel too much. You've got my eyes bandaged. What's wrong with my eyes?"

"They were burned slightly by the explosion. The ophthalmologist said that they'll be fine in a week or so."

The explosion. Now he started to remember. When he was leaving the restaurant with Habib, he heard the explosion. The force of the blast apparently knocked him unconscious.

That was the last thing he remembered until now.

"There's no permanent damage to my legs?"

"No. You'll need a long stretch of rehab though. You're probably looking at a six-month vacation with the physical therapists."

"You know, I can't feel anything in my legs."

"That's because you've been numbed from your waist down. If you should feel pain, let me know and I'll increase the medication. By the way, your wife and your Director are waiting for you on the tarmac at Dulles."

Whitestone wondered if Habib made it.

That was an important transaction, nearly as much as the last deal they had made.

If Habib didn't make it out the restaurant alive, there wasn't going to be a deal and there wasn't going to be a deposit of four million dollars into the secret account in Liechtenstein.

Ranfield and Maxwell were going to bc disappointed when they found out that this deal wasn't going down.

"Lieutenant, do know anything about the explosion? Was anyone killed?"

"Yes, I heard the suicide bomber and twelve civilians were killed. Some of them were children. These things never seem to end.

"Supposedly the Hamas are taking credit for the bombing. They were retaliating for an attack by an Israeli gunship on a Palestinian security office in Ramallah the day before.

"Commander, it seems that you were very fortunate to have gotten out of there alive. Many of the people who were killed or injured where farther away from the bomb than you were."

"What do you mean?"

"I have read the medics report. They found you lying inside the cafe about twenty-five feet from where the bomb exploded."

"Twenty-five feet!?"

"Right. You were lucky, Commander."

"Why am I still here?"

"A man was found lying on top of you inside the restaurant. He must have shielded your body from the brunt of the blast."

"Do you know if that man was alive?"

"I don't know for sure, Commander, but I can't imagine that he could have survived being that close to the explosion.

Whitestone thought that the nurse was right. Habib didn't make it. It was ironic, he thought, that Habib was killed by one of his brothers in this unholy war from the Hamas.

As the heavy C-130 workhorse descended slowly towards the runway, Whitestone's wife, Jennifer, began to feel more and more apprehensive.

Jim Devine, her husband's boss and the Director of Operations for the Central Intelligence Agency, had told her about John's injuries and that he would be fine, but she wanted to see for herself.

After a few minutes, the plane had landed and taxied over the tarmac to the secure military terminal. An ambulance from Bethseda Naval Hospital waited nearby.

The backend ramp started to drop slowly until it reached the ground.

Two medics from the ambulance walked up the ramp and into the plane.

Soon, Jennifer could see her husband being wheeled down the ramp.

She wasn't ready to see John this way.

John lay on the gurney under white blankets with bandages around his head. A nurse held IV bags that fed fluids into his body.

With tears rolling down her face, she ran to him.

"John," She cried, "it's me, Jennifer. I love you. Everything will be fine."

He reached out to clasp her hand.

"I hear you, Jen. I love you, too."

As she was walking alongside the gurney, Lieutenant Massey said, "Mrs. Whitestone, we have to keep your husband moving. Why don't you come along with us in the ambulance? You'll have a chance to talk with him until we get to the hospital."

"All right."

Once the ambulance left for the hospital, Jennifer leaned over John and kissed him tenderly on his slightly blistered lips.

"I hope that didn't hurt you. I was so worried about you after I got the call from Langley. How do you feel?"

"Not bad, really. The doctor numbed my legs, so they don't bother me and I have some pain in my eyes. That's about all."

There was no need to upset her anymore by explaining how close she came to becoming a widow.

"It's so good to have you home. I'm looking forward to taking good care of you when you get out of the hospital. The kids are excited to see you."

"Where are the kids?"

"They're in school. They'll be finishing their classes next week."

"I guess I'm home for the summer."

"That's going to be wonderful. This will be the first time in years that we'll spend the summer together."

"Yeah, the doctor said that I'd probably be here for a few months. I didn't plan this, but I'm glad we'll have the time together."

"Me, too. Are you sure that you feel all right?"

"Yeah, but I'm still a little groggy."

"Why don't you try to get some rest on the ride over to the hospital?"

"You don't mind if I doze for a while?"

She squeezed his hand and said, "Of course not, honey. I love you. You get some sleep."

Twenty-five minutes later, John was rolled through the emergency room into the elevator and brought up to the fourth floor of the hospital building.

Jennifer thought it was ironic that they had brought John to the fourth floor, because she had worked on this floor for several years as a Navy nurse.

She didn't recognize anyone at the nurse's station as they wheeled John down the hall to his room.

Most of her friends had either been transferred to another floor or had gotten married and resigned from the service.

Jennifer was somewhat curious why they weren't putting John in the intensive care unit at the other end of the floor.

The Lieutenant would know.

"Lieutenant, should John be put in ICU?"

"No. His injuries are not life threatening at this point. He needs a specialist.to take care of his femoral artery. The shrapnel chewed it up."

"Will they be operating on him today?"

"I believe so. They don't want to waste any time getting his circulation problem resolved."

The team pushed John's gurney down the hall until they got to his room. There was a single bed inside.

They moved him to the side of the bed and together they carefully slid him onto the bed.

The floor nurse came into the room and said, "We'll be prepping Commander Whitestone in a few minutes. The surgeons are waiting for him in the operating room now."

Whitestone really didn't get much sleep during the ride from the airport to the hospital. It didn't surprise him that his body ached considering what he just been through.

His brain was pre-occupied with some disturbing thoughts about the business.

He had heard Jennifer talking with Commander Massey as they brought him to his room.

It seemed surreal to him that he was back in the states. It had been almost eight months since they sent him back for some rest and recreation with his family.

John felt fortunate to be alive, but he was disappointed the biggest deal that he had ever made fell through because of a stupid suicide attack by some misguided Palestinian teenager.

He couldn't understand what the hell those kids were thinking about when they strapped on the explosives and walked into restaurants and shopping malls and detonated themselves into body parts.

He thought of his own children. Amy had just turned twelve and was starting to hang around the local shopping malls with other kids her age.

It was hard to fathom that some teenage kids from the West Bank only a few years older than Amy would want to end their lives because a few demented adults convinced them that they would be martyrs to the cause.

There were no comebacks or do-overs for these kids from the refugee settlements. They were gone, leaving their families with the misery of having lost them.

It seemed to Whitestone that those children who chose to kill other children in Israel in retribution failed to understand the consequences of their actions or how their families would be affected by their deaths.

Their families loved them, but their handlers had convinced their children that they were doing the will of Allah. Allah would grant them everlasting peace if they became martyrs.

Whitestone thought it was all a bunch of bullshit.

If he had his way, he'd strap a few pounds of C-4 around Arafat's crotch and detonate the plastic explosive while he was having a meeting with his Palestinian security people in his seedy, shell-pocked headquarters in Ramallah.

Jennifer was standing by the side of John's bed when the Director Operations walked into the room.

"How's he doing?" He asked Jennifer.

"He's a little tired."

"I can understand that. How are you holding up?"

"I'm fine. I was a nurse before I married John. In fact, I worked on this same floor for a few years."

"That must bring back some memories."

"It does. This is where I met John. His buddy was injured in a car accident and they brought him here. John came to visit him often. That's when I got to know him."

"And the rest is history?"

"Yes. We really hit it off."

"Well, I'm glad for both of you that he made it through the ordeal in Tel Aviv. He's a tough guy."

"Thank you. You're very thoughtful."

"You're welcome. Jennifer, if it's not too much to ask, would you mind if I had a few minutes with John, in private? We have to talk about a few things before he gets fixed up."

"No, that's okay. I'll wait in the hallway."
"Thanks."

After the door was closed, he turned to the bed and said, "John, can you hear me?"
"Yes."
"It's Jim Devine. I'm the new Director of Operations. I'm glad you made it."
"Thanks. I heard about your appointment."
"How are you feeling?"
"I feel pretty beat up right now."
"That was a close call, John.
"So I heard. Thanks for coming over."
"You bet. John, I've got some bad news for you, but I wanted to tell you as soon as you got here."
"What's that?"
"Jeff Maxwell was killed yesterday. I realize that the two of you were close friends."
"Jeff was killed? What happened?"
"He was assassinated by a sniper on his way to work. This wasn't a random act. This was a professional job."
"Do you know who did it?"
"No. Not yet."

Whitestone suddenly became less concerned with the operation on his leg. This news meant there might be a more serious threat to his health than the surgery to repair his femoral artery.

Whitestone and Maxwell were good friends. They signed on with the agency about the same time.

When they were rookies, the agency assigned them to a special covert mission to gather intelligence in the Middle East. It was very dangerous work.

They were dealing with mercenary arms brokers who would double-cross them in a heartbeat.

Several times they had exchanged gunfire with rogue operatives who had reneged on deals or tried to steal their money.

This was bad news for Whitestone.

"Do you have any ideas? Was it a retaliation?"

"At first, we thought so, because there had been an Iraqi agent killed the week before. Now we don't think so."

"Why?'

"Because other facts have come to our attention that make us think otherwise."

"What's that supposed to mean?"

"All I can tell you is that we're tracking down rumors that some of our people are involved with illegal arm deals."

This was really bad news for Whitestone. He was in big trouble now. The thought that Maxwell was taken out by a pro bothered him.

He wondered who hired the professional assassin. There were a lot of independent contractors for hire.

This didn't sound like the work of anyone from the Middle East. If they wanted to take some people out, they'd get up close to kill them.

They'd be more likely to ambush a car using automatic weapons firing hundreds of rounds into the vehicle, unlike a sniper who kills with the precision of a surgeon.

"Do you think Jeff was involved?"

"I don't know. I was going to ask you the same question. You knew Jeff pretty well. What do you think?"

"I don't think Jeff would be involved with anything like that. There wasn't any reason for him to mess around with that kind of stuff. He was a wealthy guy."

"I realize that, but I have to find out if any of our people are running their own unauthorized business."

"Maybe that's where the rumors came from."

"What do you mean?"

"Maybe, there's still talk about the authorized covert operation that the agency shut down two years ago."

"That's possible, but our sources say there's been a lot of noise coming out of the Middle East the past few weeks."

Devine decided that he'd refer to the Middle East as the source for the rumors rather than to Tel Aviv, where Whitestone was stationed.

He didn't want to tell Whitestone too much at this point and he wasn't sure that Whitestone was telling the truth.

Devine felt that Jeff Maxwell was involved with some kind of illegal arms operation. That was established by the thirty-six million dollars transferred to his brother's account.

He also thought that Whitestone was stoning him. At the very least, Whitestone had to know what Maxwell had been doing.

They were tight. They were in the arms business together when it was authorized by the agency.

Even though Maxwell was stationed in Florence, he had been communicating with Whitestone on a regular basis.

Devine felt that Maxwell's best friend was involved, but he couldn't prove it.

Not yet, anyway.

"Well, I still have some contacts from the old days when I was undercover. Maybe I can contact them when I get out of here."

"That might help us, John."

"If Jeff was involved, do you think he was killed because of this alleged operation?"

"We don't know yet, but we must consider the possibility. Someone certainly wanted him silenced."

"Because of these rumors?"

"Again, it's possible."

Whitestone didn't like the idea that Jeff might have been murdered to keep him quiet. This possibility narrowed down the likely suspects who wanted Jeff killed.

Whitestone figured that the agency didn't do this.

It wasn't their style to assassinate one of their agents who was dealing guns illegally.

They'd discipline or even prosecute the guy. They wouldn't shoot him.

The rival dealers might possibly have an interest in taking over the operation.

It certainly was making millions for all of them since they had established a virtual monopoly on the ordinance and munitions trading in the Middle East.

They had a lock on the business with the Hamas and Hezbollah. With the tensions mounting throughout the region and skirmishes increasing around southern Lebanon, the arms trading business was booming.

"Do you think the bomb was meant to kill me?"

"It's possible. Why do you think that someone would want to kill you, John?"

"I don't know. It seems strange that the bomb exploded on the same day that Jeff was shot?"

"That's a coincidence, but I don't believe that there's a connection between the two events."

"Well, I thought I might be a target because I worked in the Embassy. The militants have vowed to kill Israelis and Americans. They would consider killing an American intelligence officer a great victory for the their holy war."

"I don't think so, John. If they were going to target you, they'd probably gun you down outside the Embassy building or better yet, they'd rather slam a truck loaded with explosives right into the compound."

"I guess you're right."

"You know what, John? If someone wanted to keep you from talking, they'd make sure that the job was done right. They'd use a sniper to take you."

"Yeah, snipers are more reliable than bombs."

Whitestone didn't like the tone in Devine's voice. The question seemed more like an accusation.

Whitestone thought that Devine was baiting him.

He wondered how much Devine actually knew or how much he was guessing.

It didn't help Whitestone that he told Devine about his contact in the Hamas.

Devine would figure the Hamas contact was an arms broker.

Whitestone had to tell him because he had probably checked out his story with his boss in counter-intelligence.

"John, what were you doing in that restaurant?"

"I had a meeting with my contact in the Hamas."

"Is he one of your informers?"

"Yes. We had cultivated this guy when we were running the authorized operation. He's been a reliable source for us."

"Has he heard any of the rumors about Americans running an arms operation?"

"No. We've been talking mostly about the Palestinian situation, trying to keep current on their security people."

A nurse entered the room with a tray full of vials.

"Commander Whitestone, it's time to get you ready."

"John, I'll see you after the operation. Good luck."

"Tell that to the surgeon."

After a few seconds passed, he slipped into a deep dreamless sleep.

--NINETEEN--

Inside the International Terminal at JFK Airport, Brent's limo driver, Victor, spotted Leanne waiting in line to get through customs.

He waved at her until she saw him.

She smiled and waved back.

Victor thought that she looked good, even after a seven-hour flight from Tel Aviv. She was a very classy woman.

He had known her for almost a year, since the time she and Brent started going out together.

It was good to see Brent develop a relationship again.

Four years was a long time to spend mourning for Tiffany and his two children. They had perished in a horrific head-on collision with a pick-up truck on the Southern State Parkway.

Tiffany had been taking the children to her parent's summer home out in Southhampton for a weeklong visit.

It happened on a rainy Friday evening.

The pick-up truck, driven by a guy with a 2.2 alcohol level and traveling in the eastbound lanes suddenly swerved into the median strip and crossed over into the westbound lanes.

The truck sideswiped a mini-van and crashed head-on into Tiffany's shiny black four-door Mercedes-Benz.

The three of them were killed instantly.

Brent was devastated. He loved his wife and cherished his children. The reality of their deaths had been difficult for him to accept. The accident took them away so quickly that it took Brent months to fully comprehend what had happened.

Victor knew Brent's ordeal first hand.

He had driven Brent to work at his office in Lower Manhattan by six o'clock in the morning and drove him back to his apartment usually before midnight.

Brent had become a workaholic.

He spent long hours at the office and traveled around the country immersing himself into the minutia of the financing business.

Brent became so personally involved with the financings that he had irritated many of his own associates for working so hard on the deals.

They didn't realize that he was merely trying to work his way through his pain.

Leanne came into the picture a little over a year ago when Brent's firm hired her as a consultant.

After they had worked together for a few months, Brent took her to lunch.

Victor had noticed how Brent reacted to Leanne. He could sense that something might be brewing between these two.

Leanne was single and apparently a wealthy young professional art dealer.

Victor felt concerned that women would be after Brent for his money.

He was defensive for Brent, especially after the tragedy that he had finally accepted.

It seemed that Leanne had come along at just the right time. Victor didn't know very much about Leanne's background, but he had a good sense for people.

He had seen enough phonies in the investment business to last a lifetime. He knew good people when he saw them.

Clearly, she wasn't on the make for Brent. She seemed to respect him as a person.

Brent seemed to be the one moving this relationship from a business mode to a personal one.

Neither one of them seemed to be rushing headlong into any kind of commitment.

As frequently as Victor drove them around on their dinner and theater dates, he could sense they were slowly getting to know each other.

There was something about Leanne he couldn't quite put his finger on.

There was something about her that was so different from the other women Brent had dated casually.

Leanne was her own woman.

She exuded an attitude of independence with an air of confidence.

Leanne didn't seem to need anything in her life, including a man.

Victor could hear their quiet conversations in the back of the limo and it appeared, even though she was thirty-two, that she wasn't bringing any baggage with her.

Victor watched as Leanne finally got through the customs line. She was dressed in a plain black pant suit with a white open neck blouse. A large black leather bag was slung over her shoulder.

Leanne smiled as she got closer to Victor.

"Hello, Victor, it's good to see you. How've you been?"

"Fine, thank you, Leanne. How was the flight?"

"Pretty uneventful. I was able to get some sleep after we took off from Tel Aviv."

"That's good. You look terrific."

"Well, thank you, Victor. I didn't want to look like a zombie when I see Brent later."

"Leanne, it's going to be along time before you'll look anything like a zombie. Don't worry, you look fine."

Victor smiled.

He liked the way Leanne's face lit up when she talked about Brent.

She seemed to love him very much.

"Do you have any other baggage?"

"No. All my clothes are in my shoulder bag."

"You travel light, Leanne."

"Well, I really don't need a lot of clothes. I see so many different people on these marketing trips that I can get away with one business outfit and a travel outfit."

"That's pretty smart. Now we don't have to go to the baggage claim area."

"That's always saved me time, especially when I have to go through customs."

"Well, let me have your shoulder bag."

"Thanks, Victor."

"Brent was hoping that I'd be able to get you up to the apartment by ten o'clock. We might be able to make it."

"That sounds good to me."

They walked out of the terminal into a sticky summer night in Queens. Victor had put his VIP airport courtesy parking pass inside the windshield on the driver's side of the limo.

As they got to the vehicle, a New York City policeman, standing on the curb, threw them a casual salute.

Victor smiled. He would salute the officer back, but his hands were full. He thought it was good to have friends in high places.

Victor walked faster than Leanne, opened the trunk with his remote, put her bag inside and opened the limo door just as she stepped off the curb.

"Thank you, sir." She said, in mock formality.

"You're welcome."

After she got comfortable in the back seat, Leanne stayed quiet until they had gone through the Queens-Midtown Tunnel.

"Victor, I talked with Brent on the flight home. He told me about his brother."

"Leanne, I can't believe it happened. I've known that boy his whole life. It's been a terrible blow to the family."

"You know, Victor, I've never met Jeff. Brent talked about him quite a bit, but we didn't get together with him."

"You would've liked him, Leanne. I can't say that he's Brent's baby brother because he's only two years younger than him. Physically, they worked each other over pretty good when they were growing up."

"Brent told me they played ball together at prep school and the University of Virginia."

"That they did. They were both All-Americans in college, but Jeff was the better athlete."

"That's hard for me to believe. I've gone skiing with Brent and he's pretty amazing on the slopes."

"Jeff turned out different than Brent."

"In what way?"

"Well, Brent was a pretty quiet kid growing up. He was very close to his dad and they spent a lot of time together. Jeff liked to do different things than Brent. He was always looking for excitement. I guess Brent must have told you about him."

"He did talk about him, mostly about their playing ball and a little about the times they'd sail together. I saw a picture of the two of them on their parent's sailboat, but it was so far away that I wasn't able to see his face clearly."

"Don't get me wrong, Leanne. Jeff was a good kid. He just liked to have a good time. His parents thought that if he could go through Virginia without self-destructing he'd be okay."

"Well, I feel so badly for everyone in the family and for you Victor. You've really been such a big part of the family."

"Thanks, Leanne."

By this time, they had driven across town on 86th Street and were crossing Madison Avenue. It was a little after ten o'clock.

"We're almost home, Leanne."

"Victor, I hope I can help Brent tonight. He sounded so upset on the phone today."

"Leanne, there's not much you can do. You know, this is going to bring back memories. Are you going to be all right with that?"

"I thought about that on the plane. I'm a little ambivalent about talking with Brent about Tiffany and the children. What do you think?"

"Let him talk it out with you. You and Brent are going to have to work it out at some time. You can't ignore what happened to Brent."

"I hope we can get through this, Victor."

"You will, Leanne, you will."

Victor pulled up in front of Brent's apartment building on Fifth Avenue between 83rd and 84th facing Central Park.

This was a serious high-rent district, although no one paid rent in these parts of town.

Most of the apartment buildings on Fifth Avenue on the Upper East Side had been converted to condominiums thirty years ago.

Now they owned their apartments and these weren't merely one or two bedroom units.

These homes were anywhere from three to six full floors of living space.

Interior designers became millionaires pampering to the vagaries of their rich and famous owners.

Victor carried Leanne's bag as they walked past the security guards stationed in the lobby.

"How you doing, Victor?" One of them said.

"I'm doing well, Richard. How 'bout you?"

"I'm fine. Mr. Maxwell hasn't been through here yet, Victor."

"That's okay, Richard, he should be here any minute."

"Victor, Mr. Maxwell has a delivery here. Looks like dinner. Do you want to take it up with you?"

"Sure."

Victor went over to the desk and picked up the dinner delivered by Georgio's.

The meal had been put in a large insulated vinyl pouch to keep it warm.

When he picked it up, he smelled the rich distinctive aroma of the fragrant sauce on the Fettuccine Alfredo.

"This smells good, Leanne. Is that from Georgio's?"

"Yes. Brent phoned it in."

They took the elevator up to Maxwell's apartment on the tenth floor. Victor followed Leanne out of the elevator into a large foyer and went over and put Leanne's bag on a small Chippendale settee.

"Is it all right to put your bag here, Leanne?"

"That's fine, Victor. Thanks."

"Well, Rich was right. It looks like Brent hasn't gotten home yet. Do you want me to wait around until he gets home?"

"Victor, didn't he tell you he'd be coming home sometime around ten o'clock?"

"Yes, he did."

She glanced at her wristwatch.

"It's only a little after ten o'clock now. He should be here any minute."

"I'll stay if you want me to."

"I'll be all right. You go ahead, Victor. I'll probably see you tomorrow morning."

"All right, Leanne. Good night."

"Good night, Victor."

--TWENTY--

After the door closed, she took another pill for the unrelenting migraine.

It hadn't gone away.

The pounding in her head was also making her feel sick to her stomach.

She filled a plastic bag with ice, lay down on the couch with the bag on her head and hoped she would feel a little better before Brent came home.

Thank God this job is almost over, she thought. This business had become a nightmare for her.

Leanne didn't want any part of it, anymore.

She thought she understood why her attitude about the job with the CIA had changed over the years.

It wasn't that Leanne was immature when she signed on with the agency. On the contrary, she was a well-rounded, well-educated and talented woman.

Her priorities had changed as she went through several new phases of her life during the past twelve years.

Leanne had spent her entire childhood with her father living in base housing at Camp Lejeune, near Jacksonville, North Carolina.

Those were her formative years.

Leanne lived in a community of military families that shuttled through the camp every few years.

Military kids adjusted well to new surroundings and friends because they didn't have a choice.

She grew up in a society governed by its own set of laws, rules and regulations which were far more comprehensive than any state's civil and criminal statutes.

The Uniform Code of Military Justice allowed the armed forces to administer their own form of justice.

Leanne learned about rules, regulations with an unquestioning obedience and loyalty to her father and to the Marine Corps.

When she had left this narrow world to attend Yale, she felt as if she had arrived in a different country.

The agency recruited her in her junior year at Yale when she was twenty years old, only two years on her own away from her father and the restrictive confines of Camp Lejeune.

If Leanne knew then what she knew now, she never would have signed on with them.

It seemed like the right thing to do at the time.

The recruiters convinced her the country needed her. She was a world class shooter and there was a need for shooters to protect intelligence agents during covert operations.

It didn't take long before she fell asleep.

A half-hour later, Maxwell walked into the foyer looking for Leanne.

"Hello?" He called out.

There was no answer.

He put his briefcase down on the imported tiled floor and walked into the family room.

Leanne was curled up on the couch asleep.

He leaned over, kissed her on the cheek and whispered, "Leanne, I'm home."

She stirred, opened her eyes slowly and said "Hello, Brent, it's good to see you."

"I'm sorry I'm late. That last meeting went longer than I expected."

"That's all right, sweetheart. I was just trying to get rid of this stupid headache."

Brent sat down on the couch beside her.

She moved over and put her head on his lap.

"Is your headache still bothering you?"
"Yes, I can't seem to get rid of it."
"Would like something to drink?"
"Just some water, please."

Brent got up and went to the wet bar next to the wall-size entertainment center, poured a scotch for himself and a Perrier for her.
Leanne sat up as he came back to the couch with the drinks.

"Here you are, sweetheart."
"Thanks, Brent."

He sat down beside her and put his arm around her. Leanne couldn't help but notice Brent's sigh as he sat back on the couch.

"Are you all right?"
"No, not really."
"I'm so sorry about Jeff. I wish there were something I could do for you."
"I'm glad you're here."
"I'll always be with you, Brent. I love you so much. I couldn't stand being away from you now."

Brent smiled and kissed her.

"I love you, too, Leanne. It's so good having you with me."
"Do you want to talk about it?"

He downed the scotch and got up to make another one.

"Yes and no." He said, as she watched him top off his tumbler with more Chevas Reigal.
"I'd like to talk about it because I'm really angry about what happened to Jeff."
"I can't imagine how painful this must be for you."

"Leanne, he was murdered! I can't believe it. You know, being in an accident is one thing, but Jeff was murdered."

"I thought about it after I talked with you on the plane. This whole thing is awful."

"The frustrating part about it is why anyone would do something like this."

"I understand. Why don't you tell me what happened?"

"He was shot to death."

"Oh, that's horrible. Where was he, in D.C.?"

"No, he has been working over in Europe the past few years."

"I thought you told me that he was working for a research think tank down in Washington, D.C."

"I did tell you that he worked in Washington. Leanne, there's something that I have to tell you.

"I've never told you before because I wasn't allowed to tell anyone what he really did for a living.

"It's been a secret for a long time. Only my parents and I knew what Jeff was doing.

"Remember I told you about Jeff going to flight school after he got out of the University of Virginia."

"Yes."

"Well, he spent six years as a fighter pilot with the Navy. After he got out, he went to work for the CIA down in Langley, Virginia.

"They assigned him to the counter-intelligence department. The agency told us that we shouldn't tell anyone that Jeff worked for them.

"They told us to tell people he worked for a research institute in Washington. That was the cover story.

"I'm sorry to have misled you, but until now, I had to keep it a secret."

"I understand, Brent. It's okay."

"During the last couple of years, Jeff had been working as an intelligence officer in Europe. Yesterday, he was killed in front of his office in Florence."

"In Florence?"

"Yes. He was shot by a sniper."

Brent put his head in his hands and started to weep.

In Florence, my God!
Could this be possible?
It can't be possible!

Gasping for air, Leanne managed to put her arm across his back and said, "I'm so sorry, Brent. This is horrible. I feel so badly for you."

Leanne felt herself starting to gag. This was more than her system could handle.

"Brent, I've got to go to the bathroom. I'm going to get sick."

She got up from the couch, walked quickly to the bathroom and closed the door behind her.

It wasn't long before Brent heard her retching violently into the toilet.

He went to the bathroom door and asked, "Leanne, are you all right?"

"Yes." She said weakly. "I'll be out in a while. I'm going to take a shower."

"All right. I'll be here. Let me know if you need some help."

Leanne was sick because she now knew the terrible truth.

She had killed his brother.

--TWENTY-ONE--

Jennifer waited anxiously for her husband to get back from the operating room.

She had experience with patients with circulation problems similar to her husband's.

Before she married John, she had spent six years at the Bethseda hospital as a Navy nurse.

She knew that John's injuries weren't life threatening but they had to be treated quickly. Although the surgical procedure for repairing the severed artery was simple conceptually, it had to be performed skillfully by a specialist.

Anything could happen on an operating table.

The hallway door opened and Dr. Bjorn, John's surgeon, walked into the room.

"Well, Jennifer, you have nothing to worry about. He'll be fine. The operation went well."

"Thank God."

"Jennifer, we were fortunate to get him here so quickly."

"Yes, I know. Doctor, besides the circulation problem, is there anything else we need to worry about?"

"Not really, Jennifer. Your husband has some cuts and bruises. There's nothing here that time and rest won't cure. I'm amazed that he wasn't more seriously hurt."

"I know. Thank God for that. How long will you keep him?"

"We'll keep him here for a few weeks."

"What about the bandages on his eyes?"

"We'll take them off in a few days. His eyes are too sensitive to light right now."

"That's good news. When can I see him?"

"You can see him now. Why don't you wait for him in his room? They should be bringing him back from the recovery room any minute now."

"All right. Dr. Bjorn, I want to thank you for all that you've done for John."

"You're very welcome. It was good to see you again, Jennifer, even under these circumstances."

As she sat down next to his bed, she remembered when she had met him for the first time.

She had been stationed on this same floor.

John showed up to see his friend, who had been injured in a car accident.

The Navy pilot asked her out after the second time he had visited his buddy. It wasn't long before the relationship became serious.

The two nurses who were bringing John into the room interrupted her thoughts.

They slid him from the gurney to the bed and arranged his IVs.

"We'll leave you alone, Mrs. Whitestone. If you need anything, just press the buzzer over there by the head of the bed."

After a few minutes, John began to stir.

"John, it's me. Can you hear me?"

"Uh, yes."

She reached over and took his hand.

"You're going to be fine. How do you feel?"

"Not so good."

"Do you feel sick to your stomach?"

"A little bit. It'll be all right."

She bent down and kissed him.

"It's still good to see you, John."

"I wish I could see you, Jennifer. Have you talked with the doctor?"

"Yes. The operation was a success. You should be back on your feet in a few weeks."

"I was lucky, Jennifer. When I left that restaurant, all I could remember was that I got slammed in the chest by something really heavy and then I landed on the sidewalk.

"A nurse told me there were twelve people killed in that explosion.

"Most of them were standing close to me when the bomb went off. All I got were some cuts and bruises."

"Well, John, the severed artery could have really been serious if they didn't get you back here in time."

"I wonder how the Israeli medics found out who I was?"

"They probably called the Embassy in Tel Aviv. It only took the station chief an hour to get you on the hospital plane."

"Thank God, you're home. I've missed you."

"I missed you, too, Jennifer."

"Who was responsible for the bombing?"

"Hamas, I think."

John knew that he had to talk to her.

He was in trouble.

Whitestone thought that Devine was getting very close to nailing him for being involved with the arms business.

He was convinced that Jeff Maxwell was part of the operation.

It wouldn't be much longer before Devine confronted him.

He couldn't talk to Devine anymore until he could find out if Maxwell's brother, the banker in New York, knew anything about the operation.

Whitestone was bothered by the notion that if Jeff was killed to keep him quiet, than they might want to keep him quiet too.

He had to explain some things to her.

"Jennifer?"

"Yes?"

She recognized the tone of his voice.

There was something wrong and he didn't sound like he wanted to get into it.

"Do you remember Jeff Maxwell?"

"Yes. He came to our Labor Day party last year."

"Right. He was murdered yesterday in Florence."

"That's awful. Were you close?"

"Yes, he was a very good friend. We had worked together for the last five years."

"I'm sorry, John."

"Jennifer, I need your help. I have to talk with Jeff's brother right away."

"What's wrong, John. You sound like you're in trouble."

"I can't talk to my people."

"Why not? Is there something you're hiding?"

Whitestone knew that he would jeopardize her if he went any further.

But, whoever killed Jeff might want to kill him.

He needed help.

She was the only person he could trust.

He decided to tell her.

"Yes. We were involved in some things that they didn't know about."

"What do you mean, they didn't know? Who are they, John?"

"The agency."

"What were you doing?!"

Jennifer was starting to get heated up about where this conversation was headed.

It sounded like John was doing something he wasn't supposed to be doing.

"Let me explain a couple of things. The agency set up this operation..."

She interrupted him.

"Are you sure you should be talking about these things with me, John?"

"I wouldn't be telling you about this if I didn't think that I was in trouble."

"All right. What about this operation?"

"Four years ago, the agency set up an operation to gather intelligence on the militant Islamic groups. They had electronic equipment and some high-tech sensors, but they didn't have anyone on the ground to gather intelligence."

"Were you involved with it?"

"Jeff and I were assigned to run it."

"But, you were rookies."

"The militant's intelligence people didn't know about us, but they did know about our agents who were operating in the Middle East. We went to Florence posing as Canadian ex-convicts and started to run an arms trading business."

"I had no idea that you did that!"

"I couldn't tell you then."

"Why are you telling me now?"

"Well, the agency shut it down after we established a network of informers throughout the Middle East. They decided they didn't need to continue the operation."

"What's the problem, John?"

"We went into business for ourselves and didn't tell the agency about it. We made millions dealing with those people."

"John, are you crazy? You can go to jail for this!"

John had seen the Irish in his wife many times before. Whenever there was trouble with him or the kids, she'd vent on them until they promised to do the right thing.

"Our supervisor told us that the Director wouldn't find out about it."

"Why did you go along with this nonsense?"

"So that we could make money, honey. Besides, we were risking our lives every day and the supervisor told us that we deserved to make some extra money."

He didn't want to tell her just how much extra money he made, although she'd find out, if anything happened to him. Right now he needed her help, not her wrath.

"I can't believe you did this!!"

A terrifying thought suddenly hit her.

"John, do you know who killed Jeff?"
"I don't know."
"How was he murdered?"

She knew a little bit about the intelligence communities and how they operated. There was something here that didn't seem right.

"He was shot to death by a sniper."
"You mean, he was assassinated. On the same day you were hurt in the explosion?"
"Right."
"Did you think that somebody killed Jeff because he was involved with this operation?"
"Maybe."
"I mean, would they kill him for the money?"
"I don't know. Maybe."
"If they knew about Jeff, wouldn't they know about you?"
"They might. I just don't know for sure."
"Then doesn't it make sense that somebody might be trying to kill you for the same reason?"
"That's possible."

Jennifer was disappointed in him because he had made a bad decision that not only hurt him, but might also hurt his family.

She was angry with him because he made a stupid decision to get involved with this operation in the first place.

He had jeopardized himself and possibly his family, but she realized that she couldn't undo what had already happened.

Even though Jennifer was angry with John, she knew she was the only one who could help him. Right now, in his condition, he was practically helpless.

"John, I'm going to help you get out of this mess."
"I'm sorry, Jennifer. I didn't mean to get you involved, but with this thing with Jeff, well, everything has changed."

"I understand. What do you want me to do?"

"I need to contact Brent Maxwell, Jeff's brother, to tell him that I need to see him as soon as possible. We have to find out how much he knows about the operation."

"Where can I reach him?"

"In Manhattan. He works at a securities firm called Hamilton-Montague."

"All right. I'll go outside the building and call him on my cell phone. I'll be back in a few minutes."

"Jennifer, one other thing. You'll be taken care of if anything happens to me. There's a lot of money in my account in Zurich. They've been told to send it to you if I get taken out."

Jennifer really didn't want to hear that.

Outside in the parking lot, Jennifer called the number she got from information.

After reaching the main number, she was transferred to Maxwell's line.

Angie answered the phone, "Mr. Maxwell's office."

"I'd like to speak with Mr. Maxwell, it's very important. It's about his brother, Jeff."

"May I ask who's calling?"

"Yes, my name is Jennifer Whitestone. My husband and Jeff worked together in the government. I must speak with him right away. It's an emergency."

"Well, Mr. Maxwell is away from his office at the...wait, he just walked in."

She put her hand over the receiver and whispered to him.

"Brent, you should take this call."

"What's it about?"

"This woman says it's urgent. It's about Jeff."

"Okay, I'll take it inside."

"Hello, this is Brent Maxwell."

"Mr. Maxwell, I'm Jennifer Whitestone, I'm calling for my husband, John."

"Hello, Jennifer, what's this about?"

"My husband and your brother worked together in the Middle East. John was injured in Tel Aviv the same day your brother was killed.

"He thinks he may know who killed him.

"John wants you to meet with him as soon as possible."

"What? Is your husband with the agency?"

"Yes."

"Where is he now?"

"Bethseda Naval Hospital. Mr. Maxwell, John has to talk with you as soon as possible."

"I understand. Jeff will be buried at Arlington tomorrow. I'll come over to the hospital after the funeral is over.

"That should be around two o'clock.

"What's John's room number?"

"He's in room 428."

"Well, I'll look forward to talking with him."

"John will look forward to meeting you too. Thank you very much, Mr. Maxwell."

After Jennifer finished the call, she walked slowly back to the hospital entrance.

--TWENTY-TWO--

Leanne and Brent hadn't made love the night before.

Neither of them had slept well. Their distressful thoughts wouldn't allow them a good night's sleep.

Brent felt deeply depressed about losing his only brother. They had shared so many good times growing up and going to school together. He was going to miss him terribly.

Brent was frustrated because he didn't know why anyone would want to murder Jeff. The agents thought that Jeff was killed simply to keep him quiet.

That seemed so inane to him.

What was so important that the killer felt the need to cover up the operation?

How was he ever going to find out who killed Jeff?

He promised himself that he would never stop searching for the killer until he was found.

Leanne could only express her sorrow for Brent's loss, while suppressing her own feelings of guilt for what she had done.

She felt overwhelmed by the confluence of unruly emotions that were tearing up her insides.

Her feelings of guilt for killing Jeff made her feel awful.

She felt now that she had betrayed Brent by not telling him sooner that she was a contract assassin for the CIA.

If Leanne had told Brent about it, she probably would've resigned from the agency.

That way there wouldn't have been any secrets between them.

If that had happened, she wouldn't be in this mess now.

Leanne felt confused because she had obeyed orders that resulted in this tragedy.

She also felt angry because her superiors had betrayed her by knowingly assigning her to kill her fiancee's brother.

Leanne was frustrated because she didn't know how to deal with Brent.

What they needed now was time to talk things out and try to heal their emotional wounds.

Leanne's thoughts had continued to run rampant long after Brent dozed off.

What's happening to her?

Why was she ordered to kill another agent?

It didn't make sense.

Why was Jeff a target?

He was an intelligence officer and a decorated Navy pilot.

Did he do something wrong?

He was wealthy. There's no apparent reason for him to do anything wrong.

That didn't make sense either.

Did the assignor make a mistake?

The orders seemed properly drafted.

The e-mail message was coded properly.

The dossiers on both targets contained standard data.

What's happening at the agency?

There had been rumors that different intelligence agencies were squabbling about how to monitor militant activities in the Middle East.

Do they have some kind of an internal problem?

There was no way to know about that possibility.

Was the assignment authorized?

The Director of Operations would know.

But, could he be trusted?

Maybe. She didn't any other option. She had to trust him.

Was she in danger from her own people?

She'd have to find out from the Director.

Why did they assign two targets on the same day?

There was no answer.

In two different countries?
That didn't make sense!
Why was the guy in Tel Aviv a target?
There might have been a connection between he and Jeff.
Was he an agent too?
She hoped not....

She finally fell asleep with precious few satisfying answers to her troubling questions.

Brent awakened to the muted sounds of early morning traffic rising up from Fifth Avenue.

This morning they laid in bed with Brent on his back and Leanne nestled up against him. She had her head on his shoulder with her long hair covering her face.

He was glad to have her back with him. He loved her and she was there for him. She helped him to deal with the pain of losing Jeff.

Brent thought that Leanne was a sensitive, thoughtful woman who empathized with his hurt.

Brent heard her moan as she started to stir.

"Are you awake?" He whispered.
"Sort of." She replied quietly.
"Does your head still hurt?"
"Yes."

He held her close with his left arm around her shoulders and began to gently massage the back of her head with a slow soothing motion.

She felt the tension releasing from the muscles in her neck near the base of her skull. Brent had such wonderfully strong hands.

He massaged her temples to help ease the throbbing she felt on the sides of her head.

"That feels so good, Brent."

She caressed his chest with slow strokes that moved lower as she sensed his body responding to her. It wasn't long before they were making deep passionate love, losing themselves in the moment forgetting about the pain of his loss and the pain of her guilt.

Later, they left the apartment and took the limo downtown.

They were able to talk a bit as Victor drove them to Leanne's gallery on Fifth Avenue.

Traffic was heavy, but he was usually able to make the trip in fifteen minutes.

"Are you feeling any better this morning?"

She didn't want to tell him how she really felt because it would only upset him.

"Yes, I do. I'm sorry about last night. I just don't know what happened to me."

"It's okay, there's no need to apologize. I'm just glad you're feeling better."

Leanne wanted to change the subject.

"Are you going to be busy today?"

"Yes. We're underwriting a convertible bond deal for a major telecommunications company this morning. I'm sure that it'll be pretty hectic.

"I've got to check the arrangements for the family coming to the funeral tomorrow."

"Do you still want me to go with you?"

"Yes. I do. I need you."

She gently kissed him on the cheek.

"I'll be there for you, Brent."

He put his arm around her.

They were getting close to Fifty-Ninth Street and Leanne's Gallery.

"Leanne, I got a strange phone call yesterday. I almost forgot to tell you about it."

"What was it about?"

"It was from the wife of an agent who worked with Jeff. She said he might know who killed him."

Leanne hoped he didn't feel her body starting to tense up.

"What did she want?"

"She wanted me to meet him tomorrow."

"At the funeral?"

"No. At the Naval Hospital in Bethesda. The agency has just brought him back from Tel Aviv."

Oh, no! This was more than Leanne could take.

"Brent," she asked hesitantly, "What happened to him?"

"He was injured in a car bomb explosion."

Leanne was stunned.

By this time, Victor had pulled up in front of the gallery.

"I'll pick you up tonight around six-thirty." He said.

"All right." She gave him a quick kiss.

"I love you, Brent."

"I love you, too. I'll see you tonight."

Leanne got out of the limousine and walked to the front door of her gallery, feeling overwhelmed by this latest development.

Leanne was too pre-occupied with the prospect of meeting the Tel Aviv target the next day, that she never noticed the tourist watching her from across the street.

The one wearing a Red Sox baseball cap.

--TWENTY-THREE--

Kent sat in his chair, deep in thought. He smirked when he thought about the arms business.

It had been four years since he had left the agency.

When he was the deputy chief of counter-intelligence, he had advocated establishing an operation dealing weapons and munitions with extremists in the Middle East in order to gather intelligence.

His superiors approved the covert operation and authorized him to run it.

After they built a network of informers, the agency closed the operation down.

Kent seized the opportunity to go into business for himself without the agency either knowing or approving it.

The business grew so quickly that he recruited three agents to help him.

He convinced them to take part in the operation by explaining how much money they could make and by convincing them that they deserved the extra money for risking their lives.

He emphasized that the operation would be top secret. They were the only ones to know that this arms operation existed.

There was no need for the agency to know about their extracurricular activities.

It was unfortunate that these rumors had started to circulate in the past few weeks.

They started in the Alcohol, Tobacco and Firearms agency when one of their intelligence officers thought that there was an illegal arms business being conducted in the Middle East.

Kent didn't know where the agent heard about it, but it created an unfortunate situation that had to be dealt with quickly.

The rumors amplified through the rest of the intelligence community with conjectures that American operatives were running the operation and that active American intelligence officers, possibly CIA field agents, were involved

Even though Kent liked Maxwell and Whitestone, these rumors had made them liabilities for him.

After Kent left the agency, he began the first phase of his plan to fraudulently accumulate billions of dollars from unwitting investors.

He had skillfully maneuvered into a position of power in a leading investment banking and brokerage firm on Wall Street without anyone being the wiser.

Kent had gained control of the firm's capital markets and its investment banking department.

His brilliant scam was up and running without anyone knowing it was happening.

The scam had generated millions of dollars for the firm without raising a single regulator's eyebrow.

Kent considered an investment bank as Wall Street's golden goose producing prodigious revenues during the IPO bubble.

By now, the stakes had become a thousand times greater than the money he been making from the illegal arms business being operated by his three partners in the Middle East.

Kent's field of expertise was international economics. After he had left the agency, he became increasingly intrigued by what was happening on Wall Street.

As an economist, he foresaw the possibilities of how the internet could impact the economy.

The browsers were getting better, the software was improving and the hardware was getting easier to use.

Technology was improving rapidly. The old economy companies didn't drive the technological revolution.

The new economy companies were leading the change to digitization and electronic commerce.

Kent knew that although no one could predict how the new economy would work, there would be hundreds of companies that would need billions of dollars to get their businesses started.

He knew that trillions of dollars flowed through Wall Street everyday, but developing a plan to tap into that money would be a challenge.

Kent needed a way to access the capital markets on Wall Street.

It didn't make any difference if the method was legal or not.

He knew that venture capital companies and investment bankers would make the big money when the new issue market heated up.

Kent knew that he had a problem.

He didn't have the time to set up a legitimate venture capital firm. The technology revolution was happening and he needed to be in the action now.

His plan was simple, brilliant and illegal.

Kent set up a venture capital firm in Chicago to create bogus start-up companies.

Kent planned to sell stock in these companies to the public through an investment banking firm. He would make billions.

There was only one way to make that happen.

He had to somehow take control of an investment banking firm to make the scheme work.

Kent preferred targeting a partnership, rather than a public corporation, which was held to greater disclosure requirements by the regulatory agencies.

Once he gained control of the investment bank, he could manipulate the sale of billions of shares of worthless stock to millions of unsuspecting investors.

Kent needed to convince or compromise a chief executive officer to allow him to get inside the firm.

That was the key to the success of the scam.

He had an answer.

The answer was George Wilson, his classmate at St. James and Princeton and currently the chief executive officer of Montieff, Lancaster, a privately owned securities firm in Manhattan. Wilson was a long-time member of Kent's yacht club in Annapolis.

Kent doubted that he could convince Wilson to get involved with the scheme.

Wilson didn't need the money.

His family was wealthy.

More importantly, Wilson wouldn't want to jeopardize his position of power by doing anything shady.

Kent decided that the best approach to control Wilson was to compromise him.

He knew Wilson better than Wilson knew himself.

Wilson was raised as a pampered Mommy's boy up around Darien, Connecticut.

When he first ran into Wilson down at St. James, Kent saw a wimpy, skinny little kid who goofed around in school and got trashed on his boat on the weekends.

While Kent, at six-one, weighing two hundred pounds, was smashing thc snot out of his teammates on the football practice field, Wilson, at five-foot seven, weighing one hundred and thirty-five pounds was practicing some new ways to perform oral sex with his girlfriend in the backseat of her SUV.

Besides booze, drugs or other assorted chemicals, girls and sailing, Kent knew about something else that Wilson loved to do.

Wilson loved to play cards.

Wilson started playing cards at St. James. He liked the action and the company of his friends.

For Wilson, at prep school, it was a toss-up whether he liked playing poker or hearts.

Hearts intrigued him more than poker because there was an opportunity to either win the entire pot or destroy someone else who was trying to capture it.

Wilson felt there was a sense of adventure in playing hearts that he could never replicate in real life.

It was easier for Wilson to fantasize his role as a hero or as a villain in the game of hearts than to be a hero or villain in the real world.

Poker was more a game of probabilities and odds. When Wilson played friendly games of poker at the prep school, it was easy for him to count cards and cheat a little.

Wilson really didn't demonstrate his aptitude in mathematics in the classroom, but this wealthy and youngest child in the Wilson family certainly understood the concepts of math.

He understood the balance and symmetry of mathematics.

Algebra made sense to him.

Division was the opposite of multiplication.

Addition was the opposite of subtraction.

Wilson didn't need to study advanced algebra, because he understood the concepts.

Kent wasn't invited into Wilson's crowd at prep school because they considered Kent a low-rent redneck country boy.

They did their best to ostracize him without getting him pissed off at them.

Wilson's cronies at St. James had never in their life run across someone like Kent.

He didn't play their silly social games.

Kent wouldn't let them walk away after uttering snide and denigrating remarks.

The nose-in-the-air attitude would work with their friends and their families, but it wouldn't work with Kent.

Kent would call them on it.

He would express his feelings with fists and without expressions of indignation.

One punch in the mouth said a thousand words.

Kent was able to establish the rules of sociability at St. James, at least as it affected him.

If you treated him with disrespect, he would hit you in the face and hurt you.

If you treated him with respect, he would not hit you in the face and you wouldn't feel any pain.

It didn't take too long before the boys and girls at St. James reached an understanding with young Mister Kent.

An interesting phenomena developed from this new social interaction.

The girls really dug Kent.

They felt butterflies in their stomach whenever they saw him, because Kent stirred up their animal instincts.

These young nubiles hadn't experienced these feelings with any of the other boys.

This mysterious man-child was driving his fifteen-year-old female classmates into a frenzy.

After three months at St. James, there wasn't a single girl who didn't want to date him.

Kent didn't disappoint any of them.

These girls didn't need classes on their sexuality because they felt their sexuality every time they saw this tough waterman from the Eastern Shore of Maryland.

One of Kent's friends owned a vacation home on Paradise Island in the Bahamas.

He frequently invited a small group of his friends to spend weekends there to play cards, sail, drink and meet some special young ladies.

The former Chairman of a large property and casualty company had extended an open invitation to Kent to come down to his place at any time.

His wealthy guests played high stakes poker, with millions of dollars changing hands.

Kent had flown down to the island several times after he had resigned from the agency. He was sure that his friend would allow him to use his palatial compound as part of the plan.

The former executive knew Wilson and didn't like him. It had to do with some of his former dealings with George's father. Kent figured that the old man would jump at the chance to embarrass George and his family.

Kent realized that he had to be patient setting up the trap on Wilson.

One day, down at the yacht club after a race, Kent casually asked Wilson if he'd be interested in joining him over the weekend at his friends home on Paradise Island.

It would be a chance for them to get in some sailing, screw some different women and play cards.

Wilson jumped at the chance.

They went down the following weekend. Wilson was hooked on the scene. Away from home with new faces and new bodies, Wilson felt that he could lay back and enjoy himself.

In the evening of their first day at the beach home, Kent and Wilson sat down at one of the tables in the large game room to play poker.

After four hours of cards, Wilson excused himself for the night in order to play doctor-nurse with one of the thong-covered girls who had been serving him drinks.

Kent smiled to himself as he watched Wilson teetering upstairs with his new friend. He knew that Wilson would want to come back here again.

Kent had to bring him down on several weekends before Wilson felt completely at ease with his new card-playing friends. George was so distracted with the girls and the other activities that he failed to notice that the betting limits were being raised higher each weekend.

It didn't seem to bother him because he was still winning some pots. He felt that he was better than any of the other players at his table.

Kent sensed that George was getting a little cocky in his play and that he was taking some unnecessary risks. Kent felt that it was time to spring the trap.

It was time to set up the fixed card game.

Kent had already decided how he was going to do it.

He conferred with his host and explained that he was going to set up the game for the following weekend.

Kent would have two of his people at the table.

One of them was a professional dealer from Atlanta and the other was a professional poker player from Las Vegas.

They would play the entire Saturday night session. When the players agreed to no limit, open betting, the two hired hands would work their magic on Wilson.

They were going to create pots that would reach several million dollars.

This professional dealer was a magician with the cards and could easily rig the hands.

Wilson wasn't able to detect that the dealer was setting him up.

The idea was simple. George would be dealt hands that won a few pots to build up his confidence.

When the time was right, George was dealt a very good hand, normally enough to win any game.

The dealer made sure that the prop player would be dealt an even better and more improbable hand. Wilson would never anticipate that.

The other players kept raising George's bets. George was so sure he had the best hand at the table that he raised them back.

After they had finished betting, the players laid their cards on the table.

Fully expecting to win, George was shocked when the pro from Atlanta showed a better hand.

It suddenly dawned on George that he had lost over six million dollars.

Wilson didn't have the money to pay off the debt, which Kent already knew.

As a friend, Kent offered to cover Wilson's debt until he could pay him back.

Wilson accepted the offer.

After a few weeks, Kent made Wilson an offer that he couldn't refuse.

Kent owned a shopping mall outside of Dallas and he wanted Wilson's real estate department to buy it. Wilson's firm could package it into a real estate investment trust and then sell it to the public.

Kent promised to use the proceeds to pay off Wilson's gambling debts and pay George two million dollars more to make the deal happen.

Wilson agreed to the proposition.

His firm did the deal. Kent and Wilson got their money. The real estate investment trust went bankrupt six months after it went public.

Wilson was compromised and Kent had gotten control of him.

--TWENTY-FOUR--

The problem needed to be solved immediately.

The instructions were simple.

Make it look like an accident.

The bird was scheduled to fly into JFK International, Thursday night at nine-ten Eastern Daylight Time.

The packet contained the photograph and physical description of Leanne Anderson.

Twenty-five thousand dollars had been deposited into a Cayman account, and twenty-five thousand dollars more would be deposited when the project was completed.

This was a lot more money than he was making driving a school bus in Hempstead.

He had waited for her at the airport and watched as she came through customs. She walked directly to a man who seemed to be waiting for her.

He looked like he might be her driver because after they shook hands, he took her bag and walked slightly ahead of her as they left the terminal.

There didn't seem to be any security for the bird.

It seemed clear that the driver didn't expect any trouble either because his body language didn't indicate any apparent concern for the target's safety.

After he picked up her bag, he didn't look around to see if anyone was watching them.

When he left the terminal and put her bag in the trunk of the limo, he didn't bother to scan the cars double-parked in front for any possible tails.

The target wasn't vulnerable, yet.

He followed them as they drove north on the Van Wyck to the Long Island Expressway.

Traffic was light.

Following them was easy.

After they went through the Queens Midtown Tunnel, they picked up the FDR Drive and got off at Eighty-Sixth Street.

A few minutes later, the limo had parked in front of an apartment on Fifth, between Eight-Fourth and Eighty-Fifth.

He knew that the target lived in a brownstone down in the fifties off Madison. This wasn't her place.

This prèsented a problem for him.

There was much more security up here than there was in her neighborhood.

He parked across the street at a bus stop and watched as the driver and the target went into the apartment.

There was no way that he would have a chance to earn the extra twenty-five thousand dollars tonight.

He had to wait for a better opportunity tomorrow.

He arrived at Rockefeller Plaza, a little before eight o'clock the next morning.

He looked like a tourist, wearing a dark-blue Boston Red Sox baseball cap and tinted sunglasses.

A rumpled, dirty shoulder bag crammed with maps and tourist guides hung across his chest.

He held a cheap camera with an expensive and powerful zoom in his hand.

He didn't need the camera to take pictures.

He needed the zoom for target identification.

He sat down on a granite wall near a small garden that was diagonally across the street from Leanne's gallery.

The intersection at Fifth Avenue and Fifty-Ninth Street was always busy because Central Park ran from Fifth-Ninth to One-Hundred and Tenth Street between Fifth Avenue and Eighth Avenue.

North and southbound traffic either traveled through the park, or on Fifth Avenue or Eighth Avenues.

He preferred crowded streets and heavy traffic for his particular method of assassination.

He projected the target would be coming to work sometime after eight-thirty.

There was time for breakfast.

A sidewalk vendor on the corner was making breakfast on a propane grill.

He could smell the aroma of fried bacon and onions that filled the air.

It was irresistible.

He went over to the dirty aluminum wagon and waited in line. When it was his time to order, he was salivating as he told the first-generation Armenian short-order cook what he wanted for breakfast.

Two large Kabasi dogs with mustard, extra cheese and thick wads of sauerkraut.

Large black coffee and two large cheese danish.

As usual, when he bit into the overloaded bun, a blob of mustard and a clump of sauerkraut dropped down onto the front of his white sports shirt.

He thought that the stained shirt would be the right look for a tourist.

He had just finished inhaling his breakfast when a limo pulled up in front of the target's gallery.

It was a little before nine o'clock.

He wiped his mouth on his sleeve and trained the zoom lens on the vehicle.

He scoped the license plate.

It was the same limo as last night.

The windows were tinted.

He couldn't tell if she was alone.

He waited.

After a few minutes, the driver got out of the limo and opened the passenger door for the target.

As she got out of the car, he peered intently through the zoom lens.

He recognized the target from her photograph.

She didn't appear to be concerned.

She waved goodbye to someone in the limo. She didn't seem particularly concerned that someone might be following her.

Then she walked straight to the gallery and went inside without looking around her.

He didn't see any security hanging around the building. It would difficult for him to detect someone because of the crowds and the heavy traffic.

The limo waited until the target went into the gallery and then merged into the fast-moving flow of traffic.

He was convinced that since there wasn't any security around the target, that he might have an opportunity take care of business sometime today.

Unknowingly, Leanne had become very vulnerable.

The conditions were almost perfect, but he needed to get her on the street.

He had to wait until she was alone, but he didn't know when that would be.

He had to stay close to the gallery without drawing attention to himself.

He spent the next three hours browsing through the expensive antique and designer stores, asking questions, while constantly watching the entrance to her gallery.

This was demanding work.

A little before noon, he caught a break.

Leanne walked out of the gallery and headed south on Fifth Avenue.

He wondered where she was going at this time of day.
Maybe, she was going to meet someone for lunch.
He started to follow her from across the street.
She seemed to be walking with a sense of purpose.
Unfortunately for him, he didn't know where he was going, but she did.
Fortunately for him, she was walking at the same pace as the other pedestrians on the street.
That gave him an edge.
It allowed him to catch up with her.
She was a half-a-block ahead of him on the other side of Fifth Avenue.
He needed to get closer.
He didn't know how much longer this opportunity to strike would last.
She stopped at Fifty-Seventh Street and waited for the traffic light to turn green.

He loved to stalk his victims. It was such a rush.

He walked faster.

As he got closer to the intersection, the light changed.
It turned green for her, so she crossed Fifty-Seventh.
It turned red for him, so he couldn't cross Fifth Avenue.
He missed the chance to get on her side of the street.
He'd have to catch up to her at Fifty-Sixth Street.

He pushed his way through people to get to the next intersection before she did.
He was gaining on her.
This time, he was going to get her.
She had no idea that he was stalking her.
He had to get over to her side of the street!
He walked faster.
Leanne was getting close to Fifty-Sixth Street.
This time, he crossed Fifth Avenue and edged his way through the crowd until he was directly behind her.

Leanne seemed pre-occupied as she waited for a green light.
She still had no idea that she was being followed.
He was so close to her that he could smell her fragrance.

The taxis and the delivery trucks going cross-town were speeding through the intersection trying to beat the light.
This was typical New York City traffic.
It was always difficult to make time driving cross-town during the workweek.

The light turned yellow.
The cars went faster trying to beat it.

He bent his knees slightly.
Out of the corner of his eye, he saw a taxi flooring it trying to get through the light before it turned red.
This was his chance.
He rolled his knuckles back and cocked his wrists into a karate position and rammed the heels of his hands into the small of her back. The leveraged blow lifted her off her feet and into the oncoming taxi.

Instinctively, she threw her hands in front of her.
She hit the side of a speeding taxi and pushed off.
That was the last thing she remembered.

The bystanders were stunned as she bounced off the side of the taxi and landed hard on the street.

The taxi crossed Fifth Avenue and came to a stop.

Leanne lay unconscious in a filthy curbside gutter with her arms and legs spread open.
As traffic snarled the streets, mesmerized pedestrians could only gape at the sight of the woman's hair pillowed in a widening pool of blood.

The blaring sirens from FDNY rescue vehicles could be heard coming towards the scene of the accident.

New York City policemen had already backed off the curious crowd before the medics arrived.

"Let them through!" One of the policemen ordered.

The medics hurried from their vehicles and began working on Leanne.

"What do we have here?" A medic asked his partner.

"Head injury, cuts, bruises, nothing appears broken. Her vitals are okay."

"You need help?"

"Yeah. Brace her neck, but be careful. I can't tell if she has any injuries back there."

One of the medics placed a gauze pad on the gash and wrapped an bandage around her head.

The other medic gave her intravenous fluids.

Standing in the front edge of the crowd, the assassin watched anxiously as the medics worked on Leanne.

He didn't like what he saw.

She was trying to raise her arm.

She was conscious.

A slender old man, standing near him and leaning on a knurled hickory cane, asked a question to no one in particular.

"Do you think she is all right?"

"Yes." he answered.

"She was very fortunate."

As he worked his way out of the crowd, he felt disappointed.

He wasn't going to get the other twenty-five thousand dollars.

--TWENTY-FIVE--

As soon as he heard that the SEC had launched a formal probe into the trading practices at several Wall Street firms, Henry Ingersoll, Hamilton-Montague's managing director, called a meeting to discuss the ramifications of the investigation with his department heads.

He glanced around the conference table and noted the looks of concern on their faces.

Now was the time for them to play show and tell.

"As you all know by now, the SEC has started an investigation at three of our major competitors. At the moment, the scope of the probe seems to be limited to improper trading practices and conflicts of interest by research analysts.

"I'll get right to the point.

"I want to know if there is anything going on in your departments that would create liabilities for this firm.

"If we have any problems, I want to deal with them now, before the SEC decides to pay us a visit.

"Does everyone understand?"

There were nods of understanding from everyone around the long oval table.

"Brent, let's start with you. The SEC is focusing on the question of whether there was a conflict of interest by analysts who supposedly issued unwarranted recommendations to buy new issue internet stocks simply to maintain the investment banking relationships with those companies.

"Fortunately, Henry, we've avoided the problem because we didn't want get involved with those deals. First of all, they were too risky to bring public.

"Secondly, the kids running them had zero management experience.

"And thirdly, we couldn't see how they were going to make any money."

"Well, Brent, I think that you've put your finger on the problem facing our competitors.

"The SEC suspects that the only way they could have sold those stocks was to hype them to the investors and then manipulate stock prices in the aftermarkets."

"Henry, that's has been going on for a long time.

"The investment banking system really got caught up in the mania of creating instant millionaires in late 1998, not only for investors, but also for the venture capitalists, the institutional portfolio managers and themselves.

"There certainly was a food chain in the investment banking system that demanded attention.

"The prices of new issue stocks were going up over a thousand percent on the first day of trading.

"Institutional accounts put a tremendous amount of pressure on us to get involved in the new issue markets because they wanted performance for their funds."

"Brent, fund managers get paid for the amount of assets under management.

"The easiest way to attract new money to their funds was to show the big gains they had made in the new issue markets.

"Brent, what's driving the investment banking business now that the dot.com bubble has burst?"

"Henry, our clients need a tremendous amount of capital to digitize their business and develop their electronic commerce.

"It's critical for them to increase their productivity in order to stay competitive.

"The economies around the world are integrating rapidly and our clients realize that the faster they develop their technologies, the faster they'll dominate their markets."

"You're right, Brent. The size of these financing deals is mind boggling.

"Wasn't that eight billion-dollar corporate bond deal we did for the Midwest phone company a record in terms of the size?"

"Yes, but we have a corporate bond deal in the pipeline now that will be over ten billion dollars.

"Henry, I think that we made the right decision to stay focused by maintaining the solid relationships we've had with our Fortune 500 clients."

"You did a good job staying the course."

"Thank you, Henry."

Ingersoll turned his head towards the Head of Equity Trading.

"Matt, you're next. The SEC suspects that new issues stock prices were manipulated in the aftermarkets.

"Did your traders make markets in any of them?"

"Yes, we did, Henry. Even though we didn't participate in the deals, our institutional clients expected us to provide liquidity for them."

"Did you know that our competitors were pumping up stock prices after they were free to trade?"

"Yes. I noticed that back in late 1998 when the frenzy for buying IPOs began."

"Like what?"

"Well, some of our institutional accounts gave us orders to buy big blocks of stock at prices two or three times higher than the initial offering price."

"There's nothing wrong with that."

"I know, but we couldn't fill their orders."

"Why not?"

"Because they created such a large imbalance on the buy side that when the stock finally opened, it was four or five times higher than the issue price."

"I see where you're going with this, but I don't think that establishes manipulation.

"What do you think, Ira?" He asked the Director of Compliance.

"Not yet, Henry. The imbalances on the buy side were common occurrences in those aftermarkets.

"The more important question is whether the institutions and the trading desks were in collusion to drive up the prices. Collusion is very difficult to prove."

"Have you spoken with anyone at the SEC about this?"

"Yes. They're questioning why these problems have become endemic in investment banking.

"They want to make substantive changes in how capital is raised. The SEC wants something that will effectively protect the public."

"Do you see any conflicts of interest with our research analysts and our investment bankers?"

"Absolutely not. As Brent mentioned earlier, our investment banking clients are solid, highly capitalized corporations. They don't need to be touted by any of our analysts. They simply need an honest evaluation of their enterprises."

"Ira, what do you think the SEC will discover during this investigation?"

"I think they'll find out that there were some arrangements that were made between the institutional accounts and our competitors. Nothing formal, just understandings that developed over the past three years."

"Do you want to explain that?"

"Sure. I think our competitors agreed to allocate new issue stock to certain fund managers if they agreed to pump up the price of the stock when it was free to trade.

"Is that manipulation of the markets? Maybe, but the SEC won't be able to prove it."

"What else?"

"I think the SEC will find a rather unsavory relationship between their recommendations and their corporate clients.

"They're going to be fined for that mess.

"There were too many individual investors who lost money when the price of those stocks plummeted.

"Investors relied on the analysts who recommended buying those stocks."

"Well, we don't have those problems here.

"I want to thank you everyone here for your time.

"Now, let's get back to work and make some money."

--TWENTY-SIX--

As he was passing through the reception room on his way back to his office, Brent glanced at the landscape by Andrew Wyeth that he had bought from Leanne.

The masterpiece by the Pennsylvania painter had brought back memories of the day, almost a year ago, when he agreed to purchase the two million-dollar painting.

While Victor was driving him to Leanne's gallery to finalize the purchase, Brent sat in the back seat of his limousine absorbed in a proposed financing for the construction of a plant in Mexico for an important client.

The firm had been in the selling syndicate for an earlier corporate bond deal by them, but this was the first time that Hamilton, Montague was hired as their lead underwriter.

Victor drove the black Lincoln Towne Car north on the FDR Drive, got off at the 59th Street exit and headed west toward Fifth Avenue.

As he got closer to 59th and Fifth, he said, "Brent, were almost there."

Victor stopped the limo next to fire hydrant in front of the gallery.

"This is expensive territory, Brent. Is that her building?"

"Yes. Pretty impressive, isn't it, Victor? She's really done well. She'll do even better when I approve the sale."

"Are those paintings worth all the money you're paying for them?"

"I guess so, Victor. They always seem to go up in value."

"I like most of the paintings you have in the office, but I don't understand the modern stuff. They look like something my daughter would do in arts and crafts." He said, with a laugh.

"Well, maybe Andrea has artistic talent. If she's that good, maybe Leanne will sell them for her."

As he got out of the car, Brent said, "We should be finished by noon. I'll call you if were running late."

"All right."

Victor was right. This was expensive territory.

The gallery was located in the most exclusive shopping area of New York City, surrounded by high priced antique dealers and designer stores.

The Plaza Hotel and the St. Moritz were around the corner across from Central Park. Rockefeller Plaza, The Playboy Club, Tiffany's and F.A.O. Schwartz were all within walking distance.

When he opened the door to the gallery, he could see Leanne waiting for him in the atrium.

During the prior two years, their business relationship had developed into a friendship. They looked forward to seeing each other.

"Hi, Brent, it's good to see you." She said pleasantly.

"You, too, Leanne." He said, as they shook hands. "This place looks great."

Rays of sunlight were shining through the glass roof filling the four floors of exhibits below.

"Did you design the interior yourself?"

"Yes. It took six months, but I loved doing it. An Italian shoe designer owned the building. She used the first floor as a retail store and the top three floors for storage. When her designs went out of fashion, she put it up for sale. I bought it right away."

"It must have cost you a fortune."

"It did, but I couldn't get any better location in Manhattan, especially since my paintings are so expensive."

"Is your business mostly retail?"

"It's about half retail and half contract work like yours."

"Well, whatever you're doing, you're doing it well."

"Why, thank you Brent.

They walked to the back of the gallery and went into a large room with lounge chairs facing a large flat projection screen.

"Is this your private theater?" He asked.

"Yes, I think you'll like this. We have a software program, which enables us to create a virtual image of the paintings in your office, before we actually mount them. I've placed them throughout your office to make the most favorable impression on your clients. I've tried to create a feeling of wealth and power."

"That's what we want."

"This gives you the flexibility to change a painting from one office to another or replace a painting that you don't like."

"Good idea."

"Our clients like this program. Most of our paintings aren't masterpieces, but they're still very expensive.

"People want them to look good in their homes. They want to make sure that they look just right."

Reviewing the plans took almost an hour.

"As usual, Leanne, you did a great job. I really appreciate your help. You'll make me look good to my Board of Directors." He said, with a smile. "I was wondering, would you like to have lunch with me? You know, we could celebrate the deal. That's, if you have the time."

"I'd love to. Give me a few minutes to grab some things."

"Great. I'll just browse around here until you're ready."

After a short ride, they pulled up to Ristorante Georgio's. The small narrow restaurant was packed. The Matre de spotted Maxwell and walked past the waiting customers to greet him.

"Good afternoon, Mr. Maxwell. It's good to see you again. Your table is ready. Right this way please."

He led them to a small table in the back corner of the restaurant. "This is lovely. I've heard a lot about this place, but this is my first time here."

"I use it quite a lot for business. We have several clients with offices in this part of Manhattan and they like the food here. Would you like a glass of wine? I don't usually drink at lunch, but this is a special occasion."

"Yes, I'd love a glass of wine. I usually work on the gallery floor during lunchtime."

After ordering glasses of white Zinfandel, He said, "I really want to thank you for doing such a great job setting up the office."

"I enjoyed doing it. It was fun."

"What got you interested in the art business in the first place?"

"Well, I guess it started in high school. I painted some landscapes as a project for art class and my teacher suggested that I enter them in an art show."

"Did you win any prizes?"

"I won a first place ribbon for a seascape of Parris Island."

"Isn't that where the Marine Corps has their boot camp?"

"Yes, it's where I grew up."

"Were your parents in the Marines?"

"Just my dad. My mother died when I was a baby."

"I'm sorry to hear that."

"That's okay. My dad raised me. He and I are very close."

"Is he still in the Marines?"

"No. He put in his thirty years and retired, but he still lives on Parris Island. He spends most of his time fishing with his buddies."

"What happened after high school?"

"Well, Yale accepted me into their fine arts program. It was the first time I was away from my dad. It took me a while to get adjusted to civilian life."

"Civilian life?"

"Yes. It's a world apart from life in the military. The military is a highly structured society. There are rules and regulations for everything and they are strictly enforced. Their world is based on responsibility and accountability. You are told what to do and when to do it without questioning authority."

"Wow, and then you went to Yale?"

"Yes, it was a real culture shock for me. I learned how to think for myself and do the things I enjoy doing. How about you? How long have you been in the investment business?"

"Fourteen years. It's the only job I've had since I left the University of Virginia."

"Do you have a family?"

He paused, looked down for a minute, and said, "I lost my family in a car crash four years ago."

"Oh, I'm so sorry, I didn't mean..."

"It's all right. You had no way to know."

"I'm so sorry, Brent."

She reached across the table and touched his hand.

As Brent sat down in his office, Angie, his secretary, interrupted the reflections of the lunch with Leanne.

"Brent, here's the list of the institutional accounts you wanted to see."

--TWENTY-SEVEN--

While Brent was in his office reviewing the account list, Leanne was stretched out on a gurney in the emergency room at Midtown Hospital.

She was awake.

Leanne felt pain in her head, shoulder and wrist.

An intern, standing next to her, asked, "How do you feel?"

"I feel sore."

"You should feel sore. You landed on your side after the car hit you. Your right collarbone and wrist were fractured. You also have a nasty gash on your head."

"Do I have a concussion?"

"No. You were lucky."

Leanne knew better. It wasn't luck. It was an instinctive reaction developed after hours of learning how to fall in the martial arts classes at Langley.

"I can't move my neck."

"It's in a brace. Standard procedure. The rescue squad didn't know if you had any neck or spinal injuries. We'll take it off soon."

Leanne could still feel the force of the hands that pushed her into the traffic.

That wasn't an accident.

Someone tried to kill her.

But why?

This had to be connected to the assignments.

Who wanted her dead?

The agency told Brent they didn't know who killed Jeff.

Were they lying?

It didn't make sense that they'd kill one of the agents. They would discipline a rogue agent, but they wouldn't kill him.

Leanne felt that she had to contact someone at Langley, but only someone she could trust.

Who could she trust?

She had to stay away from the counter-intelligence people because that's where the orders originated.

Leanne had to contact someone higher up in the organization.

She needed help....someone might still try to kill her.

Leanne had to get out of that hospital and fast!

"Can you tell me how much longer I'll be here?" She asked the intern.

"Probably about two hours."

"Can you finish any faster than that?"

"What's the rush?"

"I have to get out of here soon."

"Is something wrong?"

"Yes, there is, but I can't talk to you about it. I need to make a phone call right away."

"Well, if it's that important, you can use the phone here."

He walked to the wall phone, picked up the receiver and brought it to her.

"Do want some privacy?"

"Yes, thank you."

"I'll check back with you in a few minutes."

After the intern left the room, she dialed the number at Langley.

"Langley."

"Director Devine, please."

"One moment, please."

"Director's office. How can I help you?" Devine's secretary answered pleasantly.

"I must speak with the Director immediately. It's an emergency."

"Who is this, please?"

"Leanne Anderson. I work in operations, counter-intelligence section. I've got to speak with the Director. There is something he needs to know, now!"

"Leanne, this is Barbara Doyle. Remember me? I was working at the training school when you went through. Hold on, I'm pulling up your file."

"Barbara, I'm in big trouble. I've got to talk with Devine."
"Leanne, what's your code-name?"
"Ten-X."

Only competitive shooters knew that the small circle inside a bull's-eye was called a ten-x.

"You're top secret. I can't access your file. Listen, Devine's in the office. I'll put you on hold and get him to pick you up."

"Thanks, Barbara."

Devine was on the line in seconds. "Leanne, its Devine. What's the problem?"

"The problem is that somebody just tried to kill me. What's going on?"

"What happened?"

"Someone deliberately pushed me into traffic near my gallery."

"Are you sure it wasn't an accident?"

"I'm sure. I was definitely pushed. Jim. I'm concerned that we may have a major internal security problem and it may be related to the events in Florence and Tel Aviv."

"How did you know about that? Never mind, don't answer. Where are you now?"

"In the emergency room at Midtown Hospital."

"Are you okay?"

"Broken wrist and collarbone. Will you please tell me what's happening?"

"When I see you. Leanne, stay put. Do not leave that hospital. I'll send a team from our midtown office to protect you. Do you hear me? That's an order."

"Yes, sir."

"I'll be there in an hour."

--TWENTY-EIGHT--

Montieff, Lancaster's private dining room was as exclusive as any restaurant in New York City.

World-class chefs managed a kitchen that served politicians, presidents and corporate powerbrokers from around the world.

There wasn't a more conducive ambiance to close billion dollar deals, especially after savoring an exquisite meal washed down with rare wines.

The only members of the firm allowed on the dining room floor were the top managers, senior partners and members of the Board of

Directors.

The lower echelon traders, analysts and salesmen were restricted to the fast food cafeteria on the capitals markets floor.

"Good afternoon, Monsieur Wilson. And how are you today?" Said the Matre'de.

"Very well, thanks, Henri."

He glanced around the room for familiar faces.

"Any special guests today, Henri?"

"Yes, Monsieur. The Vice-President of the United States is dining with Mr. Morgan in the Washington Room and Sheik Abdullah, the Foreign Minister of Saudi Arabia is our guest of honor in the large conference dining room."

"Very good. Has Mr. Kent arrived yet?"

"Yes, Monsieur, a few minutes ago. He is waiting for you in the Lincoln Room."

He nodded to several senior investment bankers who were entertaining important corporate clients as he walked to the private dining rooms overlooking the Hudson River.

The moment he walked into the Lincoln Room, he could sense Kent's irritation.

"Where've you been? You're late."

"Sorry, I got tied up with the compliance people."

He walked straight to the bar and made a vodka and tonic for himself.

"How'd that go?" He asked casually.

"They're reviewing the documents that we filed with the SEC. You know, the prospectuses for the new issues."

"Why the hell do they want to do that? There's nothing relevant in the registration filings."

Wilson had always felt intimidated by Kent. The feeling started in prep school and had become progressively worse over the past few years. They weren't kids anymore, but Wilson still felt completely powerless dealing with him.

"They want to see if there was any misleading information in them."

"Those idiots. There was no misleading information in any of the documents that we filed with the SEC.

"Those companies we brought public had no revenue or earnings history.

"We put disclaimers on all the documents, especially in the prospectuses. What else are they looking at?"

"They're looking at all the deals that came in from Atlas Venture Capital. Jack, are you sure that the SEC won't find out about us?"

Kent fixed such a hard look on George's face that it made him cringe.

"Not us, George. You!"

"What do you mean, Jack?"

"Just what I said, George. If the SEC stumbles onto that phony real estate deal from Atlas, they're only going to find out about you, not me."

"But, you told me that we were both listed on the Board of Directors of the corporation."

"I lied, George."

"What?"

"Atlas Venture Capital is not a corporation. It's structured as a partnership.

"Guess who is listed as the general partner?"

"Oh, no...."

"Oh, yes. You are!"

George downed the rest of his drink.

"Let me put you straight on something, George. The SEC won't be looking to us, they'll be looking at you."

"Wait, a minute, I didn't set up Atlas, you did!"

"That's not what the books show, George. You'll be in a tough spot if he SEC finds out the connection between Atlas and the firm.

"That won't be a civil case, that case will be criminal."

"You bastard! I thought that you were my friend!"

"I am your friend, George. I just needed some protection in case you started talking to the wrong people."

"I'm not going to say anything, Jack. I don't understand why you didn't trust me?"

"Don't take it personally, George. I don't trust anyone."

Jack understood that George was starting to feel a little desperate, but there was no need to get confrontational with him now.

"George, you have my support and I'll help you any way I can. But you better realize how tricky this gets if they decide to pursue a criminal investigation. You have to be very careful what you say to people. And I don't want you to do anything before you consult with me. Do you understand?"

The ringing from Kent's cell phone interrupted them.

"Hello."

"It's me."

Kent recognized the voice of Rich Ranfield, the deputy director of counter-intelligence.

"George, this call is going to take a while. Let's forget the lunch. Why don't you go back downstairs and see what the compliance people are doing."

"All right. I guess I'll see you down at the Yacht Club tonight?"

"Yeah."

Kent waited until he left the room.

"Okay, go ahead."

"The project in New York was not successful."

"What happened?"

"There was a traffic accident."

"Was anyone seriously hurt?"

"No. One person was taken to a hospital."

"Which hospital?"

"We don't know yet."

"We have to change our plans. It will take some time to regroup."

"All right."

"How about taking a few days off? I understand duck hunting this time of year is pretty good. I'll be in touch when we are ready to start up again."

"All right. I'll wait for your call."

Now, Ranfield had become a liability.

And Leanne, if she can, will talk with her people.

When she tells them that she was the Florence assassin, they will certainly suspect that Ranfield ordered the kills without their authorization.

Ranfield knew how to issue the orders and he could eliminate Leanne after she returned from the mission.

If they question Ranfield, he could implicate Kent in the arms business. This was an unacceptable situation.

Kent decided it was time to activate Ranfield's exit plan.

Kent's conversation with Ranfield contained coded instructions. "Time off" told him what to do. He must leave Washington immediately. "Duck hunting" told him where to go. Get down to the safe house on Kent Island near the Chesapeake Bay Bridge.

He had to get to Ranfield before Devine's people did.

--TWENTY-NINE--

The resident intern tried to reassure Leanne as he wrapped her wrist and forearm with a roll of wet plaster.

"You'll be fine. The wrist bone is cracked, so you don't need pins or anything like that. The cast will keep it immobile so it can heal properly."

"How long do I keep it on?"

"Six weeks."

"And my collarbone?"

"That was a clean fracture. I've set that already. But you'll have to wear a shoulder sling for a few weeks."

She reached up and felt a bandage on her head.

"Did you have to cut off any of my hair?" She asked.

"Just around the wound. Don't worry. You're hair is long enough to cover the bandage."

"Will there be a scar?"

"No. I used a lot of stitches to close it up. You'll never know that you were cut."

Just then, the door of the treatment room opened and a hospital security guard walked in, followed by two men in civilian clothes.

"Excuse me, Doctor, these gentlemen are here to see your patient. I wanted you to know that they are authorized to be here."

"Thanks, Scott." The intern said, as the security guard left the room.

The taller one said, "Hello, Leanne, the Director sent us over to see you."

"Who are you guys?" The intern asked.

"I'm Agent Ferragamo and this is Agent Hombrook. We're with the government."

They reached inside their coats and pulled out their identification cards.

The intern scanned them and said. “You’re with the CIA?”
“That’s right. We’ve been assigned to look after Leanne.”
“How much more do you have to do here?”
“Not much. I’m almost finished.”
“We’ll wait outside until you’re done.”

Within an hour, Jim Devine’s helicopter landed on the roof of the hospital.

Walking towards the stairwell, he worried about the seriousness of the situation.

One agent murdered, another injured and a third nearly killed by an unknown assailant.

Why?

What was going on inside the agency?

Was there someone dirty in counter-intelligence?

Devine took the elevator to the emergency room on the ground floor. He spotted Ferragamo standing outside one of the treatment rooms.

He walked up to him, and said, “Is she in there?”
“Yes, sir. Hombrook’s with her now.”
“Okay. I want to talk to her in private. You stay here. I’ll send Hombrook back out with you.”
“Yes, sir.”

Devine opened the door and motioned for Hombrook to leave the room.

“Leanne, I’m Jim Devine, Director of Operations. How are you feeling?”
“Okay, I guess. I didn’t expect to see you so soon.”
“Well, we have to talk about a few things. Tell me what happened to you.”
“I wanted to take a break from the gallery. It was lunchtime.

"So I decided to go down to a deli on Fifty-Fourth Street, pick up a sandwich and bring it back to the gallery.

"I was walking down Fifth Avenue when I had to stop for a red light at the corner at Fifty-Fifth.

"I was standing on the curb, waiting for the light to turn green, when I was shoved into the traffic."

"Are you sure you were shoved? Maybe someone just bumped into you?"

"Oh, no. This guy got both hands on the small of my back and shoved me into the street."

"Were you hit by a car?"

"Not exactly. The guy misjudged the speed of a taxi coming up to the intersection.

"He shoved me into it just as it was going by me. I was able to get my hands on the hood and push off."

"Well, I'm sorry this happened to you, but I'm glad you're all right.

"Do you have any idea who did this? You mentioned Florence and Tel Aviv.

"How does that play into this?"

"I think that someone in the agency was responsible for this. Someone who had the authority to issue orders for me to kill Maxwell and Whitestone."

Devine was shocked. He couldn't believe what Leanne had just told him. This situation had suddenly become far more serious than he could have imagined.

"You killed Maxwell?"

"Yes, in Florence last Tuesday and I just missed taking out Whitestone in Tel Aviv later that afternoon."

"You were issued orders to kill Whitestone?!"

"Yes. I was in a hotel room just down the street from the target area in front of a restaurant. I had him in my sights when he walked out on the street. The bomb exploded and you know the rest."

"This is unbelievable, Leanne."

Devine thought that there was something terribly wrong happening in his department. The idea that someone under his command was issuing orders tc kill his own intelligence officers was very disturbing.

"Aren't you engaged to Maxwell's brother?"

"Yes!" She said, trying to hold back her tears.

"Didn't you know it was his brother when you received the assignment?"

"No. The dossier had the normal information. Target time, location, physical description, shooting site and photograph, but no name. There was never a need for me to know names."

"Didn't you recognize him from the photograph"?

"No. I never met Jeff and I only saw a picture of him when he was sailing with his brother. It was taken too far away to get a good look at him."

"Did you have any reason to believe that the orders were unauthorized?"

"No. The procedures and codes were authentic.

"I thought that it was odd that I was given two assignments in one day."

"Leanne, I checked your file before I got here. You haven't had many contracts over the past four years."

"I know. That was one of the things that concerned me. The orders to shoot twice in one day in two different countries really bothered me, too. I've never done anything like that before."

"Leanne, this just isn't right."

"Since you've read my file, you probably noticed that over the years I've exhibited post-traumatic stress symptoms. Those symptoms can affect my shooting."

"I understand about your headaches. I get migraines too, but they're caused by my allergies."

"When I was coming back from Tel Aviv, I questioned the authenticity of the orders. Even though they were unusual, they seemed all right.

"After someone tried to kill me this afternoon, I was concerned that someone in the agency was responsible.

"I didn't know who to trust, but I had to tell someone about what happened to me.

"So, you took a chance and called me."

"Right. I figured that since you've only been Director for a few months, you might not be aware of a possible internal problem."

"Well, I'm glad you went with your instincts. By the way, does Brent know that you work for us?"

"No. I haven't told him anything about it."

"Well, I've got a problem here.

"Listen Leanne, I believe you, because your involvement in this was a big surprise to me. I'm the Director of Operations and I should have been informed of your assignments. I wasn't.

"I didn't know anything about it.

"Based on what you've told me, the orders were properly issued. This means I have a problem in my organization.

"One of my people must have used you to kill Maxwell and Whitestone.

"If that were true, then they'd have to kill you."

"But why?"

"Because eventually, you would know the orders were unauthorized and who issued them.

"There are very few people who know what you do and how to activate you.

"It shouldn't be difficult to find out who was responsible for this."

"What do you want me to do now?"

"You're banged up right now.

"When you're feeling a little better, you can file a formal report of your activities during the past week.

"We'll need to check out all the details of this mess. It's going to take some time."

"Brent wants me to go to Jeff's funeral tomorrow at Arlington."

"That's all right, I'll be there too."

"After the funeral, Brent wants me to go with him when he sees Whitestone at Bethesda."

"How'd he know about Whitestone?"

"His wife called Brent yesterday. She told him that he thinks that he may know who killed Jeff. By the way, I remember Whitestone. He and I went through training together. He'll probably recognize me tomorrow."

"No, he won't. His eyes are covered with bandages."

Devine was thinking hard.

He had talked with Whitestone yesterday at the hospital and Whitestone didn't say anything to him about that.

Devine thought is was strange that Whitestone wanted to talk with Maxwell instead of him.

He wondered if this has anything to do with the arms business.

Why did someone in his department direct Leanne to assassinate two of his agents?

Leanne interrupted his thoughts.

"What do you want me to tell Brent?"

"I don't want you to tell him anything.

"Go with him to the funeral and then to the hospital. Find out whatever you can from Whitestone."

"All right. I'll call Brent and tell him that this was just an accident."

"That's right. There's no need for him to know anything yet. Where will you be tonight?"

"I'll be at his place."

"We'll have a surveillance team on both of you. Don't worry, I'm not going to let anyone get close to you."

She was feeling better about Devine. Maybe they were trying to protect her after all.

"Thanks, Jack."

--THIRTY--

Kent thought that there was no need for him to stay in the office any longer.

It was almost three o'clock on a Friday afternoon. The traffic would be heavy. People would be trying to take off early and enjoy the summer weekend.

He figured that Wilson would probably hang around the office as long as the examiners were reviewing old registration documents and prospectuses.

There was a good chance that the examiners would call it a day, if they didn't find anything unusual or blatantly misleading in the mounds of paperwork in front of them.

Kent planned to talk with Wilson later down in Annapolis during the Friday night pre-race party at the yacht club.

He thought that it would be a good idea to keep the pressure on Wilson to keep his mouth shut.

Kent's main concern was that the SEC's civil investigation would lead the examiners into more serious matters.

He felt that the Atlas's sale of the practically worthless piece of commercial property located a hundred miles outside Dallas-Fort Worth to Montieff-Hamilton's Real Estate department for ten million dollars would certainly implicate Wilson.

At this stage of the civil investigation into alleged manipulative stock trading practices, it shouldn't be necessary for the examiners to delve into the firm's real estate transaction.

The transaction enabled Kent to compromise Wilson. Wilson was so concerned about the gambling debts that he became desperate to pay them off as quickly as possible.

Wilson had become extremely concerned when Kent explained that he would be facing jail time if the SEC discovered the conflict of interest situation.

Kent smiled as he remembered the cringing look on George's face at lunch.

It was priceless.

George was a man without a spine.

He had become the perfect pawn to front for him at Montieff-Hamilton while he flawlessly executed the plan to steal thirty billion dollars.

There was nothing that Wilson could do now to jeopardize Kent's plan to exit the country next week.

George couldn't afford to talk about the bogus real estate deal with anybody.

All the money realized from the sale of stock of the bogus companies had been transferred to safe accounts in the Cayman Islands, Liechtenstein, Monaco and Yemen.

The regulatory agencies would never be able to follow the intricate trail he constructed.

There were too many layers of shell corporations and private trusts in countries which had little, if any, banking regulations.

Now that the money had been safely absconded out of the United States, Kent had only one more thing to do.

He had to get himself out of the country safely.

Kent needed to concentrate on Ranfield.

Now, he was the wildcard in this game of trying to get out of the country without being detected.

A chartered helicopter flew him down to Annapolis in less than an hour.

Kent checked into the Marriott, changed clothes and went down to the marina.

His J-105 was secured in a slip near the end of a private floating dock.

He wondered what he'd do with the boat after he left the country. Probably, he'd leave it there.

Most of the boats never left the marina anyway.

Kent motored out of the congested harbor until he got into open water.

It was a good time to think about his options for dealing with Ranfield.

He could send him overseas to work for the syndicate, but that might pose a problem if the agency decided to track him down.

The only viable option was to eliminate him.

That was the only way to prevent Ranfield from implicating him in the arms business.

He didn't trust Ranfield to keep his mouth shut.

After he returned to the marina, he called Ranfield from his cell phone.

"How's the duck hunting?"

"Quiet."

"Do you want to get a bite to eat?"

"Sounds good. Where do you want to go?"

"There's a restaurant near the airport in Queenstown. The place with the live band."

"The one on the water?"

"Right. I'll be there in half-an-hour."

"All right."

Kent got to the restaurant before Ranfield.

He waited in the back of the parking lot.

After a few minutes, Ranfield pulled up next to his truck. They got out of their trucks and shook hands.

"I'm glad you made it." Kent said.

"Yeah, but that asshole I contracted to hit the shooter really screwed up."

"Tell me about it."

"I've used him before. This is the first time he messed up."

"Yeah, that's too bad. Look, let's go down to the house. I have to give you some money and the passports."

"When's the plane coming in?"

"About an hour. We have time."

Kent talked with Ranfield as he drove down to his waterfront house.

"Look, I've got a job for you when you get to Zurich."

"Really?"

"Yeah, we need someone to take over the money laundering operation. The business has really grown over the last year. We need someone with your experience to run it."

"That sounds good to me."

"After things quiet down here, we'll be able to send your wife and kids over to you."

"That'll be great."

As they drove down the private road to his boathouse on the river, Ranfield wondered whether he could trust Kent's offer to go to Zurich.

They got out of the truck and began walking down a darkened path towards the boathouse.

Suddenly, Kent pulled out his gun and shot Ranfield twice in the head.

The execution was silent.

Kent had screwed a silencer into his Glock nine-millimeter pistol.

He grabbed Ranfield by his ankles and dragged him down the dirt path to the boathouse.

Kent pulled the body onto the boathouse dock and then rolled it into his eighteen-foot Whaler.

He went to the storage shed, got two spare anchors and some rope and stepped into the boat. Kent quickly tied one anchor around Ranfield's neck and the other around his knees.

He untied the lines, coiled them neatly next to Ranfield's body and started the engine.

It was dark, but Kent didn't need to put on the running lights. He knew the Wye River like the palm of his hand.

He ran slowly and quietly past the houses that lined the riverbanks until he got into the Chesapeake Bay.

Then, he moved the throttle up a notch until he was about two hundred yards offshore.

When he figured the water was deep enough, he put the boat in idle, picked up Ranfield by the ropes around his neck and knees and dumped him into the water.

He thought that the anchors would weigh him down for at least a week.

By that time, he would be gone.

--THIRTY-ONE--

A little after dawn the following day, Jack Kent sailed out of Annapolis Harbor.

The sky was clear, the sun was rising from the east and a soft warm breeze swept over the idyllic scene.

Sleek sailboats and expensive cabin cruisers shared space along the sides of the wharf in the downtown district of the historic capitol of Maryland.

Hundreds of sailboats, moored overnight to small numbered buoys, lay still in the water all pointing in the direction of the current and light wind.

The exclusive marinas were jammed with non-resident out-of-state visitors that were typical for a summer weekend in this popular tourist attraction.

The streets were still quiet.

Only young joggers and elderly walkers felt the need to be out this early in the morning

A few outdoor cafes had opened and several waitresses were wiping off the overnight dew from the outside tables.

They were preparing for the onslaught of tourists who were expected to descend into this narrow section of town looking for a good cup of coffee and the morning papers.

There were only a few other boats heading out into the Chesapeake Bay this early in the morning.

Most of the sailors moored in the harbor were still sleeping after the heavy partying the night before.

As Kent sailed south towards St. Michaels, his mind wandered back to the days of his childhood growing up on the Eastern Shore of Maryland.

His home was a rundown trailer on a creek just south of Chesterton.

Kent was the son of a father who worked as a marine mechanic at a Chester River marina and a mother who tended bar at a shots and beer joint on Route 13.

As he was growing up, he and his younger sister thought that their life was pretty good.

Although they didn't have any money, it didn't make any difference to them. None of their friends had any money either.

They were all poor and lived in trailers like theirs or in ramshackle single story houses.

The kids spent nearly all of their free time on the water. It was their playground. There were plenty of fun things to do, like fishing, crabbing and playing in their small boats.

They grew up learning about the waters of the Chesapeake Bay in the tradition of their ancestors.

On his eighth birthday, his father gave him a present which, when Kent reflected back on it, probably changed the course of his young life forever.

His father took him to the marina where he worked as a mechanic and showed him an old, ugly vestige of what appeared to have been a twenty-eight foot sailboat.

It was lying on its hull in shallow water near the edge of the inlet wedged down in the muddy sediment.

The partially sunken shell lay tilted on its side with a shattered wooden stump for a mast, with its cockpit door hanging off a single rusted hinge.

All it needed, his father had told him, was just a little work.

During the next few months, the two of them worked hard to recondition the boat.

The owner of the marina didn't mind letting them use his equipment to fix up the wreck. The boat had been abandoned for years and had become a weary eyesore for his regular tenants.

Whenever they needed parts and materials, his father simply stole them.

It was a lot cheaper to "borrow" them from the parts department at the marina than buying them from expensive places like West Marine.

They got their sails from one of his father's drinking buddies, a sail maker in Annapolis.

He often bought more sailcloth than was necessary to fill orders for custom sails from wealthy yachtsmen.

There was plenty of free sailcloth to give to his friend across the Bay.

The boat was a wreck.

Kent and his father practically had to build the boat from scratch, but they did it after two months of hard labor. Kent had learned a little bit about the art of building a boat.

When the boat was ready, he took his first sail with a great deal of pride in what he and his father had accomplished.

Kent didn't fully appreciate what his father had designed for him until a few years later.

It appeared fairly ordinary above water, but below water his father had constructed the hull that was configured for sailing in the Chesapeake Bay waters.

After that, he sailed every day in all kinds of weather, gaining self-confidence and a sense of self-reliance.

When he was on the water, he felt free of the restrictions of school and the confinement of the trailer.

By the age of twelve, he had become a fearless, talented all-weather sailor.

Anxious to compete against the prep school kids across the bay, he started entering the free junior races sponsored by the local racing association.

Kent became unbeatable.

These young part-time social sailors were no match for him.

During the next few years, a certain mystique about him developed in the racing circles around the Chesapeake Bay.

After he won a race, he would accept his trophy and sail back up the bay towards Rock Hall. No one knew where he lived or where he kept his boat.

By the time he was sixteen, Kent was a strong six-foot one, one hundred and ninety-pound athlete.

By his junior year in his regional public high school, he was drawing the attention of college football and lacrosse coaches throughout the Mid-Atlantic and New England regions.

The high school scouting reports were touting him as blue-chip Division One prospect in both sports.

NCAA rules prohibited colleges from talking with him, but not the prep schools.

Kent had no interest in leaving the bay area.

Sailing meant too much to him. It didn't matter that they offered financial aid.

It didn't matter that he could get into college.

Kent had no interest in college, because there was nothing he wanted to learn.

The buzz about Kent had filtered down to Bob Gibbons, the coach of the sailing team at St. James, a prep school in Annapolis.

Gibbons knew about Kent.

For the past few years, Bob had seen him race in the Junior Class races against the kids who were on his sailing team. Kent had clearly overwhelmed his team.

Coach Gibbons had seen Kent move up into the open class races, even though he was still young enough to have continued racing in the Junior Class events.

In the beginning, Kent was able to hold his own against his older competitors often placing in the top ten finishers.

By the end of his second sailing season, the fifteen year-old was winning some races.

Like many others who were born and raised in Annapolis, Coach Gibbons was an inveterate sailor.

He had lived in Annapolis for his entire life.

Gibbons knew that Jack Kent, this young waterman, would never leave the Eastern Shore.

The water of the Chesapeake Bay was in his blood.

The coach wanted a sailing championship and Kent could help him get it.

The school offered Kent and his family a substantial financial package to attend on the condition that he would take an aptitude test.

Kent's high school transcript was terrible and his grades were awful.

Teachers didn't bother to flunk him because they didn't want Kent to repeat another year with them.

In his first year at the public area high school, Kent went to school a few times a week and only during the football and lacrosse seasons.

For the rest of the time, he couldn't be bothered to go to school at all.

Kent thought that high school was stupid and that he'd only be wasting his time going to class.

He had a job working as an apprentice marine mechanic making nine bucks an hour and whatever he could steal from the shop.

The high school officials wanted to expel him from school for truancy and failing grades, but the new football coach pleaded with them to keep Kent in school.

The football program had been in shambles. There were some big, strong farm boys walking around the corridors in school, but they had very few skill position players.

The scouting reports told the same old story. Good size, no speed.

The athletic director wanted someone inside the building to coach the football team and selected a young History teacher who had been an All-American quarterback at the University of Maryland.

When the new coach was merely a History teacher, he had seen Kent play as a freshman on the junior varsity team.

The former star for the Terrapins hadn't seen this kind of raw power and aggression since his playing days in the Atlantic Coast Conference.

This was a fourteen year-old who hadn't developed any football skills, yet. If he were coached properly, he would be a devastating football player.

Although Kent was big, strong and fast, he was a raw talent. The thought crossed his mind that at the high school level, a good football coach could build a team around Kent.

Potentially, he could develop into a player.

The coach conceded that Kent was a truant and that he failed his core courses, but he argued that the kid wasn't stupid and that he had missed classes because he was working. He needed the money.

The football coach needed Kent.

There was no sense admitting him to St. James if he couldn't handle the work.

The test results surprised everyone, including Kent, becausethey were extraordinary.

Kent had a brilliant mind, but he never bothered to use it.

The athletic director began salivating with dreams of the unthinkable.

Three championships for St. James. In football, lacrosse and sailing.

The transition from his public school to the prep school catering to the children of wealthy families was rocky and violent.

The cultural differences between Kent and his new classmates were as great as the Chesapeake Bay that separated them.

For nearly two hundred years, before the Chesapeake Bay Bridge was built, the Eastern Shore was virtually inaccessible to mainland Marylanders.

It seemed to some of the older families on the mainland side of the Bay that people on the Eastern Shore were living in a time capsule. The watermen kept plying their trade from Rock Hall down to the mouth of the Bay near Norfolk.

The Chesapeake Bay, the largest estuary in the United States, had provided watermen with a way to make a living for over two hundred years.

Although ten million people lived along or near the shores of the Chesapeake Bay and millions more vacationed in Delaware, Maryland and Virginia, the watermen kept to themselves.

They were a breed apart, so Kent came to school with an attitude.

Kent didn't like rich people and he especially didn't like the rich kids he raced against for the past four years.

On the first day of school, he went down to the marina where the school docked their boats.

Several members of the sailing team were working on their boats. One of them, an upperclassman, approached him and asked, in a superior tone of voice, where he came from.

Kent sensed the boy's disrespect and dropped him to the dock with one punch.

He sent a message loud and clear to the rest of the school that no one was going to mess with him.

Once he stepped inside the lines of a football field, he was the toughest player they had ever seen in the private school league.

Time and again, his coaches tried to get him to ease up, but he wouldn't do it.

The best day for his teammates was game day. Instead of punishing them, he'd punish opposing teams.

Coach Gibbons realized that Kent wasn't going to make the transition on his own.

Kent was too rebellious.

If he wasn't going to conform to the rules and regulations at St. James, the Headmaster would throw him out.

Gibbons didn't want that to happen. He might as well kiss the sailing championship goodbye.

Coach Gibbons decided that he would try to mentor the boy and help him adjust to a very different way of life than across the Bay on the Eastern Shore.

This was going to be a project. Kent had an attitude. The only way Kent was going to succeed in this new culture was if he understood it.

One day after sailing practice, Gibbons sat down with Kent and explained what he could gain by working within the system.

"Jack, there are two kinds of people in this world.

"Those who have a great deal of money and those who don't have a great deal of money.

"Most people, like us, we're in the second group.

"The kids who go to school here are in the first group.

"Do you understand what I'm saying to you?"

Kent was sitting on the edge of the dock near his boat while Gibbons sat cross-legged in the middle of the dock a few feet away.

"Sort of."

"Try to understand what I mean about wealth and money. Millions of dollars, Jack. Have you ever thought about making a lot of money?"

"Not really. I get by."

"I don't want to talk about how you get by. Would be interested in making so much money that you could buy anything in the world for you and your family and do it legally?"

"Sure."

"The first thing you have to do is get into the right schools, like this one."

"Why?"

Gibbons was grateful that Kent was starting to get a little interested in the topic.

"Because wealthy families send their kids only to the right schools and there aren't that many around the country that they consider acceptable.

You see, these prep schools cater to wealthy families because they finance and control the schools. They'll never admit it, but they only want their own kind admitted."

"I'm not their kind. Why did they admit me?"

"Because you're a great athlete. They'll put up with you because some people around here figure you're going to bring a few championships to the school. That includes me, Jack. I haven't won a sailing championship since I took over the team four years ago."

"Well, at least you're honest with me."

"That's why I'm having this talk with you, Jack. I want you to understand that you have a chance to make good things happen, not just in sports now, but later after you get out of college."

"College, are you kidding?"

"No. You've got to go the right college to be able to play the game. That's where you make the contacts with rich and powerful people."

"What kind of game are you talking about?"

"A game of making lots of money. It's about powerful people accepting you into their world.

"You see, it's almost like the rich have created their own private system of education. The very wealthy think that only a few private schools are the right places for their children to attend.

"They expect their children to come to schools like St. James. It's part of their system, part of their society. Now that you're here, you should take advantage of it. This is the best thing that has ever happened to you, Jack. Just think about it for a minute. What other kid from the Eastern Shore has ever gotten into a prep school on this side of the Bay?"

"I don't know."

"No one, Jack. You're the first one. Jack, you're very smart. I saw your test scores. You've got a brain, but you haven't used it. You can make these kids accept you if do better than them. Kick their ass on the football field and make them feel like idiots in the classroom. They'll get to respect you and when that happens they'll accept you."

"It's all about acceptance, Jack. You got a taste of it down on the dock on your first day here.

Jack curled his lip with contempt and said, "Well, I took care of that!"

That he did.

"Here's what you're going to do, Jack Kent. First, you'll get a good education. If you stick it out here for the next two years and get decent grades, you'll get into one of the right colleges."

Gibbons mentored Kent through his junior and senior years at St. James. He convinced Kent that could be as wealthy and powerful as his classmates when they got out of college.

Kent listened and learned. He discovered that it was easy to get good grades. After the first term ended, his teachers put him into the honors program.

--THIRTY-TWO--

Friends and family packed the Church of the Redeemer in Falls Church, Virginia for a funeral service for Jeff Maxwell, a former intelligence officer with the CIA, Navy fighter pilot and an heir to the Maxwell family fortune.

News of his tragic death circulated quickly through the corporate and financial worlds where his family had been such a powerful presence for decades.

The pews were filled with senators, bankers and corporate leaders who were related to the large extended family by blood or marriage and who were paying their respects to this old blue-blood industrialist family from New England.

Hundreds of friends of the Maxwell brothers from the University of Virginia and the Choate School were assembled together in the middle of the church trying to fathom why Jeff had to die so young.

A closed flag-draped casket had been placed by the front of the altar.

Most of the mourners understood why there wasn't a viewing, but few spoke about it.

Leanne and Brent sat in the second pew immediately behind his parents and only a few feet from the coffin.

Brent didn't need to see his mother's face to know that she was crying.

Normally she was emotionally strong when dealing with a crisis, but this was different.

This time, she was overwhelmed with grief.

When the funeral mass began, Leanne turned towards him and whispered, "Are you all right?"

He whispered back, "I'm okay."

Brent wasn't telling her the truth.

It was difficult enough for Brent and his parents to cope with losing Jeff, because they were reliving the terrible tragedy, fours years ago, that took his wife and their grandchildren away from them.

Brent grieved a long time after Tiffany and the children were killed in the car crash, but eventually he accepted the reality of their deaths.

This funeral brought back too many sad memories of four years ago when he had to bury them.

When Leanne came into his life three years later, he was emotionally ready for another marriage and a new family. Brent had fallen very much in love with Leanne.

Although their backgrounds were so different, they discovered that they had a great deal in common.

They were bright, articulate and successful in their professions.

A mutual respect and trust had developed in their six-month business relationship which became the foundation for their flourishing romance.

Leanne felt uneasy sitting so close to the casket.

There wasn't any solace knowing that she had been tricked into shooting Jeff.

She'd rather deal with physical pain any day, than try to cope with the emotional anguish she felt now.

How was she ever going to be able to talk to Brent about her situation?

How could she ever explain to him the guilt that she felt?

Devine told her she had to be patient and to keep the information to herself, even though she wanted to tell Brent about everything that had happened.

He needed more time to find out what was happening at the agency.

There were still too many unanswered questions about the identity of the operative responsible for ordering Leanne to kill Maxwell and Whitestone.

Brent didn't need to know about the internal problems they were having at the agency or Leanne's connection to Jeff Maxwell's death at this time.

Leanne felt that she at least owed him that much.

When those problems at the agency were resolved, she could tell Brent.

She didn't think that it was fair not being able to tell Brent about working for the agency part-time.

Since her contract with the agency was going to expire in a few months, Leanne thought that there wouldn't be any harm done to their relationship if she told Brent about it.

Even if she only told him about some of the things that she did, but not about the contracts. That would too difficult for Brent to understand.

There wasn't any need to tell him exactly what she did.

Like many other wealthy old families from New England, his parents had sent the boys to the University of Virginia, a good place to make connections, to play ball and to party hard.

The University had a reputation over the years for producing powerful leaders in the world of business and politics.

It wasn't a coincidence that many of the old wealthy aristocratic families from the industrial Northeast adopted Virginia as the right place for their children to go to school.

Their parents fully expected that Brent and Jeff would attend graduate school, preferably Harvard or Yale, in order to get their Masters degrees in Business Administration.

They could opt for a law degree, but that would take a year longer and it wouldn't be as relevant to running an investment banking firm as a MBA in Economics or Management.

Their father expected that much of them, because he wanted them to work their way up the corporate ladder by the time he retired.

His father, like other old money fathers, groomed his sons to preserve the family's wealth.

He looked forward to transferring to Brent and Jeff the power to run the large investment banking and trading firm controlled by their family.

Jeff had other ideas.

The prospects of working with Brent in the family's firm really didn't appeal to him.

He didn't need the money. He had plenty in the trust fund that his parents set up for him.

He wanted to do something more adventurous, something that had some risk involved, like land F-14s on nuclear aircraft carriers.

Jeff got what he wanted, as usual.

After completing flight school at Pensacola Naval Air Base, he spent the next six years flying for the Navy.

Most of his time was spent aboard the USS Enterprise, a refitted nuclear aircraft carrier, which traveled extensively around the Mediterranean Sea.

After he was discharged, his father asked him if he was ready to join his brother Brent at Hamilton-Montague.

After six years of landing at a hundred and thirty miles an hour on top of a rolling carrier in the dark, the thought of working on Wall Street seemed tame.

Jeff wasn't about to trade in his seat in the cockpit of his F-14 for a cloth swivel chair on the firm's trading floor.

He was looking for more action.

The CIA wanted people like Jeff.

They recruited veterans because they would be able to easily assimilate into the military-type structure of the agency.

They especially liked the attitude of fighter pilots who lived every day as if it was their last.

Jeff was a perfect candidate to become an intelligence officer in Special Operations.

He was bright, street-savvy and loved action, but the agency had a minor reservation about him.

After their psychological profilers interviewed Jeff, they reported that he was mentally fit to function in the field in life-threatening situations.

However, there was a concern that he might turn out to be somewhat irresponsible, too much of a cowboy, in the field.

The profilers saw Jeff as a person who had been taking greater risks as he grew older. By the time he was flying F-14s, Jeff was considered by some of his squadron buddies as border-line certifiable.

In fact, they pointed out, the candidate, with little regard for his own safety had pulled a dangerous aerial stunt over a civilian resort on the Costa del Sol in southern Spain a month before his discharge.

There were no formal charges filed against him, but the incident was duly noted in his service record.

Jeff was perceived as a free-spirited thrill-seeking individual who could understand orders and would obey instructions, but wouldn't back away from unnecessarily dangerous situations.

The recitation of the twenty-third psalm by the congregation brought Brent back to earth.

--THIRTY-THREE--

Annapolis had awakened by the time Kent returned from his solitary morning sail.

The activity in the inner harbor seems as frenetic as the action on the narrow streets that sloped down to the wharfs.

Kent skillfully navigated his colorful Jay-105 through the moored sailboats, past the plodding water taxis while avoiding any collisions with the dinghies that were crisscrossing through the narrow end of the harbor like large frantic water bugs.

The early post-dawn breeze had become more brisk, which Kent thought would bode well for the big race in the afternoon. The stronger the winds, the better he liked them.

The solitary sunrise sail allowed him to mentally prepare for the day. There was a mission to accomplish and failure was not an acceptable option.

Whitestone must be eliminated quickly.

The events of the past week had forced Kent to take action on his own.

Still, Kent was looking forward to the race, since he knew that this would be the last time he'd sail on the Chesapeake Bay for a very long time.

The Hospice Cup was a prestigious race in the schedule run by the local racing association.

The irony of the race was not lost on Kent, since he'd be visiting someone shortly who was in imminent danger of death.

After he secured the boat, Kent walked on the floating docks towards the clubhouse.

As he entered the lounge, a voice called out to him.

"Good morning, Jack, sure is good to see you. You been out early today?"

Henry had known Kent since the teenager first came over from Chesterton to go to St. James.

Henry was a waiter in the yacht club. He met Kent while he was bussing tables at the club to make some extra money.

"Yeah, Henry, you know it's my favorite time of day. How've you been?"

"I've been feeling fine. Crabbing's good, tips could be better. How're your folks doing? I haven't seen them in a long time."

"Dad died late last year. Lung cancer."

"Sorry to hear that."

"Smoking too much, Henry, he never would quit."

"That's a shame. How 'bout your Mom?"

Not wanting to bring up that subject, he said, "She's doing okay, Henry."

There was no sense hanging out the family wash. Henry didn't need to know about Mom's little drinking problem.

If she kept spending her time hanging around the local gin mills, she'd probably drink herself to an early death. She hasn't been sober since Dad died.

"Well, give her my best."

"I will."

Kent thought that if he did speak to her anytime soon, that she wouldn't understand a word he said.

"Jack, you want some hot coffee?"

"Yes. Would you bring it back to the locker room for me?"

"Yes, I will."

Henry thought that it was nice to see a local boy make it big. He remembered when he came over from Chesterton that he didn't have two nickels to rub together.

After Kent bussed tables in the restaurant for a while, Henry realized the boy was a hard worker.

He also knew that Kent was sneaking steaks and roast beef out of the building after the restaurant was closed.

It was all right with Henry.

No one else in the club thought the boy was swiping food out of the freezer except the chef, who lived near Chesterton and happened to know Kent's parents.

He thought that Kent must have done something right to get where he was now, a member of the club.

Henry wondered if the admission committee knew that this big shot from Princeton had worked right here bussing tables when he was a kid.

He didn't think so.

Drinking hot coffee in a steaming shower was the best feeling after an early sail.

He spent thirty minutes stretching with the hot water pulsing on his back muscles. Physically, he was ready for the tasks ahead.

Killing and sailing.

Kent finished his shower, toweled off and got dressed.

He put on a pair of slacks, a cotton sweater, a pair of dockers and an Orioles baseball cap.

Then, he slipped out the side door of the club unnoticed.

Kent walked briskly to the upper deck of the parking garage and got into his black Tahoe.

He started the engine, drove down the ramp from the upper level and slowly merged into the heavy downtown tourist traffic on Water Street.

Kent headed east towards Bethesda on Route 50.

He was careful to maintain the speed limit because he didn't want to be stopped by a state trooper today.

There was no need to rush. He had ample time to complete his mission.

Kent thought that Whitestone most likely would be in his room alone.

Ranfield had said there were no agents assigned to protect him.
That was odd, he thought.
They should know by now that he's a target.
Kent thought he would have had the floor secured.
Maybe they haven't figured it out yet, but they will soon.

The visiting hours at Bethesda Naval Hospital on Saturday mornings were the busiest of the week which would make it easier for Kent to remain relatively unnoticed.

He scanned the crowded parking lot for just the right vacant space and found it in the middle of the row between a black Suburban and black Explorer.

From a distance, the Tahoe would blend indistinguishably with the other two black vehicles.

There were only a few people who were walking towards the hospital's main entrance.

Since the morning visiting hours were scheduled to end at eleven, anyone visiting Whitestone would probably be leaving by now.

Everything Kent needed was in a gift wrapped box inside a decorated shopping bag, something a thoughtful relative would bring. This caring brother would be bringing a special present to him today.

When he walked through the sliding doors, he saw the restrooms on the left by the gift store.

Kent walked into the men's room, went into an empty stall and locked the door behind him.

He opened the gift box, picked up a white-haired wig and mustache and carefully put them on.

Then, he slipped into a long white doctor's coat that had a fake identification card clipped to the upper pocket.

Finally, he put on a pair of large frame tinted glasses.

Kent picked up a plain vanilla folder containing blank papers and the weapon, a syringe loaded with sixty milli-equivalents of potassium chloride.

After he put the shopping bag in the trash, Kent walked into the main foyer and past the security guards to the elevators.

When the elevator doors opened on the fourth floor, he went through several people waiting to take the elevator down.

The nurses at the station were too distracted to see him walk down the hallway towards Whitestone's room.

A woman came out of the room and walked towards him.

That must be his wife, he thought.

She looked at him briefly as he passed by.

Kent kept his eyes down.

She walked to the elevators and waited to go down.

He walked past Whitestone's room, hesitated and looked at the blank pieces of paper in the manila folder.

Jennifer went into the elevator.

The doors closed.

Kent turned and walked back into Whitestone's room.

"Is that you, Jennifer?" Whitestone asked.

"No. I'm here to check your IVs."

Whitestone thought that the voice sounded familiar.

"Oh, okay. Do I know you?"

His former colleague would certainly know him if he wasn't wearing the bandages over his eyes.

Kent took the loaded syringe from his pocket and walked to Whitestone's bedside.

Kent uncapped the syringe, stuck the needle into the tube and depressed the plunger.

"You used to." Kent said, as he watched Whitestone die in a second.

--THIRTY-FOUR--

Small white clouds hung like crumpled tissues in the clear blue skies over Arlington National Cemetery.

The aroma of freshly mowed grass filled the air.

As Brent and Leanne sat at the gravesite, amid symmetrical rows of white crosses, Navy chaplain was reciting the prayers for the dead in a numbing monotone delivery.

When the service ended, Jennifer Whitestone walked up to Leanne and Brent and introduced herself.

"Mr. Maxwell, I'm Jennifer Whitestone."

"Hello, it's nice to meet you. I'd like you to meet my financee, Leanne Anderson."

"Hello, Jennifer. Brent told me about your husband. How's he doing?"

"I saw him this morning at the hospital and he seems much better. We were able to talk for a while."

Jennifer turned to Brent and said, "Your brother and John were close friends. They had worked together for years in Europe and the Middle East. Jeff told John where you could be contacted."

"I'm glad that you did."

"Are you still coming over to the hospital to see John?"

"Of course. Did you come here by yourself?"

"Yes."

"Well, I know how to get to the hospital from here. Why don't we meet you in the parking lot?"

"That'll be fine. It'll only take about twenty minutes to get there."

A half an hour later, the three of them were walking through the hospital lobby past the security desk towards the elevators.

They got off at the fourth floor and walked through the double doors towards Whitestone's room.

Dr. Bjorn spotted Jennifer as she passed by the nurse's station with Leanne and Brent.

He approached them with a concerned look on his face.

"Mrs. Whitestone, I need a moment with you in private."

"Is everything all right?"

"There's a conference room at the end of the hall that we can use."

As he started to walk away, the doctor turned to Leanne and Brent and said, "We'll be a few minutes. Why don't you wait for us outside in the lounge?"

"What do you think that was about?" Brent asked her as they sat down on an uncomfortable vinyl couch in the waiting room.

"Something's not right."

"Why do you say that?"

"I didn't like the look on the doctor's face."

"We'll find out soon enough. How are you feeling?"

"I feel sore."

"How about your headaches?"

"They feel worse than the gash. How are you doing?"

"All right, I guess. I feel so empty. The funeral brought back a lot of bad memories. You know, Tiffany and the kids."

Leanne loved Brent and felt so badly for him. She would never deliberately do anything to hurt him.

That was the last thing she wanted to do.

Trying to cope with her worrying about Brent and whether there was someone trying to kill her was making her feel sick. She had to stay strong and console Brent.

In the conference room, Jennifer and Dr. Bjorn were sitting at the table.

"Mrs. Whitestone, I'm sorry to tell you this, but we lost John this afternoon."

"Lost?" Jennifer muttered in disbelief. "Do you mean he's dead? I saw him this morning. I talked with him. There was nothing wrong with him."

"I know. I checked him on my rounds this morning and he was fine. He even asked me when he could go home."

Tears welled up in her eyes as her body started to tremble.

"I can't believe this. John is dead? Are you sure?" She asked desperately.

His head sagged slightly as he tried, as compassionately as he could, to convey the reality of her husband's sudden and unexpected death.

"Yes, Mrs. Whitestone, we are sure."
"How did he die?"
"He suffered cardiac arrest."
"There was nothing wrong with his heart. I checked his charts. He didn't have any heart problems."
"I know."
"When did this happen?"
"It happened sometime between eleven and twelve o'clock this morning.
"When I saw him at eleven he was fine, but when the nurse found him at twelve he wasn't breathing."
"My God! I must have just missed you. I was here a little after eleven. John and I talked until I had to leave for a funeral."
"What time did you leave?"
"I left around quarter to twelve. You said the nurse found John around twelve?"
"Yes."
"Something's not right, Doctor."
"You know that we'll have to perform an autopsy on John. Maybe we'll find out why he had heart failure."
"Where is John now?"
"He's in the morgue."
"I'd like to see him."
"Of course. I'll take you down."
"I'd like to have my friend, Mr. Maxwell go with me. His brother was a good friend of my husband."
"Is he the man you came in with?"
"Yes."

"I'll go get him. We'll be right back."

The doctor walked quickly into the waiting room and stopped in front of Leanne and Brent.

"Are you Mr. Maxwell?"

"Yes."

"I'm Doctor Bjorn, John Whitestone's surgeon. I have some bad news. John died of heart failure this afternoon."

Leanne and Brent looked at him in utter disbelief.

Brent said, "Jennifer told me that he was going to be all right! She didn't say anything about a heart problem. I don't understand how this could happen."

"We didn't see any problems with his heart before or after the surgery. Right now we don't know why he suffered cardiac arrest. We're going to perform an autopsy this afternoon. Maybe we'll find some answers."

Leanne knew right away that Whitestone was murdered. Officially, the cause of death would be listed as heart failure.

She knew that an excessive dose of potassium chloride injected into the blood stream would cause the heart to fail instantly.

Leanne also knew that an autopsy wouldn't detect the overdose.

It wouldn't show any evidence of an excessive amount of potassium chloride because it would have blended into the blood stream. This was a perfect execution.

"Mrs. Whitestone would like you to be with her when she goes downstairs to the morgue to see John."

"Of course. Do you mean now?"

"Yes. I want to get down there before they start the autopsy."

"Leanne, will you be all right?"

"Yes, I'll be fine, go ahead."

--THIRTY-FIVE--

Leanne was waiting for Brent and Jennifer to get back from the morgue when the elevator doors opened and Devine walked into the waiting room.

"There you are. We've got to talk." He said, plopping down into an oversized lounge chair next to her.

"I guess you heard the news?" She said.

"Yeah, I got here as soon as I could. Where's Maxwell?"

"He and Jennifer went down to the morgue to see Whitestone. What do you think?"

"About this?"

"Yes."

"Somebody got to him."

"Jennifer told me that she was in the room with him until around quarter to twelve. And supposedly the nurse found him dead a little after twelve."

"A fifteen minute window. Well, a forensic team will be here soon, but I don't expect they'll come up with much. This guy was a pro."

"What do think, potassium chloride?"

"Probably. But we won't be able to trace that in the autopsy.

"If we're lucky, maybe we'll find a puncture in the IV tubes."

"The doctor said he checked him around eleven and that he was fine.

"If he had a visitor after Jennifer left, the security cameras would have picked him up."

"That's what I'm going to do after you and I figure out what we're going to do next."

"Do you know who did this?"

"I have a pretty good idea."

"Someone in the agency?"

"Yes. You know Ranfield, don't you?"

"Sure. I worked with him on a hostage rescue operation about six years ago in Spain."

"I found out about that yesterday when we checked your files. We wanted to see if there was any connection between you, Maxwell and Whitestone."

"And?"

"While you were working full time for us, you had nine different assignments in the Mediterranean area.

"Each time you were there, either Maxwell, Ranfield or Whitestone was also there."

She paused for a moment trying to recall the field agents involved on those missions with her.

"You're right. I remember them now. They were new guys, about the same age as me.

"In fact, Ranfield was in my training class. What do you make of that?"

"These agents have worked together for years. They're a real tight group."

"Do you suspect that they were working together in this operation?"

"Yes and my guess is that Ranfield had heard the scuttlebutt that the AFT people suspected some of our agents.

"He probably felt jeopardized that Whitestone and Jeff might talk if the ATF got to them.

"I still don't understand why it was so urgent for Ranfield to take these risks.

"Either the ATF was closer than we thought or there's something else that's going on that we don't know about."

"Have you talked to Ranfield?"

"No. He left the office yesterday afternoon around three o'clock. We sent some people over to his house in Falls Church last night, but he wasn't there and his wife doesn't know where he is.

"We still don't know where he is. He may be on the run, but we'll get him."

"I never would have believed that this could have happened. Do you think Ranfield was behind yesterday's accident?"

"Yes, I do."

"Why?"

"He had to kill you. You would have exposed him if you were left alive.

"We wouldn't have known about the bogus kill orders. You would have already destroyed them.

"After a while, we would have figured out that you were the shooter and possibly working for Ranfield.

"But we wouldn't be able to prove anything, because you'd be dead."

"There wouldn't be any trail to him, would there?"

"No. He would've stopped his arms dealing, if that's what this is about, after he had taken care of all of you.

"He would have kept on working in counter-intelligence like nothing had happened."

"Does Ranfield think I'm alive?"

"Yes, I'm sure that he does. But his plan blew up with that car bomb in Tel Aviv.

"He may try to hit you again or he may go to ground.

"Obviously, he was desperate enough to leave his wife and kids. There's one other thing that bothers me."

"What's that, Jim?"

"If Ranfield is our guy, and he knew you were alive, why would he risk killing Whitestone?"

"Maybe Ranfield hired an independent contractor to kill Whitestone."

"Maybe, but if not, there may be more to this than we think. You know, we have to tell Brent about yesterday."

"Oh, no. You can't do that, he's been through too much the last few days."

"We have to tell him, Leanne. It's for your own protection and his."

"You're not going to tell him about his brother, are you?"

"No, I'm going to tell him that you worked for us for about five years in special operations.

"You had a support function, nothing close to what you really did. He should be able to handle that."

"I hope Brent believes you. It hurts me so much to see what he's going through."

Just then, a somewhat ashen-looking Brent walked into the room.

"Brent, are you all right?" Leanne asked.
"That was rough. Jennifer is really taking this hard."
"I feel so sorry for her."
"Yeah, me too."

Devine thought he might as well as get down to business with Brent. It was time to tell him a little bit about Leanne and the agency.

"Brent, I need to talk with you, alone. It's pretty important. Leanne, do you mind if you would wait downstairs for us. We shouldn't be more than a few minutes."

Leanne got up of the couch, looked at Brent briefly with a concerned look on her face and walked to the elevators.

--THIRTY-SIX--

The Bay Cup post-race party was held at the home of the Commodore of the Yacht Club.

It was a Georgian styled mansion, surrounded by manicured grounds that sat high on a hill overlooking the Severn River near the United States Naval Academy.

Music filled the air, as guests mingled throughout the home, sampled the buffet and kept the bar busy.

Kent knew that before too long, most of them would be drifting into an alcoholic fog.

After an exhausting day on the water, there was no way they'd be able to handle all that booze on empty stomachs.

He spotted Wilson on the veranda talking with the host's young daughter.

Kent needed to get Wilson alone.

He accepted congratulations for winning the race as he worked his way towards Wilson and his young friend.

When he got to the veranda, Wilson spotted him and waved him over.

"Jack, you remember Heather, don't you? The Commodore's daughter? She just started her sophomore year at Loyola."

Heather was strikingly attractive in her low cut sundress, long blonde hair and summer tan.

Wilson was well on the way to getting fried.

After a few more drinks, he'd be asking her for a private tour of the bedrooms on the second floor.

"Certainly, I do. Heather, would you mind if I could have a few minutes with George, alone? I have to talk with him about some things."

She looked coyly at him and said, "Not at all, Jack."

After she had left, Kent said, "Aren't you pushing the envelope a little bit, George?"

"Nah, she's looking for some action. I can tell." "Well, hit on her later. We need to talk. Let's go out on the lawn, it's too noisy here."

Once they were outside and alone, they could hear each other talk.

Kent said, "I got a call this morning from a source in the U.S. Attorney's office in New York.

"The SEC has referred their findings to them concerning the allegations of stock manipulation and commission gouging at our firm. They have recommended that a criminal investigation be launched into our investment banking transactions."

"So what?"

"They found the real estate deal."

"Oh, shit!"

Wilson gulped down his drink.

"How the hell did they find out about that?"

"I told you that I couldn't guarantee that they wouldn't find out. If they dug deep enough and long enough, they certainly would have been able to find it."

"Why did they dig so deep, Jack? I did exactly what you told me. You said that would keep them away from that stuff."

"I explained that to you, George.

"Once they expanded their investigation into the venture capital business, they were bound to find out about the deal. They wanted to know why the real estate trust went bankrupt so soon after it went public."

Kent knew exactly what had happened.

"George, the firm did many too deals with Atlas Venture Capital. We did over ninety percent of our IPOs with one firm.

"There are hundreds of venture capital firms in the country. That raised red flags for the SEC auditors.

"If we had to do it all over again, we should have used more venture capital firms.

"There is nothing we can do about that now."

"You set me up me Jack! I thought you were my friend!"

"I helped you out of a jam, George. I wasn't the one running up big gambling debts.

"You were.

"If it wasn't for me, your father would have found out how stupid you were and canned your sorry ass."

"That deal was a hoax.

"Building a shopping center in the middle of nowhere in Texas? What retailer would lease space in a place like that?

"You ripped off the investors by charging too much for the property."

"What's it to you, George. Your father never found out about it. You kept your job. You paid off your debts and you've made a fortune with all the IPOs that went through Atlas.

"George, do you have any idea how much money is in your operating account at Atlas right now?"

"I didn't know that I had an operating account at Atlas. What the hell have you done, Jack?"

"I wanted to make sure that you made some money, George. You know, if you ever had any more gambling debts, you could pay them off with the money you made ripping off your investors."

"How much money is in the account, Jack?"

"Eighty million dollars."

Wilson couldn't speak.

He looked at Kent through blurry eyes and tried to decipher the words, eighty million dollars. His brain wasn't working. He needed another drink.

Wilson didn't want to hear any more about the Atlas deal because he knew that he was in deep shit.

"What's the matter, George? Aren't you happy that you have all that money? You don't need your daddy now, George.

"What am I going to do now? Are they going to indict me? And what about you?"

"Well, George, I'm not a part of any of this. I'm just an economist you hired to advise you on global economies."

"You did the Northport real estate deal! You're behind Atlas!"

"No, I'm not. You are. Don't you remember that I told you that you were the general partner of Atlas?

"You signed the papers closing the deal with your own firm. You've got a little conflict of interest problem, George."

"What? I didn't sign any papers."

"I have copies of the closing papers with your signature on them. You represented Atlas. You're in trouble, unless..."

"Unless what?"

"Unless you do exactly what I say."

"What if I don't?"

"You could have an accident. It could be serious. Maybe you'd have a heart attack. Either way, George, the result would be the same. You'd be dead."

"Are you crazy? Do you think you'd get away with something like that"?

"Yes, I'm a little crazy and yes, I will get away with it."

"What do you want me to do?"

Kent wanted to put a spin on the situation that Wilson could handle.

"George, it's too early to worry about this. Civil cases get referred to the United States Attorney all the time and never get prosecuted. You'll be all right."

"I not so sure about that."

"When is the last time that someone like you got into serious trouble? Never. You're too well connected."

Kent was really mocking Wilson.

"George, this business is based on buyer beware. We put warnings and disclaimers on every prospectus we send to buyers of our deals.

"Don't worry about the Northport deal.

"Tell the investigators that you entered that deal on the advice of a friend who you knew and trusted.

"You went through prep school and college with him. You even hired him into the firm as your senior consultant.

"Tell them that you did the deal based on my recommendation."

"You want me to blame it on you, Jack?"

"Yeah, sure. You're my friend, but we shouldn't say anything about it, unless we have to.

"I don't understand why you would want me to do this, Jack."

"Because it'll take some of the heat off you."

"I appreciate that."

"No problem, George. Go get yourself a refill and see if Heather will give you a tour of the bedrooms."

--THIRTY-SEVEN--

They were walking in the hospital parking lot towards his Tahoe when Brent said to Leanne, "I made reservations for us down at the Marriott in Annapolis. I thought it would be good for us to spend some quiet time together.

"Is that all right with you?"

"Yes, it is. I'd like to rest a little."

For the first twenty minutes of the ride, they were silent, absorbed in thought.

Leanne could understand how he might feel.

She had not been allowed to tell him about her secret work and had hoped that she would never have to tell him.

Would Brent understand why she would want to work in the intelligence community?

Did he have the right to know what she did, because they were engaged?

Would Brent believe that her feelings about her work had changed?

Leanne knew that their marriage had to be built on trust. This revelation could destroy his trust in her.

Brent was thinking about his brother.

Why did Jeff ever get involved in this arms business?

It couldn't have been for the money.

Mom and Dad had set up a huge trust fund for him when he was born.

He remembered when Jeff was a kid how excited he got by breaking rules and getting away with it.

As he got older, he enjoyed doing more dangerous things, like skydiving and taking out his hot air balloon.

Jeff couldn't be in a more dangerous line of work than operating undercover in the Middle East with his life in danger every day.

Leanne finally broke the silence.

"Are you all right? You're so quiet."

"No, I'm not all right." He said, roughly.

"I'm having a hard time dealing with all of this stuff right now. It's bad enough to lose Jeff, but to learn that my financee leads a double life makes it worse."

"I tried to explain that back at the hospital. I told you that I wasn't allowed to tell you.

"Look, Brent, I can understand how you feel. I've thought about this ever since we got engaged.

"It bothered me that I couldn't tell you what I did and I was concerned about what it might do to us.

"I took a chance because I loved you so much. I was worried you'd feel differently about me if you knew."

"Well, I don't feel very good about it right now. I mean, I don't even know what you do for them.

"If it's anything like what Jeff did, it must be dangerous stuff."

"I can't talk to you about it."

"Well, that's bullshit.

"Do you really expect me to get married when I don't know anything about this secret life of yours?

"I mean, who the hell are you?

"Are you an art dealer or some kind of spook agent?

"And why did you go into the agency in the first place?

"Don't you think that I have the right to know about that?"

"You asked me if I'm an art dealer or an agent? Well, I'm both. Do you have a right to know why I went into the agency? Yes, you do. But, please let me explain what happened."

"All right. This better be good."

"Brent, I lived on a Marine Corps base for the first eighteen years of my life.

"All I had was my dad.

"My mother died when I was a baby and I had no brothers or sisters.

"My dad was a career Marine and he raised me to be obedient and respect authority.

"He probably treated me more like a son than a daughter, because he taught me everything he knew about fishing, hunting and cars."

"What does this have to do with the CIA?"

"You'll see. I was accustomed to military life. It's so different than civilian life.

"When I went to college, I had to make a big adjustment. I left a strict, regimented life in the Marine Corps for an unstructured, freethinking life at Yale.

"It wasn't an easy transition for me.

"I did well at school, but I felt a little lost without any kind of direction.

"The CIA contacted me in my senior year.

"They said they needed bright young scholars to do research for them."

"How did they know about you?"

"They said they profiled me as someone who would be able to work in their organization.

"They said that they liked to recruit people who had a military background because they were accustomed to structure and chain of command.

"My background fit the profile."

"You must have gotten pretty good grades. I know Jeff didn't get good grades at Virginia, but he was in the ninety-nine percentile on all his aptitude tests.

"The CIA doesn't recruit dummies."

"Well, I was allowed to construct my own curriculum. Brent, their offer really appealed to me. They promised to pay my way through graduate school before I went to work for them. And after I worked full-time for five years, they would give me the money to open my own art gallery."

"That's how you were able to buy the warehouse on Fifth Avenue."

"Right. But there was one condition. They wanted me to work part-time for five years. After that, I was on my own."

"When does your contract expire?"

"At the end of this year. In just a little over three months from now."

"Yeah, and three months before we were supposed to get married."

--THIRTY-EIGHT--

Late Saturday afternoon, a team of SEC examiners sat around conference table in the offices of Montieff, Lancaster pouring through thousands of pages of documents.

They had discovered enough questionable transactions in the firm's investment banking department that they considered sharing the data with the United States Attorney's office in New York City.

"Bob, do you think there's enough evidence here to go criminal?" The brunette asked the senior examiner.

"Well, let's go over what we have at this point. Let's focus on the IPO transactions for a minute.

"Up until late 1997, we know this firm was barely a player in the investment banking business.

"They didn't originate any deals themselves, they just participated in other firms selling syndicates.

"Then all of sudden, when the dot.coms started going public, these guys became a leading underwriter of new tech stocks. How come?"

Tony, the former college wrestler spoke up.

"It was easy. Somebody here was waving in every hair-brain idea that knocked on the door. I checked the files on most of the companies they brought public. They were worthless."

"Yeah, but wasn't every other firm doing the same thing, Tony?"

"Not exactly, Bob. These guys used a different wrinkle to create business."

"What do you mean?"

"They made them up. Every one of the companies they brought public were initially financed by the venture capital company in Chicago. Doesn't it seem odd that there was an exclusive deal between Montieff, Lancaster and those guys? I mean, this wasn't a once a month type deal. They went from originating nothing to doing forty deals a month!"

"Did you check out the venture capital firm?"

"Yes. Its called Atlas Venture Capital and they work out of a small office in downtown Chicago on LaSalle Street. We figured that there are probably no more than five people working there."

"That sounds like a shell company. Did they finance real businesses?"

"No. They were all bogus companies. They were incorporated, but the principals and the description of the businesses and the financial information were all fictitious."

"How did they pull that off?"

"Montieff, Lancaster was responsible for performing due diligence on the new companies they were bringing public. Their investment bankers should have known that these deals were worthless."

"It appears that Mr. Wilson knew that they were worthless."

"He knew all right. As the managing partner, Wilson took control of the investment banking department just before he starting buying the deals from Atlas Venture Capital, his own firm."

"How did he get these deals through our examiners?"

"It was easy.

"Wilson instructed his clerical staff to file the registration forms with us, using the financial data that he gave to them.

"The investment bankers who worked for Wilson never got the opportunity to perform due diligence on the sham companies. He wouldn't let them."

"Was he the only principal at the firm who knew about the scam?"

"It appears that way. This was a multi-billion dollar lay-up for Wilson."

"This is incredible. We might never have found out about this if it weren't for the civil issues."

"What do we do now, Bob?"

"We'll set up a meeting with the United States Attorney over here in this office as soon as possible. We'll be spending the rest of the weekend putting this case together. By the way, everyone, you did a great job."

--THIRTY- NINE--

Leanne was taking a shower in their third floor room at the Marriott Hotel on the waterfront in downtown Annapolis.

She could see herself in the bathroom mirror through the glass shower door.

What a mess, she thought.

The gentle spray of hot water didn't hide the bruises that covered her arms and legs.

The trash bag wrapped around her cast to keep it dry didn't enhance her appearance either.

Leanne shut off the water, got out of the shower and awkwardly managed to dry off.

She put on a pair of white linen pants and slipped into a sleeveless coral silk blouse.

As she was trying on a bright floral straw hat, she heard the front door open and Brent calling out, "Are you here?"

"Yes." She said, walking out to see him.

He stood there soaking wet in sweaty shorts and a tank top.

"Did you have a good run?"

Still breathing hard and sweating on the carpet, he said, "Yeah, it feels good to blow off some steam."

"How far did you go?"

"Around seven miles. The streets were crowded. It seems like the whole town is out either running with their black labs or pushing baby carriages. I went to the track up at St. John's."

"You know, I was so tired that I didn't even hear you get up. Are you feeling any better this morning?"

"Yeah, a little. I'm sorry I was so angry with you last night. I guess I was taking out some of my frustrations on you.

"I still don't understand, Leanne, why you didn't tell me you were in the CIA.

"I mean, my brother told me when he joined the agency. He didn't tell me exactly what he did, but I knew that he was working in Europe.

"Don't you think you should have at least told me when we got engaged?"

"I guess so." She said, weakly. "I was going to tell you the other night when I came home, but, you know, finding out about Jeff..."Her voice trailed off.

She moved close to him, put her hand on his wet cheek and said, "Brent, I love you. I never would do anything to hurt you, you know that. You mean the whole world to me. I don't want to lose you."

He glanced at his watch and said, "It's getting late. I'll take a quick shower. We can make the Yacht Club brunch before it closes. We can talk about this later."

Brent walked to the bathroom and closed the door behind him.

Leanne walked out on the balcony that overlooked the historic harbor, feeling troubled by Brent's resentment towards her.

She sat down on the white cast iron seat wondering how much more she could afford to tell him.

There had been so much tragedy in so little time. Leanne felt that their relationship had been shattered by what had happened to them.

How could Brent ever be able to trust her?

She had lied to him.

Not directly, but she had lied by omission. She should have gone with her feelings and told him about the agency.

Brent was more important in her life than the agency.

What would the agency do to her if she had confided in Brent? The worst case would be that they would fire her.

Leanne thought that she wouldn't tell Brent about the shooting until later. She wanted to help Brent get through the next few weeks without causing him any more pain.

Twenty minutes later, they were walking into the entrance of the Yacht Club.

Brent spotted George Wilson coming out of the dining room and chatting with a man he didn't recognize.

Although they would bump into each other occasionally at various Wall Street functions, Brent and Wilson had never socialized together. Brent always thought that Wilson was a pompous ass.

When Wilson saw them approaching, he called out, "Brent Maxwell, what brings you down to old Annapolis? I'd never imagine seeing you at the club. Are you a member?"

Without answering the questions, Brent reached out to shake hands, and said, "Hello, George, how are you?"

"I'm doing very well, thank you."

His eyes shifted to Leanne.

"Are you going to introduce me to this gorgeous creature?"

"Sure. I'd like you to meet my financee, Leanne Anderson. Leanne, this is George Wilson, he's the CEO over at Montieff, Lancaster."

"It's nice to meet you, George."

"It's my pleasure. Oh, I'm sorry, this is Jack Kent. He's an economic consultant for us. Jack, this is Brent Maxwell. He runs the investment banking group at Hamilton-Montague."

"Nice to meet you, Brent."

"You too, Jack. You'll have to excuse us, George, or we'll miss the brunch."

"Sure, Brent. It was good seeing you."

As they walked towards the restaurant, Leanne became lost in thought.

She knew that face because she had seen it before.

Leanne never forgot a face.

But where had she seen him before?

It probably wasn't important.

That name was familiar, too!

Jack Kent.

It would come to her.

Brent interrupted her thoughts.

"Are you all right? You fogged out on me."

"Yes, I'm all right. The guy with Wilson seems so familiar to me, but I can't place him."

--FORTY--

While Kent and Wilson were discussing their mutual problems on the Commodore's front lawn during the post-race party, a solitary crab boat was working in the shallow waters off the west side of Kent Island.

Local restaurants had been paying the highest prices of the season for crabs. Thousands of tourists and sportsmen were flocking to the restaurants around the Chesapeake Bay creating tremendous demand for the famous Maryland crustaceans.

The crabber thought that he might as well make some extra money by staying on the water later than he usually did. It was getting dark, but he had one more line of crab pots to check out.

Suddenly, his boat snagged on something.

"What the hell is that?" The waterman muttered.

He figured that he was in about two feet of water. He picked up a pole hook, stuck it into the soft muddy bottom and pushed hard.

The boat moved off the object.

He peered into the water.

"Holy shit!!"

He almost lost his balance as he stumbled backwards.

It would be a natural reaction for anyone who had just looked into the eyes of a dead man.

The phone rang in the FBI office in Washington, D.C.

"Special Agent Brown speaking."

"Hello, this is Sheriff Black. I'm with the Kent County Sheriff's Department."

"How can I help you, Sheriff?"

"We recovered a body in the Chesapeake Bay just off Kent Island. We're pretty sure that it's that guy Ranfield you've been looking for. His face is a little pasty, but it matches the photograph you sent us."

"When did you find him?"

"Around five-thirty this afternoon. I wanted to get to you right away."

"I appreciate that sheriff. Have you determined the cause of death, yet?"

"Oh yeah. He was shot to death. He took two rounds in the back of his head."

"Thanks, we'll send some people down there to pick him up."

As soon as he heard the news, Devine called Maxwell at his office.

"Hello, this is Brent Maxwell."

"Brent, this is Devine. Something's come up, we've got to talk."

"What's happened?"

"I'll tell you when I see you. Where's Leanne?"

"Leanne?"

"Yeah, where is she now?"

"She's probably up at my apartment."

"All right. I'll be there in an hour. Brent," he said, before hanging up, "be careful."

Brent looked somewhat bewildered when he hung up the phone. He wondered what that was supposed to mean.

Brent called the apartment.

"Hello?" Leanne answered.

"Hi, it's me. Listen, Devine just called me. He's meeting us at the apartment in an hour."

"Did he say why?"

"No. But he told me to be careful. What's he talking about?"

"Something has happened. You might be in danger."

"From what?"

"I don't know. Is Victor with you?"

"No. He has the day off. I drove in alone."

"Where's your car?"

"It's in a garage down the block. Why?"

"Don't go there. Can you get a limo?"

"Sure, there's a line of them waiting outside the building."

"Brent, you have to promise me that you'll be careful. When you get on the street, don't let anyone get close to you."

"All right. I'll be there as soon as I can."

--FORTY-ONE--

Devine strode into the lobby of Maxwell's apartment, flanked by two of his agents. He walked up to the security desk and showed his identification card to the uniformed armed guard.

"I'm here to see Mr. Maxwell. I believe that he is expecting me."
"Yes, sir. You gentlemen can take the elevator over there to Mr. Maxwell's apartment. It's on the tenth floor."

The guard wondered why the CIA wanted to see Maxwell on a Monday night.

"I'll tell him you're coming up."
"Thanks."

Brent was waiting at the front door as they got off the elevator.

"You made good time." He said, shaking hands with Devine.
"You know Agent Ferragamo and Agent Hombrook, don't you?"
"Yes." He said, nodding to the men who had questioned him at the Trinity Church.

"Where is Leanne?"
"She's resting in the living room. Come on in."

Leanne sat up when they came into the room.

"Please, don't stand up, Leanne." Devine said.

Devine and Maxwell sat down while the agents stood outside in the foyer.
Devine got right to the point.

"We found Ranfield."
"Well, that's good news." Maxwell said.

"Not really, Brent. He was murdered. He was shot twice in the head and dumped into the Chesapeake Bay."

"Is that why you told me to be careful?"

"Yes. The killer didn't expect that Ranfield's body would be found so soon."

"Why do you say that?"

"Because the body was weighed down with anchors."

"Is Leanne still in danger?"

"Maybe yes, maybe no."

"She's in danger if the killer learns that we found Ranfield's body.

"In that case, Leanne might be able to establish the identity of the killer.

"She probably would not be in danger if we had not found Ranfield's body. We would have blamed Ranfield for operating the arms business and ordering the assassinations.

"If another attempt were made on Leanne's life now, then that would indicate that someone else was involved.

"We're not going to take any chances.

"We're going to protect you. We'll have surveillance on the two of you."

"Who do you think killed Ranfield?" Brent asked.

"Someone who knew him well and who was involved in the arms business. He might be the mastermind behind all of this."

"Why do you think that he was involved in the arms business?"

"He murdered Ranfield. Ranfield was the last one of his people who could identify him."

"Are you telling me that Jeff was killed just because he knew this guy?"

"That's right."

"What's he trying to hide?"

"I don't know, but it was important enough to kill the three of his partners."

"Do you have idea what it could be?"

"My guess is that he's running another illegal operation that's much different and bigger than the arms business. We won't know anything more about this operation, until we find out who he is."

"How are you going to do that?"

"These four guys worked in counter-intelligence."

"Are you sure the killer worked in the agency?"

"Absolutely. He knew too much about what was going on inside the agency.

"I've brought the personnel files of everyone who worked in counter-intelligence for the past ten years.

"Leanne, I want you go through these files and pick out anyone you recognize."

"Do you want me to go through Jeff's and John Whitestone's files?"

"No. There's no need to do that. Just give me the files of people you recognize. We're trying to make the connection to our mastermind killer."

Leanne quickly scanned through the dossiers stacked high on the coffee table.

Each one contained a large photograph of the agent attached to the inside cover.

She had already set aside several dossiers of agents who she had recognized when she suddenly leaned forward and gasped.

Leanne was holding up a file and looking intently at the photograph of an agent.

"Look at this!

"This is him!!

"I remember him from an assignment in Lebanon. My team worked with him and Whitestone on a hostage rescue mission."

"Let me see that file." Devine ordered.

"Brent, this is the guy we met at the yacht club in Annapolis yesterday. Jack Kent. I knew that I had seen him before. He worked in Operations."

She handed the file to the stunned Director of Operations.

"You what?!

"You met him?

"When, on Sunday?"

"Yes. That's the guy we met at Brent's yacht club in Annapolis.

"We were going to brunch when he and George Wilson were leaving. Wilson introduced him to us."

"In Annapolis?

"Ranfield's body was found off Kent Island!

"That's just across the bay from Annapolis."

Devine opened the dossier and looked at Kent's photograph. Devine didn't recognize him.

There wouldn't be any reason to know him because Devine had been working in a different Directorate when Kent was in the counter-intelligence group.

"Let's see if we can find out a little more about the mysterious Jack Kent."

Devine started to read out loud.

"Jack Kent.

"He was initially recruited in 1988 in his senior year at Princeton University.

"He received a Bachelor Degree in Economics.

"He attended University of Helsinki and earned a Doctorate Degree in International Economics.

"In 1991, he joined the agency and was assigned to the Research Department at Langley.

"In 1992, he was assigned to the Middle East.

"In 1996 he was promoted to assistant deputy, counter-intelligence.

"In 1997 he resigned.

"I wonder where he is now."

"Wilson told us that Kent worked for him, as his economic consultant." Brent volunteered.

"Where? Here, in New York?"

"He should be working in their headquarters at the Seaport Plaza. Do you think Kent is behind this? Is he the one who killed Jeff?"

"He might be a good candidate, but we have to find out more about him. Just think about it. Bethesda is only thirty minutes from Annapolis. He might have killed Whitestone, too.

"Brent, how much do you know about this guy Wilson?"

"He's from old New England money. The family owns a controlling interest in Montieff, Lancaster. After he got out of Princeton, the family put him on the fast track to run the company."

"Princeton, you said? How old is Wilson?"

"He's my age, thirty-five. Why do you ask?"

"Maybe they knew each other at Princeton. We'll check on that. We could be on to something here."

"Jim, you just said that Jeff's killer might be involved with another illegal operation. Isn't that right?"

"Yes, but it's only a hunch."

"Didn't you also suggest that Jeff was killed just because he knew who ran the illegal arms operation?"

"Yes, but what are you driving at?"

"Well, this might only be a coincidence, Jim, but I didn't know until yesterday that this guy Kent worked with Wilson."

"Why would you know?"

"Because they've been one of our major competitors for years and I know all the key players in their investment banking group."

"I still don't see where you going with this."

"Wilson said he was an economic consultant for the firm. I've never heard of him before yesterday. I've never seen anything that he has written. No economic reports, no forecasting, nothing."

"Does that seem odd to you, Brent? I mean, I don't know anything about your business."

"Yes, it does. Every major firm has an economist, but usually they're senior people, very well paid and highly visible. People like Kent would usually appear on all the television and cable business shows. I don't know what this guy is doing at Wilson's firm, but he seems to be very close to Wilson."

"That might be the Princeton connection, Brent."

"Well, hear me out, Jim. One of my buddies at Montieff, Lancaster called me last week and told me that the SEC had started an investigation into their investment bank.

"The SEC suspects that Hamilton's investment banking group had brought a number of questionable start-up tech companies public over the past year and a half.

"And?"

"Wilson runs the investment bank, even though he's the managing partner of the firm."

"Is that unusual?"

"Yes, it's very unusual. A managing partner needs to oversee several different departments at the same time. Wilson wouldn't have the time to run the investment banking group and manage the other departments at the same time."

"Are you suggesting that Kent might be helping him run the firm?"

"I don't know, but the street has always wondered how Montieff got so many new issue deals so quickly. They had never been a factor in the new issue business and then suddenly they're in the top five underwriters."

"That seems odd to me, Brent. What do you think Kent is really doing at Montieff?"

"I don't know."

"Let's assume that Kent is our killer and that he killed three of my agents because he didn't want to be identified. Now we know who he is, but what's he trying to hide?

"One, it has to be connected to Montieff, and two, it has to be making a lot more money than he was making in the arms business."

"You're talking about more than a hundred million dollars!"

"You better think bigger, Brent. Think billions. That's plenty of motive for killing Jeff and the other two.

"Like I said, you know this business a lot better than I do. What kind of a scam could he be running at Montieff that would generate that much money?"

"I don't know. I've seen some smaller schemes, like traders failing to disclose losing transactions or manipulating stock prices or insider trading, but I've never heard of any fraud that has generated a billion dollars.

"Well, Kent has the brains to think up something big. We'll be talking with him first thing tomorrow morning."

Devine paused and looked at Leanne with an expression that appeared both apologetic and sympathetic. Leanne sensed what was going to happen and felt absolutely helpless.

"Brent, it's time to tell you something about Leanne and you're not going to like it.

"I'm going to ask you to try and understand what's happened here, but it's time for you to be told.

"Leanne has a ten-year contract with us.

"During the first five years, she worked for us full time.

"She went on missions to Europe and the Middle East as a shooter, mostly as protection for her team, but sometimes to take out specific individuals.

"During the last five years she's been working part-time for us."

"As a shooter?" Bent asked, dumbfounded.

"Yes."

Appearing dismayed, he looked at Leanne and said, "Is this true?"

"Yes, it is." She answered nervously.

Devine interrupted.

"Our agents are sworn to secrecy. They don't tell anyone about their operations. Not even their families. I'm sure that Jeff didn't tell you anything about what he did in the Middle East."

"No, he didn't. What does that have to do with Leanne?" He said.

"Leanne was involved in the operation to eliminate Jeff and Whitestone.

"She received orders that appeared valid.

"Kent's plan, if it was Kent, was simple.

"He wanted to kill your brother and Whitestone by using one of our shooters.

"Kent told Ranfield to assign an assassin.

"He chose Leanne because she was a part-timer and would be easy to eliminate when she got back to the United States."

"What, are you shitting me?!!" Brent shouted.

"Listen to me." Devine ordered in a stern voice. "The orders looked authentic. Nobody at the agency knew the orders even existed, except Ranfield. Leanne had no idea that Jeff was a target."

"You knew this all along, Leanne?!!" Brent said heatedly.

"I knew about the assignments, but I didn't know about Jeff until I came back from Tel Aviv and saw you." She said.

"The plan started to unravel. Whitestone survived, but Leanne still had to be taken out." Devine said.

Pacing the floor with a harsh look on his face, Brent started to vent.

"Leanne, I've got a real problem with this. You should have told me that you were involved with the agency. You didn't have to tell me all the details, but at least you could have told me that you worked with these guys. We are supposed to get married in four months. Were you ever going to tell me?"

"Ah, yes, I wanted to, but you felt so bad and I didn't want to hurt you any more."

"I don't believe you, Leanne. How can I trust you anymore?"

Devine jumped into it.

"Look, Maxwell, Leanne was doing what she was told to do. She wasn't going to tell you anything that would jeopardize you."

"Well, I guess it's a little too late for that!" Brent shot back. "You've already killed Jeff!"

"That's not fair, Brent, I was just..."

"Fair?" He shouted at her. "You know what, you make me sick. I can't stand looking at you anymore. Get the hell out of here. I don't want you here anymore."

She got off the couch and started towards him.

"You don't understand, I couldn't..."

"I understand everything I need to understand! Jeff is dead and you did it. Now get the hell out of here!"

Devine looked at Brent and said, "I'm sorry, Brent, I know how painful this is for you, but you had to be told. Believe me, Leanne had no idea that it was Jeff."

Brent glared at Devine.

"I want everyone out of here. I want to be left alone."

"We'll leave, Brent, but Hombrook stays with you for protection."

Devine pointed to Ferragamo and said, "Vince, you go with her, Rob, you stay here with Maxwell. And check in with me every thirty minutes. We don't know what's going to happen tonight."

"Yes, sir!" They said in unison.

--FORTY-TWO--

Leanne lived in an expensive two-story brownstone on 64th Street, between Park and Madison, within walking distance of the gallery. While Agent Ferragamo stood guard downstairs, Leanne tried to get some sleep on a chaise lounge in her bedroom upstairs.

She felt awful about losing Brent and anxious that a killer might be outside waiting for her.

Leanne wasn't able to sleep. The tone of finality in his voice hurt her deeply.

Leanne and Brent's world had been ravaged in just a few days. Their relationship was wonderful a week ago and now it was in shambles. She could understand the hurt in Brent's heart, but could only hope that he would come to realize how much she loved him and that she would never do anything to deliberately hurt him.

The thought that it might be over for them was unbearable. Her stomach felt like it was tied up in knots.

It was such an empty feeling, to have lost him.

All through the night until dawn, these thoughts kept her awake.

A cell phone rang downstairs.

Leanne heard faintly that Ferragamo was talking with someone, but she couldn't make out what he was saying.

A few minutes later, Ferragamo called upstairs to her, "Leanne, it's time to get up. Devine wants to move you out of here now."

"I'll be right down."

She smelled the aroma of freshly brewed coffee as she came downstairs. Ferragamo had found his way around her kitchen.

"Was that Devine on the phone?" She asked.

"Yes. We're out of here."

"Where are we going?"

"You'll be going down to a safe house in Maryland for a few weeks, at least until you're safe."

"When does he want me to go?"

"Now. He's already sent a car to pick you up."

"I have to make some calls before we go."

"Well, make it quick, because they'll be here any minute."

After leaving a message for her gallery manager explaining that something came up and she would be out of town for a few days, she dialed Brent's number.

Three rings later, his recorded voice answered, "You've reached 274-5555, leave a message."

"Brent, it's me, Leanne. Are you there? If you are, please pick up. I really need too talk to you.

"I know you don't want to talk to me, but I want to tell you how sorry I am about last night.

"I'll always love you.

"I wish you were there.

"There aren't enough words to describe how awful I feel.

"I never wanted to hurt you.

"Brent, please, you've got to believe me.

"I was doing what I was told to do. I didn't know Jeff was involved.

"I really want to talk to you, but I can't reach you.

"Devine is sending me away for protection.

"I can't tell you where.

"I hope that you find it in your heart to forgive me.

"Brent, I'll always love you.

"If sometime later, you feel you want to talk with me, contact Devine.

"I don't know how long I'll be gone. Goodbye."

When the phone rang, Brent knew from the caller ID that it was Leanne who was calling, but he felt too much anger with her to pick up the phone and talk to her.

He lay back in bed and listened as she poured out her feelings to him.

Deep down he wanted to believe her, but it was so difficult to understand who she was and to understand the incredible events that had happened to them.

As she spoke longer, he began hearing the pain in her voice, reflecting how deeply hurt she was.

Pangs of anguish slowly seeped into him softening the anger he felt towards her.

Last week, he was deeply in love with her. This week, their relationship was shattered.

Brent wanted to talk to her.

He called her at the house.

There was no answer.

There wasn't even an answering machine.

He tried calling her on her cell phone.

It was out of service.

Realty really hit him hard.

She wasn't there any more.

--FORTY-THREE--

By eight-thirty in the morning, Devine and his team of agents had arrived at the Seaport Plaza Building.

He instructed his men to stake out the front doors of the building and the service entrances in the back.

Devine turned to Ferragamo and Hombrook and said, "Let's go."

As they got on the elevators, Ferragamo asked his boss, "Do you think Kent is carrying a weapon?"

"Probably." Devine answered

"What do you want us to do, when we get up there?"

"First thing you do is search him. I don't want to get into a shoot-out with this character. Second, we're going to ask him a few questions. Then we'll have to see how it plays out."

"Do we know that he's here?"

"Yeah, we called his office. His secretary said he was there."

"Well, he's going to be surprised to see us."

"I hope so."

Meanwhile, a few blocks away, two Securities and Exchange Commission investigators were walking towards the same building.

"Does Wilson know we're coming this morning?"

"No."

"Have you had any experience with him before?"

"No. Only with his compliance guy."

"Anything serious?"

"No. Churning and unsuitability. Typical cases."

"Do you think we can nail Wilson for anything criminal?"

"I'd like to, but he might have too many connections to have it go that far."

"This is going to be an interesting day."

--FORTY-FOUR--

A little after seven o'clock on Monday morning, Kent sat at his desk browsing through the morning papers.

A headline in the business section of a New York newspaper caught his attention.

"SEC To Probe Conflicts of Interest On Wall Street"

"The Securities and Exchange Commission has launched a formal inquiry into the possible conflicts of interest by Wall Street analysts.

The SEC, together with the United States District Attorney's Office for the Southern District of New York, will investigate whether financial analysts at several leading Wall Street investment banking firms had mislead investors by issuing favorable recommendations on certain companies in order to maintain their investment banking relationships with them."

Kent knew this was going to happen eventually.

The practice of recommending stocks in order to keep their investment banking relationships intact had become an endemic problem within the investment banking system.

Corporations expected their investment bankers to bolster the price of their stock by continually issuing buy recommendations.

Since the bulk of the CEO's compensation was options to purchase the company's stock, there was substantial self-interest to keep pushing up the price of their stock.

The investment bankers expected their corporate clients to continue paying exorbitant fees for this not-so-subtle marketing service.

The regulators needed to make changes now that would protect investors in the future.

This meant trouble for Kent.

The investigation would certainly uncover all the bogus companies that the firm had purchased from Atlas Venture Capital.

The SEC would learn that the company was a shell operation and that George Wilson was listed as it's general partner.

Kent worried that Wilson wouldn't be able to keep his mouth shut when the District Attorney's Office threatened him with criminal prosecution.

Kent realized that there was no reason for Wilson to take the fall for him.

The lame excuse that he allowed those deals to go through his firm on Kent's advice wasn't going to fly either.

The investigation might jeopardize Kent's plan to escape to France on Friday night.

After he finished reading about the upcoming investigation, Kent picked up the Washington newspapers to see if there was any coverage of the weekend yacht races.

He nearly missed a small squib in the News- in -Brief column.

"Man's Body Found In Chesapeake Bay"

"A man's body was dredged up yesterday afternoon by a crab boat in the Chesapeake Bay near Kent Island.

The Anne Arundel County Sheriff's Department issued a statement that the unidentified man was a victim of a homicide."

The agency will know that the man was Ranfield.

They might even know now.

It would be easy for them to make the connection between he and Ranfield.

If that were the case, they would be after him.

They might even be coming to get him this morning.

He had to escape.

Kent called his secretary sitting in the outer office.

"Mary, would you please get a fresh carafe of coffee from the restaurant for me?"

"Certainly, Mr. Kent. Would you like anything else with that?"

"No, Mary. The coffee will be fine."

Kent needed to leave the office without Mary seeing him.

He had prepared for this situation.

Kent went to his closet and pulled out a long sleeve white maintenance shirt and a pair of blue khaki trousers.

After quickly slipping on the shirt and pants, he put on a plain blue baseball hat and walked to the wall safe behind a painting by Marc Chagall.

Kent took out a packet of false identification papers, passports and foreign currency and closed the safe.

It was time to get out of the building now.

Kent walked briskly past Mary's desk into the hallway. As he approached the front foyer, the elevator doors opened and three men walked out.

They had government written all over them.

He stopped, turned his head away from them and pretended to talk into his cell phone.

They were agents. Their body language gave them away. Their eyes scanned the foyer and the hallway as they walked with a sense of purpose straight to the receptionist's desk.

Kent thought that their suits were far less expensive than the custom-made suits normally worn by the executives on this floor.

When they started talking with the receptionist, he started walking towards to the elevators still mumbling into the cell phone.

With his back towards them, he depressed the down button, waited and hoped that they had not gotten a close look at him.

Kent couldn't hear what they were saying to the receptionist, but he was able to hear her responses giving them directions to his office.

They had walked past him and down the hallway towards his office when the down arrow light blinked on.

As he entered the empty elevator, he glanced quickly down the hall.

They had already turned the corner.

There was a need to get out of the building quickly.

Kent knew that there would be agents covering all the exits. He had to take the chance that he could walk by them undetected.

Kent had no other choice.

The agents upstairs would soon find out that they had just missed him.

When he got to the lobby floor, Kent saw Devine's people stationed at the front doors monitoring people leaving the building.

Now, the only way out of the building was through the lobby and out the revolving front doors.

Kent quickly thought about his options to get past the agents without being recognized.

Simply walking to the front door wasn't going to work. They certainly knew his face from his photograph in his personnel file.

He could try to create a situation that would distract the agents, but Kent couldn't think of anything and he didn't have any more time to loiter in the lobby.

The agents upstairs would soon discover that he had slipped past them. He had to get out of the building before they alerted their people at the doors.

Kent decided to attract their attention.

It was time to do a little play-acting. He wanted to make sure that the agents noticed him.

Still holding the cell phone on the side of his head, he sauntered to the security desk and turned his back to the agents.

"Hey, how goes it?" He asked the security guard sitting behind the desk.

"Good." She said. "How you doing?"

"Busy. We had a real mess on elevator twelve."

"What happened?"

"You know that deli down the street?"

"Yeah."

"Some guy was delivering coffee and donuts and he dropped the whole load in the elevator. That coffee really stained the carpets."

"I can imagine." She said, somewhat disinterested.

Kent's excellent peripheral vision enabled him to observe the agents at the doors.

They were watching him.

Good. They had no reaction.

It appeared to the agents that this man, whose face they couldn't see, was indeed a maintenance man. Security seemed to know him. He wasn't the man they were looking for.

Kent knew that he was running out of time. He had to get out right now.

Kent glanced again at the agents.

They weren't looking at him any more.

Now was his chance.

He had them set up.

They wouldn't look twice at him when he walked out of the building.

Meanwhile, upstairs on the executive floor, Devine and his two agents had gone to Kent's office at the same time that his secretary had come back from the executive restaurant with the fresh coffee.

"Can I help you?" She said, as she put the carafe down on her desk.

"Yes," Devine said, "we're here to see Mr. Kent. Is he here?"

"Yes, he's in his office. Is he expecting you?"

"No. We're with the federal government."

"Do you have some identification?"

Somewhat impatiently, Devine flashed his card and said, "Miss, this is a very urgent matter. We're going into the office right now!"

Devine opened the office door and walked inside. There was no one there. They checked the private bathroom and the closet.

"When did you last see Mr. Kent?" He asked Mary.

"About ten minutes ago. He wanted fresh coffee."

"Do you have any idea where he is now?"

"No. I thought he would be in there."

"Jim, look at this. It's about Ranfield." Ferragamo said.

Ferragamo was pointing to one of the newspapers on Kent's desk Devine read the News-In-Brief section in the Washington Post.

"Kent knows we're on to him. We must have just missed him. Wait a minute! The building maintenance guy we passed coming in here. He was pretty good size. Did you get a look at his face?"

"No. He was waiting to get into an elevator. He had his back turned to us."

Mary overheard their conversation.

"Did you say you saw a maintenance man on this floor?"

"Yes. He was standing at the elevators when we came back here to see Mr. Kent. Why are you asking?"

"Because we don't allow maintenance personnel on the executive floor during our normal business hours."

"Oh, shit." Devine muttered.

He depressed the button on his hand held radio. "Reilly, this is Devine. You copy?"

There was a little static on the line. "Reilly here, I copy."

"Our man is dressed as a maintenance man. You see anybody like that down there?"

"Yeah. A guy went out of the building a few minutes ago. He seemed okay."

"Reilly, that's our man, go after him!"

"Yes, sir."

Devine turned to his two agents.

"Kent just left the building. I hope we didn't lose him."

--EPILOGUE--

Six months later

An article appeared in the business section of a New York newspaper on December 23, 2000.

Investment firm agrees to settle SEC suit

Montieff, Lancaster will pay $150 million
in allegations of IPO abuses

WASHINGTON -- Montieff, Lancaster has agreed to pay $150 million to resolve regulators' allegations of abuses in its distribution of hot new stock offerings, the government announced yesterday.

The Securities and Exchange Commission alleged that Montieff, Lancaster, a major investment firm, gave favored investors a larger number of shares of initial public offerings, or IPOs, and on other stock trades, got a share of its clients' IPO profits in the form of inflated commissions.

Montieff, Lancaster neither admitted to or denied the agency's allegations in agreeing to settle the SEC's civil lawsuit filed in federal court in Washington and a related action by the self-policing arm of the National Association of Securities Dealers.

The SEC has been investigating for about six months Wall Street's dealings in IPOs during the tech-stock boom of 1999 and 2000.

As the lead underwriter of hot IPOs for many start-up companies, Montieff, Lancaster had control over the allocation of most of the shares in the IPOs, the SEC said. In exchange for some of the highly coveted stock, Montieff, Lancaster "wrongfully extracted" from certain customers a large share of the big profits those customers made in quickly reselling the

IPO stock they got from Montieff, Lancaster, according to the agency.

It said that between April 1999 and June 2000, Montieff, Lancaster allocated shares of IPOs to more than 100 customers who, in return, funneled between 30 percent and 60 percent of their IPO profits to the investment firm. The customers typically resold the stock on the day of the IPO, often gaining tremendous profits, then transferred a share of the profits to Montieff, Lancaster in the form of excessive brokerage commissions.

In a statement, the New York-based firm noted that theSEC and the NASD did not allege any fraudulent conduct by the firm.

"Today's settlement allows us to move forward," said Thomas R. Towers, Montieff, Lancaster's recently appointed chief executive officer. "We are strongly committed to upholding the highest standards of conduct at Montieff, Lancaster."

Besides paying the $150 million, the investment firm also agreed to refrain from future violations and to tighten its practices to prevent future improprieties in selling IPOs.

The firm also said it was taking disciplinary action against the employees involved, including fines, suspensions without pay, and suspensions from supervisory duties.

In a related matter, the United States Attorney's office announced that they have dropped all charges of criminal fraud and collusion against Montieff, Lancaster, citing insufficient evidence.

A brief announcement appeared in a monthly Investment magazine on December 28, 2000.

People in the News

Top Tier Investment Advisors, a privately owned investment management group, announced today that George W. Wilson, formally Chief Executive Officer of Montieff, Lancaster has been hired as an investment adviser for the Greenwich, Connecticut based firm.

On December 29, 2000, the Director of Operations for the Central Intelligence Agency placed a call to Brent Maxwell, the Director of Investment Banking at Hamilton-Montague in New York City.

"Brent, it's Jim Devine. How've you been?"

"I can't complain. How about you?"

"Good. Did you read about the settlement at Montieff?"

"Yes, I did. You were right, Jim. You said that Wilson would get off easy."

"Wilson was fortunate to be a member of a very wealthy family. They have strong ties to some very powerful people in the government."

"Did Wilson cooperate with the DA?"

"Oh, yeah. Wilson was looking at serious jail if he didn't. He told us how he got set up by Kent and why he let Kent run the scam on his firm. Wilson still doesn't understand why Kent screwed over him."

"Why did he?"

"Because Kent could control him. Kent knew that Wilson was a weak stick and could be manipulated. The man was a genius."

"Any more about him?"

"Not much. After he escaped from the Seaport Plaza, he stole a boat from a marina right around the corner from the building. Our people had searched for him after he got away, but they never thought about checking the marina."

"I'm sorry you missed him."

"We're still looking for him. We found the stolen boat down on Kent Island, near a small airport. We figure that he flew out of there sometime that Monday afternoon."

"I assume you checked his flight plan."

"We did. Kent registered the plane under a fictitious name. The flight plan showed that he flew to Toronto. We found the plane in a privately owned hanger."

"Did you get any leads from that?"

"Not really. The hanger is owned by someone with the same fictitious name. It's Kent. He probably flew out of Toronto on a commercial plane."

"Do you have any idea where he is now?"

"Nothing specific, but if I had to guess, I'd say that he's on the Mediterranean."

"Why the Mediterranean, Jim?"

"He's a waterman."

December 30, 2000

At Ristorante Georgios, Leanne Anderson was finishing her luncheon meeting with an events manager from the Plaza Hotel. Brent Maxwell arrives some time later with two senior executives from a local broadcasting company. After a while, he looks across the room and sees her. She was signing the check and getting ready to leave. She sensed something, looked up and saw him. Their eyes met. He excused himself from the table and walked over to her table.

"You look good. When did you get back?"

"I got back last month. They thought it was all right."

"Are you still with them?"

"No. They gave me early discharge."

"That's good. How do you feel?"

"I'm all right. I'm trying to get the business back on track. How are you, Brent?"

"I'm all right. I've been trying to sort some things out. Are you still living in the same place?"

"Yes."

Leanne looked at Brent, smiled and said, "Would you like to sit down?"

"No, thanks...I have to get back, you know, business."

Trying not to show her disappointment, Leanne said, "I understand, it was nice to see you again."

As Brent looked into her sad green eyes, he realized that he still loved her.

"It was good to see you too, Leanne, take care."

Leanne watched Brent walk away and felt her stomach sink again. She knew she would have to move forward in her life and hoped that one day Brent would come back to her.

ABOUT THE AUTHOR

David Traynor was born and raised in Brooklyn, New York. After graduating from Brooklyn Prep, he attended Holy Cross College in Worcester, Massachusetts. An honors student, an All-American lacrosse player, and nominated for the Rhodes Scholarship, Traynor graduated with a Bachelor of Arts degree in English Literature and was commissioned as a Second Lieutenant in the United States Marine Corps.

He served two and one-half years as an infantry platoon commander with the First Battalion, Ninth Marine Regiment, stationed at Camp Schwab, Okinawa and six months as a range officer and weapons instructor at the Camp Pendleton, California rifle range.

After an Honorable Discharge from the Marine Corps, he attended Fordham University School of Law and graduated with a Doctor of Laws degree. Traynor clerked briefly at LeBoeuf, Lamb, Green and McCray, a prestigious Manhattan law firm, before joining Salomon, Smith, Barney as an institutional salesman.

For the next twenty-five years, Traynor enjoyed a highly successful career with Morgan, Stanley, Prudential Advisors and Salomon Smith, Barney.

Currently he is President of Traynor Management, a firm that represents professional athletes and celebrities.

Printed in the United States
782800001B